NOT DATING MATERIAL
Accidental Love
Book 2

SAXON JAMES

Blurb

MOLLY

Moving to Seattle is supposed to be all about getting a fresh start and leaving the bitter man I was becoming behind.

I have new roommates–quirky, sometimes strange, roommates– a nosy, next door neighbor and a grumpy kitty for company, but even surrounded by people, I still don't feel like I belong. Plus, it turns out the men in Seattle are exactly the same as the ones I left behind, and my string of romantic *dis*connections continues.

It's not until one of my roommates, Seven, hits me with some hard truths that I realize where I was going wrong.

Maybe the men aren't the problem.

I am.

And there's only one way to fix that.

SEVEN

Being found tied up naked to my bed by my cute new roommate isn't an ideal way for us to start a friendship.

But apparently a quid-pro-quo is.

He keeps his pretty lips zipped about the compromising position, and I step in as his dating coach. We go out, I point out where he's going wrong, and he magically becomes dating material.

The problem is, between my codependent brother Xander and a new best friend I can't get rid of, Molly and I are the target of a matchmaking scheme. My life is way too busy to add another person to it, and Molly is the kinda guy who needs to be made a priority, which I just can't do. Xander's medical anxiety takes up too much of my time, and I've never found a partner who doesn't resent it.

I'm determined to help Molly find his ever after.

But that guy will never be me.

Content Warning

TW: mention of past physical and sexual abuse of a minor (no details). Character with trauma due to neglect. On page non-consensual photographs.

Chapter 1

SEVEN

I can't see, thanks to the blindfold, and I can't move, thanks to the handcuffs at my wrists and ankles, but there's nothing to stop me from hearing the telltale "click" of a motherfudging phone camera.

And I'm completely stark naked.

"Yo, I didn't consent to that," I say, injecting as much firmness into my voice as I can. Considering the position I'm in, I highly doubt my hookup is quaking in his ... well, yeah, boots, actually. Seeing as how I'm the fool who got naked while he stayed fully dressed. Normally, that'd be hot. Not right now though. "Delete it."

"Mmm ... no," he says in that simpering voice that originally caught my attention. Soft, silky, pretty, exactly my type.

I jump as something brushes my chest, but he's only dragging a feather down the middle of my torso. "I think it's time you untied me. We clearly need to go over boundaries again."

His cute laugh has an edge to it. "Oh, honey, no. That would be counterproductive to what's happening here."

"And … what exactly is happening?"

"Revenge."

I jerk against the handcuffs. "*Revenge?*"

"You were dating my friend, then ghosted him, and the next time he saw you, you were out dancing with some bald woman."

Bald woman? Oh … he's probably talking about Elle, the sister of my roommate's husband. Who, ridiculously, I've never hooked up with. We bonded hard and fast as morons-in-law, but anything further than that never happened. Whoever his friend is though, even without Elle, there have definitely been others since.

"Listen," I try to reason. "I don't know what you've been told, but it's all horse patties. I don't date. I make that very clear up front. It's a staple of my 'boundaries' conversation."

"You don't sleep with someone for a month if you're not dating them."

I have no clue who he's talking about. "Of course I do. If everyone's having fun, why shouldn't I?"

Pretty boy scoffs, and the camera clicks again.

"*Stop. Taking. Photos.*"

"Make me."

"This is illegal." Probably.

"Not calling people back is illegal."

I snort. "No, it isn't."

"Well, it should be." Another click. "Good to know you find this so funny."

"I hope you're getting my good side," I say dryly. But this whole situation isn't okay. I'm getting really uncomfortable. Really. I might like to play helpless in the bedroom, but playing and being are two totally different things.

I've *been* helpless. Actually. And I promised myself that would never happen again.

Well, well, Seven. Haven't you gone and screwed that right up?

2

"Oh, don't worry," he says. "I'm getting *all* your sides."

My stomach turns. "Get. Out."

"You're not going to say please?" The sweet tone makes it so much worse.

"You're violating my privacy. Unlock me and leave. I won't ask twice."

"Ooh, big man, throwing around threats. Good luck with that."

I'm not a violent person, but in times like this, I really wish I was.

Instead, I force one of those ridiculous meditative breaths Madden taught me and close my eyes behind the blindfold. I ignore everything … I want to say Colt? … says and try to stay relaxed until I have a way out of this situation. None of my roommates are home, otherwise, I would have already yelled out.

Nope, it's just me and the creep.

Who I'm actively trying to tune out. Kinda hard when he's monologuing harder than a '90s-era action villain.

"You know, I have a lot of regrets. Now I've seen you naked, I wish I didn't agree to this plan at all."

I grit my teeth.

"Your body is …" He makes a kissing noise.

I clench my fists.

"But no matter, these pictures will do the trick." His footsteps move toward the door. "Eddie says hi, by the way."

Then he's gone. I listen to him make his way down the stairs and to the front door, but for a second before it closes behind him, I swear I catch another voice.

And footsteps.

Please let it be one of my friends and not some other wannabe photographer with a grudge.

"Hello?" I holler. Sure, I'm not thrilled at one of them finding me dick and balls out, but while I'll have to endure everyone teasing me for the next few weeks, at least I'll be free of these cuffs. That's the great thing about living here. These guys are my brothers; we've all been there for each other when we've hit rock bottom, and while we annoy the crap out of each other, we don't judge.

I'd trust these guys with my life.

And, uh, in all my naked glory.

"Hey," I shout. "Come give me a hand."

Given Madden, one of my roommates, is a nudist, we're all used to seeing a bit of peen. It's more the embarrassment of being so easily manipulated that's sitting wrong, as well as the … well, the pictures. The helplessness. *Urg, don't think about it.*

"Hey, what's—*oh my god!*"

Oh nooo.

Out of all the guys I live with, that horrified tone is barely recognizable, which makes it easiest to pick.

Molly. The new guy.

Okay, so not *all* of my roommates are brothers to me. Gabe didn't move out that long ago, and Molly is so quiet I forget he's here half the time.

I try for a winning smile, even though this definitely isn't a winning scenario, and hope he's still there. "I've gotten myself into a situation."

"Holy shit." And he must run across the room because one moment, his voice is by my door, and the next, his soft, cold fingers are pushing up the blindfold, revealing big eyes filled with concern. "Are you okay?"

"How about you ask me that again when I'm not starfishing naked for you?"

"Right. Yes." He goes to glance downward but rips his eyes back to my face. "What do you need?"

"The keys are in the drawer." I nod toward my bedside table, and Molly hurries to it.

"How did you end up like this?" he asks, digging through the mess, floppy mop of brown hair falling over his forehead.

"A hookup gone bad."

He throws me a sympathetic look before delicately moving my Fleshlight to the side. "What the hell happened to make him leave you like this?" Molly successfully finds the keys and comes back over to the bed.

I try to shrug, but it's too hard with my hands secured over my head. "Didn't call his friend back or something. It's so—"

"Oh." Molly straightens, face pulling tight. "So you deserve this."

"Wait? What?"

He mouths wordlessly at me for a moment. "What *is it* with men?" he explodes, and it's only this uncharacteristic tone that stops me from pointing out that he's a man too. "You go on a nice date, send them flowers, show up at their work to surprise them with lunch. You call and send texts and make sure they *know* you're interested, then the second you have sex with them —*pow*! All over. Like they never existed. I'm sick of the games. You're all the same." Then Molly tosses the keys on the bed and stalks toward the door.

"Wait! Whoa, hold up!"

"You're part of the problem."

"I didn't ask someone to tie me up and take naked pictures of me, okay? There's no excuse for that, no matter what I did or didn't do to his friend."

Molly turns slowly back toward me, pretty eyes still narrowed. "Photos?"

"Yeah." My gut turns over itself again. "I don't want to talk about it. Can you please just unlock my arms?"

And clearly, he's been taking lessons from Madden as well because he sucks down a deep breath and moves closer. He picks up the keys, hesitates a second, then grabs my sheet and drapes it over my groin.

5

"I'm sorry," he whispers, turning his attention to my wrists.

"Yeah ..." I cut him a look. "Me too." And because I'm not going anywhere in a hurry, I add, "I'm getting the impression you've been through something."

"You could say that." And after him word vomiting on me, he's surprisingly restrained now.

"Need to talk it out?"

My first wrist clicks free of the handcuff, and before I can tell him that I've got it from here, Molly leans over me to unlock the other. His sweet scent washes over me, and while he'd been a good boy and stopped himself from checking out my dick earlier, my gaze isn't as controlled. His shirt lifts, revealing a slice of soft-looking, lightly tanned skin hovering mere inches above me.

Now is not the time to get hard.

"I'm okay," Molly says, and I call bull crap based on all that oversharing, but what am I supposed to say? My second wrist frees, and Molly immediately turns his attention to my leg.

It's on the tip of my tongue again to tell him I've got it, but his hand on my calf stops me. I'm a sensory guy, and it feels incredible to be touched. Fingertips over hair, skimming near my ankle. After what I've been through today, I can give myself this moment, at least.

He finishes one leg, and I'm almost sad when he unlocks the other, then rubs his hands gently over my ankle before letting go.

Instead of leaving, he settles on the side of my bed. "Do *you* need to talk?"

Immediately, my face flushes red, and I curse my stupid pale skin. "I'm good."

"It's okay if you're not. I imagine it felt violating."

I sigh and sit up, pulling the sheet more securely over me.

"Yeah. A little." More than a little, but I'm not going to let on how much it got to me.

We're quiet for a moment, one of his feet bouncing up and down on the floor. "Okay. Well. If you need me …"

"Thank you." Almost forgot that. "And sorry guys have been donkey's breath to you."

His lips twitch. "Donkey's breath?"

"I prefer to get colorful with my insults rather than dropping curses all over the place."

Molly nods, brown mop swaying with the movement. "They really have been donkey's breath. I mean, I've had my donkey moments too though. But as a whole … men suck."

"Date women?"

"Gay," he says, looking miserable. "I thought dating older men would cut out the bullshit, but so far, it hasn't helped."

"Why?"

"Because either they know *more* bullshit, or … let's just say I moved for a reason, okay?"

"Ah, but now you've gotten me curious."

"Says the guy I found tied naked to his bed." He laughs and stands, and for the first time since he's moved in, I check him out properly. He's a cute little thing, kinda like my foster brother Xander, only Molly's tan and has light muscles to Xander's thin frame.

"Fair point."

Molly gets all the way to my door before he pauses again. "I know we're not friends, I guess. But if you need to talk—"

"Noted. Oh! And, hey, please don't mention this to the others."

"Why? I thought you knew everything about each other."

"And we do, but …" My eyes flick up to meet his soft ones. "I don't want to talk about it."

"I get it."

"Thanks. And really, Molly, I owe you."

Chapter 2

MOLLY

"How are you settling in?" Madden asks from his yoga mat on the grass beside me. Only when I shift into downward dog, I don't realize I'm setting myself up for a front-row view of his legs in the air, ass spread open.

I sigh. "Aren't you afraid of getting skin cancer in your crack?"

"Nah, five minutes of sun a day is good for the soul. The ass-soul."

"What did you do during winter?"

"Same thing." He lifts his head to grin at me from between his legs. "I just had to recover my balls when I was finished." Those same balls that I'm trying very, very hard not to notice right now.

Madden and I went to college together, and even though he was better friends with my bestie, Will, we haven't lost contact since. So when I called him one night after an epic fuckup that was totally my fault, he suggested I pack up my life and move across the country for a fresh start.

It feels like I've run away from all of my problems, but my hometown was feeling too small. Too stifling. I had no idea what I was moving *to*, but I've only been here a few weeks, and I already know I'm going to like it.

Madden lets out a long groan and releases his ankles, feet dropping back onto the mat. "Can't help but notice you avoided my question about settling in. Anyone giving you shit?"

I laugh and straighten, stretching out my back before sitting down cross-legged beside him. "Nothing like that. I'm just very much the outsider here. I feel like I'm living with someone's ghost."

Madden frowns. "What the hell does that even mean?"

"Like … the room was always Gabe's. He's gone now, and Christian's traveling. Rush is …" I pause, not even sure how to describe Rush. "Unpredictable with when he'll show up. Seven and Xander are like …"

"Brothers?"

"They seem closer than that."

"It's not romantic if that's what you think."

"No. And I know. I actually think it's super sweet, but like, you all have your place in this house. You all fit. I'm not saying I don't appreciate being here, because I definitely do. I think it'll just take some adjusting."

"That's what I love about you, Mols. Always so positive."

If he knew about my mini breakdown before I left Kilborough, I doubt he'd be saying the same thing. "Not as much recently, but I'm hoping to get that back."

"Don't put too much pressure on yourself. We all go through changes in life."

"I'll say." I reach out a foot to nudge his bare thigh. "Nudist, huh?"

"Nudist, naturalist. Whatever you want to call it."

"I never would have picked this in college."

"Yeah, but in college, I was headed for the MLB and so uptight about my future and making it. After the injury, the more I looked into holistic medicines and natural living, it made me happy, you know?"

"Full-blown hippy."

Well, as hippy as a dude-bro can be.

Madden lets out an enormous laugh that hasn't changed. "Totally am. No shame in my game."

"I think it's cool."

"Thanks. It's always nice when people try to keep an open mind rather than assuming I'm weird."

"Oh, no. You're definitely weird. But not because of the naked thing."

Madden shoves me. "That's it. I'm not introducing you to any of the Daddies that I work with."

"Urg. Mean." I pretend to pout, but he's already set me up on a blind date with one of them next week. The guy's not an actual Daddy, thankfully, because I'm not into kink, but I do like my men older. Or at least, I thought I did.

I don't know what to think anymore.

Madden shifts, and his dick falls against his thigh. I've been doing so well to not stare at him naked, but the movement triggers a memory I've tried to lock down tight.

Seven. Spread-eagled on his bed. Immobilized. Large, tattooed body on full display ... along with a sneaky little surprise.

I lick my lips and flick my gaze to Madden and away again. "Hey, random question ..."

"Shoot."

"You, uh, ever ..."

"Hmm?"

"Have you been with someone who has a Jacob's ladder piercing?"

Madden slaps a hand over his mouth and points at me. "You talking about Seven?"

"You *know*?"

"Of course *I* know," he says like it's the most normal thing in the world. "How do *you* know?"

Okay, this is a question I didn't see coming, and even though I don't know him well, I'm not about to rat Seven out when I promised I'd keep his secret. "I ... walked in on him in the shower."

Madden's eyes squint up. "I still don't get—"

"He was hard," I rush out, my cheeks getting hot. "Okay? Can we just ... move on? Please."

"Did you have sex with him?" Madden asks. "Is that what your question was about? Because, dude, I told you. We don't sleep with each other. I can allow you the one freebie—like a welcome gift—but we're a family here. That's ... it's weird. And it doesn't work if we want things to stay simple."

I flop back on my mat. "Let's pretend I never asked. Better yet, can I move back to Kilborough? I'm done. I'm sooo done."

Madden cracks up laughing. "Fine. Relax. You didn't sleep with him. I almost want to tell you that you *should* since you're suddenly so interested in it. I gotta tell you, it's gonna be a whole lot harder to find an older guy with one of those if that's suddenly what you're interested in, but I'm up for the challenge."

"I don't want someone with a piercing. I was curious. Like, doesn't it hurt? How does it not get ripped out? Can you even *do* anal with them? How doesn't it hurt ... *someone*?"

A cool chuckle comes from the back porch, and I glance up to see one of our other roommates there. Xander is adorable, with blue hair and freckles and super-pale skin. Out of all my new roommates, he's been the easiest to get to know because Xander doesn't have a filter.

He jogs down the stairs and wriggles into the gap between me and Madden before pulling Madden's arm around his shoulders. "I've asked Seven all about it if you want to know."

Aaand of course he heard all that.

"It wasn't … I didn't mean Seven. I was just … curious …"

Xander snorts. "I was curious too, which is why I used to perve on him changing when we lived with our fosters."

I blink at him, waiting for him to drop the part where he's joking.

Xander smiles back innocently.

"You used to *spy* on him?"

"If I asked him to show me, he would have. I just didn't want to make things awkward. Besides, he only had the one piercing back then. He has two more now."

"And you've seen them?"

"Not the new ones." He leans closer, cherry-scented lip gloss invading my nose. "You wanna know what it's like?"

Him talking about Seven having sex? I want to say no, but I'm strangely intrigued by this. I've heard about the piercings before, but I've never known anyone to have them outside of porn. And come to think of it, I don't think any of the porn stars I watch are pierced either. Xander's studying me so closely I can't even lie.

I groan and cover my heating face. "Yes, tell me. I wanna know."

Xander laughs. "Seven said he's gotta be more careful when it comes to anal, but apparently, it makes everything a lot more sensitive for him, and for the guys he's with, it's like a ribbed condom—extreme edition."

"Ah, right." I peek up at him, trying to read if it's weird for him to talk about. I know Xander and Seven are close—I've seen Xander mid-freak-out and the way Seven takes care of him, and I can't stop myself from wondering if there's something there. Normally I'm not a nosy person, but turns out finding my roommate tied up naked to a bed gets me curious about the guy.

"Is that weird for you?" I ask.

"Why?"

"Aren't you ... are you—"

"Into him?" Xander guesses.

I nod, hoping my nosiness isn't about to make him pissy with me. Xander's like a cute puppy you don't want to make upset.

"Not like that."

Not like that? How do I interpret that answer?

"Well, that's enough curiosity for one morning," I say. "I need to get ready for work."

And by "get ready," I mean shower, change, and pull up at the desk I've set up in one of the bedrooms. Big-Boned Bertha, as they call the house, has ten bedrooms. There's six of us roommates, and then one room is used for Rush's atelier, one for Xander's art studio, a junk room, and an office that Seven and I are both set up in.

I've been in Seattle for close to a month now, and while I'm missing home—my dad and best friend most of all—I think I'm loving the change.

It's a beautiful city, and Madden's been taking me out to explore most weekends, but while I have it made with freelance work, I almost wish I worked in an office. With people. Outside of the house.

Until I have my date next week, my roommates will have to be it when it comes to filling my social needs. And considering how different they all are, it's working so far.

I just wish I didn't feel like the odd one out.

Chapter 3

SEVEN

The low buzz of the tattoo machine fills the room, a constant hum of background noise as I zone in and focus on my art. Being a tattoo artist wasn't on my dream board as a kid, but it suits me. Plus, I get cheap ink, which is a bonus, because the amount I have already would have sent me to the poor house.

Or … the *poorer* house.

Because I'm not exactly bathing in Benjamins each night.

Not like my roommate Christian, who met his literal Prince Charming, complete with fairy-tale-ish wedding.

And I currently have Princess Charming under my needle.

"I swear you're making it hurt more on purpose," Elle mutters from where she's lying facedown in my chair. "It wasn't like this last time."

"Last time, we started with your butt cheek. More fat there, so it didn't hurt as much."

"Wow. You're causing me physical harm *and* giving me body issues."

"Want me to start on childhood trauma too?" I ask in a baby voice. "I have a lot of experiences to draw from."

"That's one of the things I hate about you." Elle sighs. "You make my childhood look trivial. It's not good for my dramatics."

I smirk, wiping down her art so I can see it better. "Shoot, sorry, let me just pop back in time and tell my sperm donor *not* to beat me as a kid and send me into the foster system for my own protection, which actually only made things worse. Elle can't stand not having the worst childhood."

"Much better," she says, resting her shaved head on her crossed arms, British accent coming out posher than usual. "You're finally starting to appreciate how hard it was growing up with any and everything I could ever want."

When I first met Elle, we'd tried going on a date and spent the whole time one-upping each other on our crummy families. She concedes I win, but in reality, we both know it's not a competition. Crummy is crummy. There are different levels, sure, but everyone's trauma is valid.

And thankfully, Elle has as morbid a sense of humor about hers as I do mine.

It's why we immediately clicked.

It's also why we steered hard away from any kind of relationship. Messed up recognized messed up, and we're both too emotionally damaged for more than a screwy friendship. You can't build foundations on rocky soil and all that.

We're both hard edges and snark, who don't have the energy to take anything too seriously. It's left me kinda numb to a lot of things and her feeling too much that she keeps locked away until it explodes.

Honestly, we should both be in therapy, but until we pull our heads out of delusions, we have each other.

She hisses loudly. "What in the fuck are you doing back there?"

"My job."

"Your job sucks. You suck. Why did I let you talk me into this?"

"Pretty sure you're the one who was all *design me a tattoo that will immediately repel all the misogynists that sneak past my sensors, Seven*, and now I've gone and done that, you're still complaining. Can't win with you."

"I'm not going to be able to sit down tonight, am I?"

I laugh, remembering the hemorrhoid donut I convinced her that she needed the last time. It's tempting to tell her to do that again, but given I'm working mostly on her lower back, I doubt I'll be able to get away with it twice. "Nah, you shouldn't notice this too much unless you sleep on your back."

"Or get plowed up against a wall," she muses.

"Yeah, I'd suggest trying to avoid that until it's healed over." I start adding the tiny spots of color to finish it off. "Interesting that you wanted this near your bum and not your vagina though. Don't the misogynists usually go for your snatch?"

"You'd be surprised."

Yikes.

I finish the color and check the design over to make sure it doesn't need any touch-ups, but I nailed it, if I say so myself.

"Wanna see?"

"Fuck yes." She climbs off the bed, and we cross the room to the full-height mirror on the wall.

Elle turns, and the second she sees it, she *cackles*. "Oh, this is absolutely perfect, Seven."

It's a male pinup model, hairy legs, bulging jock, one nipple peeking over the top of his corset. And wrapped around the pole he's holding on to are the words *You're about to fuck a feminist, and she's rich enough to sue.* The pinup man is wearing sparkly red heels and standing on a rainbow brick road that leads all the way down over her butt.

"You really didn't peek?" I ask.

"Oh, no, I totally did. I was curious how making me look like I fart rainbows fit the brief." She turns to me with a wide smile, septum piercing almost touching her top lip, and pulls me into a hug. "I love it."

"Amazing." I shift back. "Now, do you want to put on pants?"

Elle pulls away with an eye roll and grabs her panties. "You never tell Madden to put on clothes."

"Most of the time, I don't notice he's not wearing any." Once she's back in her thong, I cover the tattoo and get started on cleaning my workstation.

"You got plans later?" she asks. "I'm free for dinner if you are."

I hum as I grab my phone to check if I have any messages from Xander. The screen is cluttered with social media mentions and nothing else, which means he's had a good day. Like it always does, the knot in my chest loosens. "Looks like I'm good."

"Excellent. You can fill me in on that twink you left with the other night."

I freeze midway to picking up an ink canister. "Ah …"

"What?"

"Nothing. It … let's just say it was a bust."

"Really?" She narrows her heavily lined eyes. "But he was so into you."

Elle's not an idiot, even though people try to treat her like one. She's currently working as a paralegal because she studied law at Cambridge and now has a bunch of hoops to jump through in order to practice here.

It's obvious she knows *something* happened, but I'm not sure I want to get into what. It was bad enough that Molly found me so vulnerable, and I've spent the last few days waiting to see if anyone in the house was going to bring it up.

So far, it seems like he kept his word.

And yet, I think out of everyone, she'd get it.

"Actually," I say, keeping my stare pinned on my tattoo machine as I disinfect it. "He wasn't interested at all. He was there as revenge."

"What in the hell do you mean?"

"Long story short: his friend was having kittens because he thought we were dating when we weren't, so twinkity tied me up and took a bunch of photos of me naked. Even after I told him to stop." Just saying the words makes my throat uncomfortably tight. I hate being weak. I hate even more having to admit that to someone. Like I've cut myself open and held up my heart for inspection.

"Excuse me, you're going to have to repeat that fucked-up story you just told because there's no way I could have heard you properly."

Her indignation makes me smile. "Nah, I think you got it."

"How goddamn *dare* he?"

I shrug. "He dared, and now it's done. Not much I can do about it."

Elle pulls me into a hug again, but this time, the extra *oomph* she puts into it makes me feel like she's trying to hold me together.

"Okay, okay," I say, stepping away and trying not to feel too awkward. "It happened. It's over."

"It certainly is not. We need to find this piece of excrement and delete those images from his phone. He has no right to do that, and not only is it morally corrupt, it's illegal. Could you imagine the public outrage if a man did that to a woman?"

"Yeah, but … I consented to getting naked. You know what people will say."

"And I also don't give a hoot what people will say. Naked or not, he took advantage of you. You're allowed to be pissed at that. We all deserve agency over our own bodies."

My neck grows hot at the acknowledgment, but it'll take more than a pep talk for me to agree with her. Externally, at least. Because I do agree with everything she's saying, but being vulnerable doesn't fit into the concept of "being a man" that I was raised with. I can recognize that's about as valid as Xander's medical anxiety episodes, where his body tricks him into thinking he's dying, but that doesn't make it any easier to shift. Habits die hard. Especially when they've been beaten into you.

It's my job to keep my mouth closed about myself and to protect everyone around me.

"You should file charges. This falls under revenge porn," she says.

"That's a thing?"

Her lips curl. "It's not a thing that's prosecuted anywhere near fairly enough, and with you being a man, there will be stigmas involved, but—"

"No."

"Seven—"

"I don't want to go through all that."

She chews on her bottom lip for a moment, and I recognize that look.

"What are you thinking about?"

"I don't think we should let this drop."

"I don't see a lot of options here."

"What's the name of the guy who thought you two were dating?" she asks.

I tell her, and it takes her two seconds to find his social media pages.

"Know where he lives?" she asks.

"If he hasn't moved, yeah."

"Then let me swing by my place on the way."

"You want to *go* there?"

"Of course I do. We're going to confront that SOB and make sure he gets his little friend to delete the photos."

"Elle …"

"Don't 'Elle' me, mister. This bullshit is *not* being allowed to happen. Not on my watch."

I love how indignant she's getting on my behalf. "I don't see how anything we say will make a difference. I mean, I could tackle him while you delete the photos, but even then— how do we know the guy sent them to Eddie? What if they're saved to the cloud? There are so many different options these days. They have the images—it's too late."

"It's never too late, come on."

Elle drags me out to her car, and after stopping by her place for long enough for Elle to tone down her makeup, put on a wig, take out her piercing, and change into a suit that probably costs more than my monthly utilities, we're on the road again.

"So …" I wave a hand over her. "What's all this?"

"This is Work Elle. And today, I'm your legal representation."

"Stuff a duck."

She snorts. "I don't recommend *that.*"

"There's no way he's going to think I lawyered up for this."

"You sure? People are pretty stupid."

"Okay, but why the wig?"

She pats it gently. "Men trust women with hair."

I laugh and direct her to the U-District because, hey, she's on a roll, and if she can get these photos gone, I'm not about to fight her on it. I had a boring afternoon ahead of me anyway, so at least this will give it some spice.

"How did you get out of the handcuffs anyway?" Elle asks as she drives.

I'm hit with a flash of Molly's bare stomach. "New roommate was home."

"Shit, that was lucky."

"Sure. Lucky."

Her face falls, clearly misinterpreting my reply. "Obviously it would have been better that none of it happened in the first place. I'm only saying—"

"It's fine." Not only do I have to remember lying there helpless, I've been having inappropriate thoughts about my roommate ever since.

When we pull up to Eddie's apartment block, his car is sitting on the street. "Looks like he's home."

"Excellent." She jumps out of her Audi, straightens her suit jacket, and waves at me to lead the way. Out of all my nightmares, this sits high on my absolutely trucking not list. Facing an ex-hookup with a grudge. Yet I walk ahead anyway, almost curious to see where this goes and trying not to feel sick over the whole situation.

Eddie's barely opened his door, all floppy hair and curious eyes, when Elle absolutely steamrolls him.

"I hear you've received illicit images of my client."

"I ... I ..."

"How long has it been since they were sent to you?"

"They ... *what* ..." He turns to me. "Seven? What's going on?"

"You sent your friend to hit on me and then take revenge pictures."

He pales so fast it's almost comical. "Oh, fuck."

"What do you plan on doing with these images?" Elle asks.

"N-nothing. I swear it." He turns his panicked expression from her to me again. "I *swear* it, Seven. I haven't sent them to anyone."

"But you admit to having them," Elle pushes.

He mouths wordlessly for a second. "Uh ... Well, I ..."

"Are you aware that the distribution of nonconsensual pornography is a federal offense?"

"I didn't distribute them."

"But your friend did, under your advisement. This doesn't look good for you."

Eddie can't answer. He's panting like he's about to hyperventilate.

I step forward before Elle can freak him out more. "I just want the pictures gone."

"Yeah. Okay." His eyes have tinged red as he scrambles for his phone, and I watch his hands shake as he opens his photos and starts hitting Delete.

"How can I trust you'll delete all of them?"

His attention flicks to Elle. "Mark used my phone, and these are the only copies. I swear."

"Finding it hard to believe you though."

Eddie swallows thickly. "I didn't mean any harm by it. I wanted to piss you off so you'd have to talk to me. That's all."

I stare at him like he's grown another head. "That doesn't make any sense."

"You don't know what it's like," he says pathetically.

"What *what's* like?"

"Seeing your boyfriend with someone else."

Even though I want to call him out for being a fulloping idiot, I soften my tone. "We weren't dating. I'm sorry if I gave you that impression, but it was never communicated. I was clear that casual was all I was interested in."

He glares at me. "Yeah. Okay."

"If you took that to mean something more, that's not on me."

"Not on *you*?" he asks, some spark jumping back into his voice. "Have you ever stopped, for just a second, and considered how you play with people's feelings? How you're sweet and kind and then go radio silent? You might say you want casual, but your actions say otherwise. And you're a fucking jerk for not picking that up." He shakes his phone at me. "They're gone. Now, get out of my house."

He all but shoves us out the door and slams it behind us.

"Standard victim-blaming behavior. Why is it so hard to find decent men?"

I ignore Elle's man hate for a second because I know it comes from daddy issues and isn't directed at me. "You think he really deleted them all?"

"Well, if you're not interested in filing charges, we have to take him at his word. He was pretty scared of me though, so there's a good chance you're fine."

I sigh and bury my hand in my hair. "That was kinda messed up."

"What was?"

"The whole thing about me leading people on."

"Nope. We're not getting into that. No means no, Seven. Don't let people convince you otherwise."

I huff a frustrated laugh as we head for the car. "It reminded me of something Molly said. About men playing games."

"*Were* you playing games with the guy?"

"*No.*" But the more I think about it, the less sure I am. "I don't *think* so."

"Well, if I can give you some professional advice … Be sure. You don't want to get into that kind of situation again."

"Yeah, yeah, I hear you."

"Good." She yanks the wig off and slides her sunglasses on. "Now, get in the car. I'll bill you for my services later."

"Sure. I'll pay you in good thoughts and feelings."

"We both know you're just as broke in those as actual funds. I'm not above you working off your debt." She pumps her eyebrows. "I could always use a pool boy."

Chapter 4

MOLLY

The man across from me smiles, lines around his eyes deepening, and I do my best to smile back. He's a total silver fox, super fucking attractive, and I have to hand it to Madden: he's given me exactly what I said I wanted.

The problem is, I don't think I actually *know* what I want.

I love the maturity of older guys, but it's so hard to find someone I can connect with. Common ground isn't something I find easily, and other than generic small talk, everything else leads to conversation that reminds me how different we are.

Gerald shifts forward, leaning over the table between us, eyes sliding down my exposed neck. "You want to get out of here?"

Heat floods my cheeks. This is never my favorite part of the conversation. "Actually, I don't, *you know*, on a first date."

"Ah." Gerald's gaze pings away from me, expression closing over. Oh, no. I recognize that look.

"I'm sorry?"

"Don't be." He holds up his hand, signaling for the bill.

"This has been fun, but if I'm honest, I don't waste time, kid. You're cute and all, but I'm not interested in, well ..." He waves a hand like he expects the silence to fill in the rest of his sentence. But it doesn't. And I can't.

Not interested in *what*? Dating? Commitment? *Me*?

And even though I wasn't sure about him to begin with, panic at being turned down takes over.

"Wait. We can. It's fine. I just know that usually when I do, men never call back, and so I was trying something different, but if that's a deal breaker for you ..." My throat is closing over, making it hard to get out the rest of my words.

Gerald's heavy eyebrows bristle. "No. If you have boundaries, you keep them. Just know that they might not always line up with what someone else is looking for."

"But I'm okay with hooking up!" I assure him, only I do it so loudly the people sitting at the tables either side of us glance over.

His posture tenses, making it clear he's noticed the attention. "Molly, that's enough."

"What? I'm not good enough for you?"

"Keep your voice down."

My eyes sting with tears. "One minute, you're asking me to leave with you, and now you don't want me to?"

"Molly ..."

"Take me home. You have my full permission. In fact, we don't even need to go that far—"

He abruptly stands and grabs his jacket.

"—they have bathrooms here!" I call to his retreating back.

It's not until I've lost sight of the back of his silver head that I realize it's gone completely quiet around me. So quiet I hear the old man a few tables over *tsk* in my direction.

All of my self-confidence tries to wither as I numbly stand and sniff those tears away. Embarrassment is not something that will fuck with me today. Shoulders straight, head high, I only need to hold the act until I'm out of here.

I'm past the staring tables.

Halfway across the dining room.

Almost to the doo—

"*Sir*. You can't leave until the bill is paid."

Fuck.

I glance over at the snooty voice, hoping it's directed at anyone other than me, but two steely eyes are narrowed my way.

I offer what I hope is a friendly smile. "The other gentleman didn't pay?" He'd specifically said it was his treat, and judging by the Rolex he was flashing around, he could certainly afford it.

"No." The server folds his arms.

"Right. Of course. Yes." I scramble for my wallet and thank the universe when I'm able to pull my card out without dropping it. "Here."

Then I'm left standing right in the walkway while he disappears with my card. I can still feel the weight of people watching me. He's sneering when he returns and hands it over.

"I assumed someone in your ... *profession* was happy with a twenty percent tip."

I have no clue what he's talking about as I take my card back. "Ah, yeah. Thanks. That's fine."

He eyes me. "I didn't realize they let people use an alias on credit cards these days. Happy hunting, *Molly*."

Then he turns and walks away.

I leave, face screwed up, confusion helping to keep the disappointment at bay until—

"He thought I was a hooker!"

The words burst from me, startling the family walking past, but I'm too mortified to care. I bolt for my car, yank the door open, and throw myself into the front seat before the tears can come.

As I sit there and sob, I can't work out what I'm so upset about. In college, I knew plenty of people who engaged in sex work to get by. Stripping and porn ... whatever. You do you. But thinking of all those eyes on me, all those people watching and judging and making assumptions about me ... thinking I'm *beneath* them.

Is that what Gerald thought too?

Holy shit. My face is burning, indignation racing through my veins and making my hands shake. Somehow, I get the car on and hit the road, heading home where I can hopefully spend the night in bed, nursing yet another broken heart.

It's not even broken over Gerald. It's broken for me and all the effort I put into dating and relationships only to never be enough. I want my person, but I'm beginning to feel like no person wants *me*.

My tears are sticky on my cheeks by the time I pull up home, and I've got a headache building behind my eyes. I park in the driveway, slam the door, then stomp my way inside. As much as I want to run and hide, I make out voices coming from a room down the hall, and I could swear Madden is one of them.

Madden, who set up this nightmare of a date to begin with.

And if I can't get ragey at *fucking* Gerald, I sure as hell can get ragey at *him*.

"What in the hell, Madden?" I gasp as soon as I reach the doorway. "Did you tell Gerald I was a ... a ... a *call boy*?"

"What?" He shoves to his feet. "What did he say to you?"

I open my mouth to relay everything, and—nothing comes to mind. "He ... he asked to leave together."

"Okay."

"And I said no ..."

Madden's soul almost leaves his body, I swear. "Did he try to force you?"

"*No*, nothing like that. He said it was fine and ended the date."

"And ..."

"*And* he was leaving!"

"Right ..." Madden's anger is being replaced by confusion.

"Without my number! He was leaving, and I told him that it was fine and I'd go home with him, but then people were staring, and he left anyway, even though I—" I clamp my hands over my mouth as the thought hits me that *maybe* I brought this on myself.

"Molly ..." Madden's lips curl at the corners. "What did you say?"

"Nothing."

A chuckle comes from behind Madden, drawing my attention to Seven and Xander.

"You *definitely* said something," Seven says.

I look from him to Xander to Madden.

"I maybe said he could do me in the bathrooms," I rush out. "And everyone heard me."

Madden's booming laugh starts first, followed by Seven's, and then ... I let out a huge breath of anxiety and join them.

"What is *wrong* with me?" I groan. "Why can't I be normal?"

"Normal's overrated," Xander says. "You're normal for you. If it helps, I would have accepted your offer."

Seven slaps his thigh. "Down, boy."

"*What?*" Xander's aqua eyes widen. "Molly's cute as hell. I would have."

"Thanks," I say around a grin, then flop onto the couch across from them. As much as laughing has helped, I'm ... tired. Ever since my college boyfriend cheated on me, I've been more than unlucky in love. It feels like I'm cursed some days.

Guys my own age are always too much of a mess in themselves for a relationship, so I made the decision to date older guys and keep striking out there as well. I don't know if I just keep picking the wrong men or the right ones aren't interested in someone like me—unless it's to spread my legs.

I thought I'd found someone back in Kilborough. Ford is one of my dad's friends. He's flirty and handsome and seemed like a no-nonsense type of guy. The kind of guy who'd treat me right. But then he went and found himself a boyfriend, and I was so bitter and petty and *over* never being enough that I'd kissed him.

Safe to say that hadn't gone well. His boyfriend had been ridiculously kind about it, and then I spent the next few months hiding from both of them until I could move here.

Where Seattle men aren't much different.

"Why am I so bad at this?" I ask no one in particular.

"You're not bad at it, Mols," Madden says, sitting down next to me. "You just haven't found your man. It'll happen."

"Not soon enough."

"How do we know he's not bad at it though?" Seven asks.

Xander's mouth drops. "Don't be mean."

"I'm not. It's a question." Everything about Seven is rough. From his dark red hair to his large frame to his tattoos and piercings, and then he looks at me with the kindest eyes I've ever seen. "You said a *lot* the other day about lunch dates and calling and messaging … In the nicest way possible, it sounded a little stalkerish, man."

"Stalkerish?"

"Don't freak out, I could be wrong. I obviously don't know you well, but if things are as sucky as you say … maybe it *is* you."

No one, and I mean literally no one, has ever even suggested that. My best friend Will is always on my side over how jerkishly I'm treated, Dad always tells me that if they're not interested, they don't deserve me, and even Madden, right now, is giving me empty platitudes.

I blink at Seven, my mouth hanging roughly around my ankles. "Me?"

"Whoa, don't look at me like that."

"Maybe you need to stop talking," Xander hisses, then turns to me. "Seven doesn't always watch his words."

He huffs. "I watch them, wiener brain. I just don't sugar-coat things like the rest of you."

"Some people like sugar."

"Then I'm not for them." Seven shrugs, and being so blatantly okay with not being everyone's cup of tea is something I wish I could have.

"Maybe it's me …" I mutter, turning it over in my head. "But how do I *know*?"

None of them have any answers. But they're listening. Supporting. Even if Seven's way of support might not be something I'm used to, it's nice that they're here for me when they don't know me that well.

"I think I'm going to go to bed, but thank you." I meet Seven's kind eyes and offer a small smile. "*Really.*"

Back in my room, I change out of my date clothes and into some pajama bottoms before climbing into bed. I showered before my date and don't have the energy to do it again.

Instead, I turn the memory of countless men over in my mind, over and over until Gerald and Ford erase the others and then … Seven.

Seven and his tattoos and muscles and blunt words.

Seven and his kind eyes.

Seven and his … *piercings.*

My cock gives a twitch at the memory, and I lift my blanket to stifle my laugh into it. I'm so immature.

Maybe that's what Gerald meant?

It's that thought that sobers me.

A soft creak and a flash of light lets me know someone's opened my door, but it closes quickly again. I squint into the darkness as light footsteps cross the room.

"What—"

My blanket lifts on one side, and then a warm body snuggles in beside me. Xander's floral scent washes over my bed.

"Are you okay?" he asks.

"You're ... in my bed?"

"I wanted to check on you."

"You, uh ... know we're not going to have sex. Right?" Because even though I don't actually think Xander was serious earlier, I want to make sure.

He wriggles closer. "I know. I know all about the rules. But also ..." His voice quiets. "I know what it's like. To feel like you'll never be good enough. Seven didn't mean what he said, and I wanted to make sure he didn't hurt you."

"He didn't," I say because I get the feeling Xander would go back out there and rip Seven's balls off. "But I think he might be onto something."

"You do?"

"Maybe." I suck in a long breath and roll onto my side to face him. "It can't be a coincidence that I keep striking out *so* much."

"Well, whatever you need, we're all here. You're only new, but you're our family now too. We look out for each other."

"Thanks. That means a lot."

His fingers find my hair in the dark. "You didn't even let us burrito blanket you. I miss Christian."

I smile at his pouty voice. "What's a blanket burrito?"

"Where we wrap you in a blanket really tight and smother you in hugs and nice words and then break out the rum."

"Christian used to need that a lot, did he?"

"Yeah ..." Xander's fingers keep stroking. "So much that I wondered if I'd develop a drinking problem."

My laugh bursts from me, quick and short. "Well, burrito blankets and rum might not be my thing, but I'm always okay with hugs."

"Right now?"

"Uh …"

Before I can answer, Xander rolls me over, crowds in behind me, and wraps his arms around my waist. "Go to sleep."

It takes me a second to work out what's happening, but then I relax into his hold. "Thanks."

"I've got you." He squeezes tighter for a second. "And, Molly? I'm so happy you're here."

I'm so happy you're here.

The worrying knot over not fitting in, over being the outsider, loosens just a bit.

I'm smiling as I close my eyes. "Good night, Xander."

"Night. Also, if I get a boner, I apologize in advance." He yawns. "I wake up with one. Just ignore it."

"Got it."

Fucking hell, these guys are so not what I was expecting.

Chapter 5

SEVEN

I cross my arms and lean against the doorframe, watching them sleep. It's no surprise to me that Xander is in here, but I'll be pissed with him if he propositions our new roomie. Molly wasn't in a good place last night, and maybe I should have been softer with my words or whatever, but … the guy is clueless as anything when it comes to dating.

If they weren't going to tell him, someone needed to.

I thought the creak as I pushed open the door would wake them up, but apparently not, so I give them another minute before knocking loudly on the wall. "Rise and shine."

There's some movement, one of them yawns, and then—

Molly sits bolt upright. "Nothing happened!"

I chuckle, and Xander joins me.

"Lies," Xander says. "We snuggled all night."

Molly's mouth drops, and he lets out a sweet, helpless noise.

"Don't worry," I assure him before he can start getting

worked up again. "Xander's snuggled with everyone in the house by this point."

Molly smirks. "Bit of a snuggle slut, huh?"

"It's about the only type of slut I am."

He's so dramatic. "One day, Z. Now, get your ass out."

Xander crosses his arms. "Why?"

"Because I wanna talk to Molly for a minute."

"And you can't do that with me here?"

"Nope."

"Rude." And even though I'm sure he thinks he's joking, he's not. Xander and I rarely keep things from each other, so even the smallest secrets hit him hard.

"There are some things that aren't your business."

He pretends to gasp. "If it's to do with you, it's always my business."

I cross the room to grab his arm and haul him out of bed. Then I throw him over my shoulder, carry him into the hall, and set him on his feet again.

Xander glares up at me.

I press a kiss to his forehead and lower my voice. "This isn't to do with me," I assure him. "And if Molly's okay with you knowing, you'll be the first one I tell."

"Okay." He turns to go but stops himself. "Be nice to him. He's … not like us."

"Like us?" I hitch up an eyebrow.

Xander twists his hands in front of him. "Damaged."

"Everyone's damaged in some way."

"Maybe, but if he is, his is like a bruise you have to poke at to bring out the pain."

"Whereas ours is like a gaping flesh wound?"

"You got it." He slaps my chest. "Be nice. And also, quick. I've been relatively healthy the last few days, so I expect I'll be dying anytime now."

Even though he's joking and even though we both laugh, my chest clenches a little as I watch him walk away. *Gaping flesh wound, indeed.*

Molly is up out of bed, T-shirt on and struggling to flatten his mop of brown hair when I step back into his room.

"You got a minute?"

"Yeah, of course." He's like an overeager puppy. All bright eyes and bouncy. I ... I don't know what to do with all that enthusiasm.

"So ... about last night ..."

"Don't worry about it. I actually think you were right. Or maybe onto something. It was valid anyway, so don't apologize for being honest."

Apologize? Huh. "Ah, I wasn't going to."

"Oh." His cute nose wrinkles with confusion, and he drops to sit on the side of his bed. "It's just ... when you said about last night, and then Xander was telling me not to worry about it like he thought you'd upset me, which you totally didn't, I guess I—"

"Maybe I should do the talking?"

Molly's mouth snaps closed against a giggle, and he hurries to nod.

I'm already regretting my idea. "I had a thought that might help you."

"Really?"

"You said you could be the problem but didn't know how to figure out if that was the case."

"Exactly. It's not like I can call all my failed dates and be like *do you have time to complete a short survey* and then start asking them questions."

"Well, no. But you can ask me."

That nose wrinkle again. "Ah, Seven? I might have seen you naked, but we've never actually dated."

And wonderful, we're bringing that up. How nice. I've already lost patience with this idea, but Molly helped me out, and I don't like being in his debt.

"The idea was that you use me as a surrogate boyfriend. We'll go on dates, you'll do everything you usually do, and I'll point out where you're—" Being clingy? Annoying? Stalkerish? "*Overenthusiastic*." How's that for thinking my words through, Z?

"You'd be my fake boyfriend?"

"Nuh-uh. No fake, no boyfriend. We're not going around pretending to keep up an act. If anyone asks, we give them the truth. But between the two of us, you'll act exactly like you would with any other guy you're dating."

He watches as he wriggles his toes into the carpet. "Sex?"

"Definitely not. Point out to me at which point you'd do it, and when you'd normally ask for it and whatever. But this is purely education. Like … training. I'm your dating coach."

"Dating coach." His smile is so big and pure I'm kinda understanding what Xander meant. Molly is *not* like us. "That sounds fun. But it's a big commitment for you. Why are you offering this?"

"You helped me, now I'm returning the favor."

"All I did was untie you."

"No, you helped me out of a gross situation and kept my secret. That's loyal as fudge."

"It's cute that you don't swear."

I scowl. "I'm not cute."

"Cute little Seven with his squeaky-clean mouth and tattoos and piercings."

I glance over at his tone. "Piercings?"

His face falls, and it's almost comical how animated he is. "Face piercings. Nose. And ears. And …"

"Dick?" I grin. "You looked, didn't you?"

"They *caught the light*."

I crack up laughing at how mortified he looks. He's tan

enough that he's not blushing, but I could swear his cheeks look darker. "Hey, if you want to catch the light as well, I'm happy to pierce you wherever you want."

"No way. It seems so painful. And you have to abstain from sex for—"

"You looked them up."

He shakes his head. "I'm going to stop talking now."

"You could just ask me, you know."

"He asked Madden."

We both turn to the voice in the doorway and find Xander there. He's dressed and smiling innocently. That damn innocent smile he gives me when he thinks it'll help him get away with anything. It usually does.

"What part of *private* don't you get?"

He shrugs. "I felt left out."

My hand scruffs through my hair as I debate whether to get mad at him or not. But … it's Xander. I understand him. I'm as attached to him as he is to me, and neither of us has been able to find a healthy balance with our relationship. Some days, I wonder if either of us even wants to.

"You can't just listen in on people's conversations," I point out, trying to be reasonable.

"But you're not people."

"It's okay," Molly says. "I don't mind."

"If you give Xander an inch, he'll take a mile," I caution.

But it's too late. Xander has already shuffled into the room and thrown himself over the bed.

"Are we still talking about the piercing?"

"How much did you hear?" I ask.

"No more piercing talk," Molly says. "Jesus. It's like you want to embarrass me."

"But it's cute when you're embarrassed." I use my best baby voice, echoing what he said before.

Unlike me, he doesn't deny it. Just bats his lashes, one hand propped under his chin. "I am cute, aren't I?"

"Oh no." I throw a look at Xander. "There's two of you."

And while they look nothing alike, the mischievous look they share is almost identical. Almost. Xander's has more of an edge to it, whereas Molly is pure sunshine.

I can't understand people like that. People whose lives aren't darkened by memories. People who let themselves be soft because they've never needed to develop armor. Xander gets me. It's why we're so close. He doesn't like being soft either, but some days, he doesn't have a choice. On those days, *I'm* his armor.

I turn and flop back on the bed as well, hit with a huff of Xander's familiar scent, along with a new, stronger one that must be Molly. It's kinda woodsy, maybe? Reminds me of the outdoors.

"Well, while you two take a nap in my bed, I'm getting ready for work," Molly says.

"No morning yoga with Madden today?" Xander asks, and I glance between them.

"You do morning yoga?"

"Some days."

"How do you know that?" I ask Xander.

His eyes drift closed, and it looks like he is, in fact, about to take a nap. "I perve on them from the porch."

"You're such a horndog. Get laid already."

"I tried. You remember how it went last time."

Yeah, that isn't a situation I want to be involved in ever, ever again.

"What happened?" Molly asks.

"He had a dirty mouth," Xander answers.

"You don't like dirty talk?"

"No, as in, his mouth looked gross. And his breath smelled. So I didn't want to kiss him, and when he told me I didn't need

38

to kiss him to suck his dick, apparently asking when he'd cleaned it last wasn't the right response."

"Aww … Xander."

"Don't pity him," I throw back, pushing up onto my elbows. "Pity *me*. He had a panic attack and locked himself in the guy's bathroom, so I had to go over there and save him from a perfectly innocent dude who did *not* have bad breath."

"Ah …" Molly grabs a pair of shorts out of his dresser. "I'm confused whose side I'm supposed to be on here, so I'm going to back out of my room and wish you both a fantastic day."

He flees, and I smile after him.

"So …" Xander says, crawling up the bed and climbing under Molly's sheets. "You guys were talking about your dick."

"Don't go there."

"Where? I don't know *what* you mean."

"How much did you hear?"

"Apparently not enough. Do you want to fuck him?"

I reach out blindly and pinch Xander's thigh. "No, you little snot."

"You should."

"We have a rule, which we all agreed to."

"It's a stupid rule."

"No, it's to make sure things don't get messy. We've got it good here. It's the first place that's ever felt like home. Even if I wanted to sleep with him, I wouldn't risk all that."

"True." He yawns widely.

"Don't you have work to do?"

"Maybe later."

I laugh and sit up, ripping the sheets off him again. "You know later is never a guarantee. Get to it. Your paintings aren't going to make themselves."

"You didn't tell me what you were talking about." His voice is sulky as he climbs out of the bed and stretches.

"I offered to help him out with this dating stuff. That's it."

"Wow."

"What?"

He whacks the side of my head. "That's stupidly thought-ful. Who would have ever known you had it in you? Well, with anyone but me."

Chapter 6

MOLLY

There's a light groan behind me, and I glance over to see Seven walk into our shared office. He's nursing a mug in one hand, flicking through his phone in the other, and isn't wearing anything other than the headphones around his neck and the sweats sitting low on his hips. Ink covers his abs, his chest, his neck, and creeps halfway up his head.

I've always had a thing for tattoos.

I tear my gaze away from shamelessly ogling him just as he glances up. He sets his mug down on his desk that's against the opposite wall of the room to mine and then approaches, gaze on my screen.

"That your work?"

It takes me a moment to follow what he's talking about.

I'd been taking a break between the web design I'm working on for one client and the logo for another to fuck around on my web comic, and an image I'm halfway through working on is sitting on my screen. "Yeah, I'm just playing around."

"Tentacle porn." He nods. "Hot."

"What? No!" I hurry to look back at my image to see how he got that impression, but Seven just laughs and ruffles my hair.

"I'm not going to kink shame."

"It's not tentacle porn, dammit."

"So what are those?" He points at the squiggly lines at the bottom of the screen.

"I'm not *finished* it."

"*Riiight* …"

I huff, clicking back over to the coffee house logo. "You're annoying."

"I've heard that before." He tilts his head, still looking at the screen. "It's good, but it's no sex fantasy."

I eat my laugh and nudge him. "Go away, I'm working."

Seven crosses to his desk and falls back into his chair. He's got a three-screen setup, gaming chair, and his desk forms a large L. Ever since I set up my workstation in here, I've been curious about what he needs all that for.

He pulls his headphones on before I can ask.

Even with him working and me apparently working, I can't stop throwing quick glances his way. His hands drum out the tune to whatever he's listening to between typing, and every now and then, he'll release a muffled laugh or scoff.

I could go and get my noise-canceling headphones as well, but I'm way too interested in whatever he's doing. Watching him, without him knowing I'm watching him, is like an anthropological study. A Seven in the wild. Relaxed and open and … *sexy*. So sexy.

I shouldn't interrupt. Obviously. He's wearing headphones for a reason. But whatever he's doing isn't work. So would it *really* be rude to say something? To creep up on him and read over his shoulder?

I chew on my bottom lip for a moment before finding his

social media profile and opening the chat box. If he's busy, he can ignore me.

> ME:
>
> What are you doing over there?

SEVEN:

Are you messaging me from across the room?

> ME:
>
> Are you ignoring my question from across the room?

SEVEN:

Never you mind, Tiny.

> ME:
>
> Ah, so it's something embarrassing?

SEVEN:

Well, it's not tentacle porn so I didn't think you'd be interested.

> ME:
>
> I'm beginning to suspect you're the one with a thing for the strange appendages.

SEVEN:

I'm an open-minded guy.

> ME:
>
> I've noticed.

His loud laugh crosses the space between us.

> ME:
>
> My curiosity is hurting. You don't want to hurt me, do you?

SEVEN:

You're talking to the wrong person if you're going for the guilt trip.

ME:

True. Madden can never resist that.

SEVEN:

Too bad I know that curiosity is good for the soul.

ME:

Mine is shriveling up.

SEVEN:

Something that bright? I doubt it.

A tickle of nerves crosses my stomach. Sure, I could get up and go over to his desk, answering my questions at once. I could take off his headphones and have a proper conversation instead of typing away and distracting myself, but talking to him like this is different. Seven's intimidating. I know he's not as scary as he looks, but it's not even that. He's … a force. Gravitational. I can't help but get distracted by his presence.

And he thinks I have a bright soul.

I'm not sure if that's something he'd ever say to me out loud, but I'm reluctant to break this little conversational spell.

ME:

Can you be bribed?

SEVEN:

Nope.

ME:

Bought?

SEVEN:

Sure. You buy me a new car and we'll talk.

ME:

Hot Wheels, okay?

His huff of a laugh comes again. It's a nice sound.

SEVEN:

Sorry, Tiny. No dice.

ME:

Tiny, huh?

SEVEN:

Hate to tell you, it's stuck now.

ME:

It's okay, I like nicknames.

I wait a minute, and even though he hearts the comment, he doesn't write back. So I take it that's a giant fucking *no* on sharing with me. I try not to let it distract me as I get back to my work.

After I graduated college, I worked in an office for two years and spent time building up my freelance clients before I moved back to Kilborough. I'm used to working with people around, I'm used to ignoring distractions and focusing on whatever's on my to-do list for the day, but Seven is a big distraction, and blocking him out is more challenging than I'm used to.

I think the main problem is that I'm so interested in him as a person. Madden told me Seven and Xander have been through some shit, were foster brothers together for a while, and that Seven's the kind of guy who'll do anything for anyone.

Will, my best friend, lived with me back home because his family were passive-aggressively homophobic, but other than him, I've never known anyone who had a horrible upbringing. It's a morbid fascination, and I hate myself for it, but I can't stop wondering about how Seven became Seven. How he and Xander grew into whatever massive thing there is between them.

My yearning to know them both deeper won't switch off.

An hour later, my chat notification sounds.

SEVEN:

So when are you going to ask me out?

I blink at the message, smile growing steadily larger until I catch on to what he's saying.

ME:

For the coaching?

SEVEN:

I figure we should start there, right? Do you normally ask out your dates, or do they do the planning?

ME:

Either works. I'm fine with both. Normally it's a mutual setup type thing where we plan to meet up for lunch or dinner, but if you want to go with a proper, planned-out date, we can do that too.

SEVEN:

I'm not a big restaurant guy.

ME:

That's okay! We can figure something else out.

SEVEN:

Well, what do you normally do on dates, though? We should probably look to make it as close to what you're used to if we want to make it worthwhile.

That's a good point, actually.

ME:

You're not going to like it.

SEVEN:

Restaurants?

ME:

At least ninety percent of the time, yeah.

SEVEN:

Come on, you can do better than that.

ME:

It's an easy go-to! And normally I don't make it past the first date, so I don't get a chance to stretch my date muscles.

SEVEN:

Fine. Just this once, the date's on me. Pay attention, grasshopper, and you just might learn something.

ME:

Now I'm grasshopper?

SEVEN:

Hey, those are tiny too.

It's my turn to heart his comment and close the chat. If we keep it up, I'm only going to push him to spill the date details, and I think I want to go into this surprised. It's not a real date, so who the fuck cares what he's actually got planned? As long as he does it because date planning isn't my thing, and if Seven wants to step up and get this lesson underway, I'm not going to fight him on it.

I chance a quick glance over my shoulder to make sure he's engrossed in … whatever … and then I open a blank page. I'm not entirely sure what I'm planning to draw when I get started, but the image morphs into an octopus with dicks instead of tentacles. Only seven of them. I draw a Jacob's ladder piercing on each appendage and then have one of the dicks holding up a sign that says, "thank you for the squid pro quo."

I'm just debating whether or not to send it or delete the damn thing off my computer when that huff of a laugh hits my ear, and I almost jump out of my chair. I didn't even hear him cross the room.

Seven leans in for a closer look, one elbow propped on the back of my chair and his other hand resting on my desk.

"You made an octo-seven."

"I was thinking of calling it a sevipus."

"It's me."

"Just need to give it a million and one tattoos."

He's grinning, staring at the screen for a full minute before his gaze drops to mine. "You're really good."

"It's a sevipus with dicks. Calm down. It's nothing special."

His kind eyes fill with amusement. "Why?"

"Because I was fucking around."

"That's what I do best." He holds out his arm at the display of random images. "Just because it's fun doesn't mean it's not art."

"That's true, but …" I wrinkle my nose and try to look at Sevipus as anything but a blob with multiple phalluses. "I don't think art is usually so pornographic."

"Tell that to the ancient Greeks."

He stands, finally giving me distance from him, but when he stretches his arms over his head, his whole torso pulls tight and long and … fuck. There's far too much body heat in this itty-bitty room.

"Can you send it to me when you're done?"

"Yeah, I was planning to."

He clasps me on the shoulder. "Look at our friendship flying ahead. We're already at the exchanging porn level."

"Oh, dear god."

"Wait until I tell everyone that you made porn specifically for me."

I roll my eyes and turn back to adding the tattoos. "And wait until I tell everyone I freed you from being tied naked to your bed."

"Oooh, harsh, Tiny."

"I might be little and sweet, but I know how to fight back."

"Good. Standing up for yourself is an important skill to have." His eyes drop briefly. "If you don't learn anything else from me, remember that."

Chapter 7

SEVEN

Give me a grind on the dance floor any night over this. One-on-one with a guy isn't my usual go-to, and while I have exactly zero clue what the hell we're supposed to talk about, I figure if I leave it up to Molly, it'll make it easier for me to give him notes. Planning the actual date isn't something I give too much thought to. I guess if it was real, I'd stress and get all up in my head over it, but it seems simple to me.

Plan something we can do together that's safe for a first date and gives Molly a chance to be ... *Molly*. The more "him" he is, the easier it'll be to see if he's the problem.

No, the date isn't something I'm worried about.

It's Xander.

The reason I don't bother with more than a hookup is because people don't get our relationship. If I'm in the middle of a date, the person I'm with doesn't appreciate being blown off because my roommate thinks he's dying, which says more about them than Xander. People call him a hypochondriac and say I shouldn't pander to him. They don't get it. Medical anxiety isn't something you can shut off, and I'm not about to abandon him because some person I'm interested in tells me to.

Our relationship is too strong. It intimidates people, and unfortunately, with how Xander is, he always has to come first. If I can't give my whole self to someone, I don't see a point in starting a relationship knowing I'll only disappoint them.

Xander and I are a package deal. No one will ever get that.

I only have to hope that Molly will understand that if I need to go, it has nothing to do with him.

Laying out ground rules is probably a good place to start this date.

I've told Molly to be ready by eight and organized for Rush, Madden, and Xander to go out together. I didn't go into details since I have no idea what Molly's telling people, and I know that if Xander senses there's fun going on, he'll want to stick around.

Even though it's not a real date, I get dressed up nice enough, then fuss with my hair and spray enough smelly shiz over myself that I'll probably remind Molly of those perfume kiosks you walk past in the mall.

It feels ridiculous as I head to Molly's room, where I told him we'd meet, just like if I was picking him up for a real date.

I've barely knocked when he throws the door open, enormous, adorable grin in place.

Oh, boy.

"Tell me you weren't standing there waiting," I say.

"Okay, but that would be a lie."

I laugh. "You look way overeager."

"I'm excited."

"It's not a real date."

"So? I'm *still* excited."

"Well, your nervous hovering got that message across loud and clear. Well done."

He cups his chin, index finger tapping the tip of his button nose. "So guys *don't* want to know that I'm excited?"

"That is kinda out of my wheelhouse, but I'd say your safest option is to play it cool. Obviously be happy to see them or whatever, but don't launch yourself at them the moment they get here."

"Right." It's like I can see the cogs working madly behind his eyes. Then he steps back suddenly and slams the door in my face.

Son of a gun, have I already scared him off?

I quickly cast my mind back over what I said, and *come on*, none of it was that bad. If Molly's going to be oversensitive—

"Please knock," comes through the door.

It takes me a good couple of seconds to realize he's serious. I lift my fist and drum out a quick tap.

Nothing.

No movement, no answer, just … silence.

It's right as I'm debating whether to knock again or head back to my room when Molly pulls open the door. His lips twitch a little, but he doesn't smile, just holds out his hand.

"Hello, nice to see you again."

Christ on a cracker, it's a do-over. "Yeah, you too." I take his hand, but instead of shaking it, I tug him in to land a quick kiss on his cheek. "You look good." And he does. His brown mop is styled, his clothes are tight but not obscene, and with him holding back his smile, his eyes forking shine.

Yeah, there's way too much goodness inside this guy.

He steps into the hall and closes his door, then clasps his hands in front of himself. There's nothing natural about the movement; it looks more like he's holding himself back.

I eye his body language and how tense he is, and then I break into laughter. "This isn't working."

"*What?*" He throws his hands up, the tension immediately

disappearing. "You said don't be overeager, so I'm toning it down, and now it's not working."

"Just … be you."

"I was being me."

"You were trying too hard."

"I *have* to try hard." He looks at me like he can't believe what I'm saying. "I'm not going to let a great guy go because I half-assed it."

"No, you're going to scare them away because you barnacle yourself to them and never let go."

Molly sags. "This is hopeless."

"No, Rachel, Omron, and Pilot's love triangle is hopeless. This is just a date."

"Who are Rachel, Omron, and Pilot?"

I blink at him with shock and betrayal. "The golden triangle of love interests? Kill Diver?"

Molly's eyebrows inch higher. "Who?"

"Wow. *Wow.* If this date was real, this is where I'd end it."

"I have no idea what you're talking about."

"Kill Diver. A video game turned book series turned movie franchise."

"Aww …" Molly links his hands together and rests his cheek on them. "Are you a little fanboy?"

"Shut up." I turn and start walking down the hall, Molly trailing after me. I'm not just *a* fanboy. I'm *the* fanboy. I've run the Kill Diver fandom site since I discovered the video game, and I have zero plans to stop. The series was there for me during the most dog breath time of my life, and now it's my happy place. The one thing I can sink into that's all mine.

"How tall are you?" Molly suddenly asks.

"Six three."

"Oh, shit."

"Gabe, the guy whose room you took, is six four. It's nice being the biggest person in the house now."

"What is with all you behemoths?"

"Childhood trauma's like fertilizer. It makes us grow big and tough."

Where I'm expecting that my comment will bring the mood down, Molly laughs. "Is that what stunted my growth?"

"Yep. A healthy family upbringing isn't good for you. Too much money saved in therapist fees and too much sleep at night when you should be up spiraling with anxiety."

"You do that often?"

"Nope. When I can't sleep, I bury myself in the internet."

"Healthy." He snorts.

"It's one of my better qualities."

We leave the house and start down the street.

"What are your other better qualities?" he asks.

It's just as I'm contemplating the question, Molly steps in close and wraps his arm through mine. I'm taken by surprise for a second, but when I look down at him and he stares patiently back, waiting for an answer, I let it go. Clearly, he gets comfortable easily on dates.

"Let's see … I'm loyal as a golden retriever, good in bed, got a nice-sized cock—"

Molly sniggers. "Now something I don't know."

I give him a nudge. "Right then, perve. I … I'll always be the first person to tell you when you have a dumb idea, but I'll one hundred percent back you if you choose to go through with it anyway."

"Ooh, that's a good one."

"And that's about all I have."

Molly squeezes my arm. "I'll see about that."

"Okay, then, what about you?"

"Good qualities?"

"Yup."

"I'm coming up empty." His whole face squishes up. "Sometimes I worry I'm not a good person."

At first, I think he must be joking until I see how serious he looks. "I'll bite. Why?"

"I'm like ... a people repellent."

"Yeah, I still need more."

"My college boyfriend cheated on me. A lot. We were going to get married and do all of those big forever commitment things, but turns out *I* was the guy on the side. He was in love with his high school boyfriend, and they never broke up. He was sleeping with us both at the same time, promising us both the same things. I'd be lying in bed with him after some really intense sex, and he'd be texting this guy how much he loved him and missed him. Obviously, I didn't know all that until after, but it was *mess-y*. Full-on Jerry Springer shitshow when it all came out."

Ouch. "That definitely sounds like a him problem though. He was a trash human."

"The thing is, I *never* would have guessed. Not in a million years. He came home with me to visit Dad and everything. Zero guilt. Zero shiftiness. Just a totally sweet guy who treated me like a prince."

"Maybe that's the problem."

"What do you mean?"

"Well, everyone has an ugly side. No one is that great all the time. Xander and I are as close as two people can be, but we still fight. I think your partner has to see the gum under your shoe of your personality, otherwise, how do they love you? This guy ... he knew his gum was nasty. He did everything he could to hide it from you. You didn't love him. You loved the guy he pretended to be."

"Hmm ... maybe."

"Hey." I tug him around to face me and stop walking. "I'm serious. There was nothing you did wrong."

He tilts his head, expression softening. "You really are loyal."

"And truthful."

"Okay, okay." Molly pulls me back along the path. "Either way, it tore me up. I wanted a mature guy, and my best friend is attracted to older men, so we bonded over going out and hooking up with proper grown guys."

"And how'd that go for you?"

"Obviously, not well."

"Just because you've been unlucky with guys doesn't mean you're repellent."

"It's not only them. I was close with Dad and my best friend, but whenever it's the three of us together, I might as well not be around."

What now?

"He'd rather Will was his son. And this guy back home who I was getting flirty with suddenly up and got himself a boyfriend. My friends from high school barely ever reached out to catch up—"

"What about Madden?"

"What about—"

"You've known him since college and haven't scared him off. Plus, you live with us now, and we stick together."

"For how long?"

"Forever. I'm serious. You're ours now, Tiny."

"How claimy of you." He hugs my arm tighter.

It sucks, though, that he feels the way he does. Maybe he's projecting and making more out of it than is there, but I learned a long time ago that feelings are valid. On a deep, intuitive level, we pick up on things, and even if we're misplaced with our assumptions, they're usually rooted in something.

Molly feels left out.

He feels like the outsider who no one wants.

I can tell him as much as I like that he's welcome with us and that we'll look after him, but words mean nothing. So we'll show him. Xander's great at that. Madden's already his friend.

I'll need to have a chat with Rush since his scatteredness can make him come across as aloof, but it's down to me and him to up our game and make sure Molly fits.

The rest of us are bonded through our sinkhole of an upbringing, but apparently, Molly isn't completely unaffected.

The sunshine boy has scars. They might not be as deep as mine and Xander's, but they're still scars.

We finish our lap of the block and pull up back out the front of Bertha. "Here we are."

Molly shoots me a confused look but doesn't question me. Just lets me lead him around the house to the back, where Madden and I nailed this date setup.

Chapter 8

MOLLY

"Umm, hello, gorgeous." My jaw drops, and I turn back to look at Seven with wide eyes.

He smirks. "You're only just checking me out now?"

"Oh no, I had that part covered as soon as I opened my door, but *this*. How did you do this without me seeing?"

Seven shrugs, hands in his pockets as he puts distance between us. "You're remarkably unobservant."

"Never been happier to be insulted."

"Not an insult. Just a fact. You look like your head's in the clouds most of the time."

"Noted." I nod, suddenly serious, trying to take the feedback on board. So far, this has been great. Mostly. I'm taking things in, but now the challenge will be whether I can put it into practice on my next date.

Though that date will be hard-pressed to beat how pretty *this* is.

Our backyard is sort of overgrown with huge trees and shrubbery, but my favorite of all of them is the reddish

Japanese maple. It has a perfect reading spot underneath that the leaves curl around, and right now, it's completely surrounded by twinkle lights.

Seven bows and pulls the hanging string of lights to the side. "After you."

I duck down and crawl under, my chest immediately filling with an *awwww*.

So I let it out.

"Seven …" I turn puppy eyes up at him as he drops onto the blanket beside me. There are cushions everywhere, and from inside the tree, it's like being surrounded by the night sky. Or inside a sparkly, leafy cave. *Oh!* Or a fairy grotto.

"What happened to playing it cool?" he asks.

"How am I supposed to play it cool when this is the single most romantic thing I've ever seen?"

He chuckles, deep and rich. "You're a cheap date."

"*Apparently*. Who needs a restaurant when you can throw me in the dark with some sparkly lights?"

"You're like a bird. They like shiny things too."

I stretch out on my side along the cushions. There's the faintest scent of wet earth, something floral, and then a whole lot of whatever it is Seven's wearing. He smells like a warm hug. "Now you have me here, are we just enjoying nature, or did you have an actual plan?"

"Wow. Suddenly, he's hard to please."

I gasp and whack his arm. "I just have more faith in you than that."

"Faith is what we're calling it, huh?" But he's smiling as he reaches for two shopping bags.

"What are in those?"

"And now we can add impatient to the list," he mutters.

"I'm going to go home with a complex tonight, aren't I?"

He glances over, sweet eyes assessing me, and without him needing to say anything, I know what he's looking for.

"I'm joking."

"Good. Because I don't want you feeling down about yourself. For what it's worth, the enthusiasm is kinda adorable, but I'm not the one trying to date you. We're looking to cover all bases here."

"Right. Yes." But I can't help craning my neck to try and get a glimpse in the bag.

Seven shoves a massive hand at my face, knocking me onto my back. "For that, I almost don't want to show you."

"If you have food and alcohol in there, I can't promise not to fall in love with you."

"Then things are about to get awkward because that's exactly what I have. Plus, an activity for later."

"*Activity?*" I perk up, suddenly excited and nervous about the thought of him bringing condoms and lube on the date. "Bit presumptuous, but I can roll with it."

"*What?*"

"I mean, I normally don't put out on a first date—"

I'm cut off by Seven's choking. "We said no sex stuff, remember? Now, get your head out of the dirty gutter and start stuffing your face."

He works quickly to pull out a huge variety of containers that he places between us and then tops up two glasses with wine. Wine isn't high on my list of likes, but it's alcohol, and I can use it at this point. I don't drink to get drunk anymore, but I like building up a happy buzz.

Seven stretches out across from me, his shoes bumping mine for a second before he pops open the first container. I help him, and I swear to Jesus, the man has thought of everything. Olives and sun-dried tomatoes, a million and one cheeses, crackers, cured meats, and sushi. Just about every berry I can think of, threaded lovingly onto sticks, whipped cream, chocolate, and an assortment of nuts.

"How many people are you expecting on this date?" I ask, peering at all the food.

"I eat a lot. I also didn't know what you ate aside from cereal, so I brought a bit of everything." Then he shakes the last container, and when he pops off the lid—

"Lucky Charms!"

He sets the container down in front of me. "Are you nine? How do you eat those?"

"Sweet tooth."

"Somehow, that doesn't surprise me."

I pick one up, and when I look over at him, he's watching me. Those sincere eyes and his soft smile are making this whole pretend-to-date thing so much easier. I throw a Lucky Charm up and catch it in my mouth.

"Nobody likes a show-off," Seven says.

I grin at him as I chew. "Admit it. You were impressed."

"Eh, I can think of better uses for my mouth."

Well, hello. I flutter my eyelashes at him. "And for mine?"

Seven's gaze drops to my lips, and I use the moment to grab another charm, hold it to my mouth, and scoop it up sexily with my tongue.

Only instead of licking it into my mouth, the charm drops, and a line of drool follows it.

"Oh my god" gets caught in my throat as I slap a hand over my mouth.

Seven loses his shit laughing. "That—whatever that was—needs to go top of your list of things to never happen again."

"I was trying to be sexy!"

"No. Hard no." He's holding his stomach now. "Molly, from the bottom of my heart, that was straight-up weird."

I pout. "Glad you're not being a dick about it."

He's still clearly struggling to keep a straight face when he reaches over and cups my cheeks. The poutiness immediately disappears at the feel of his big palms cradling me, and suddenly, Seven could say whatever he liked to me, and I wouldn't care.

His lips twitch, like he's fighting the amusement. "This is what happens when you try too hard. You're allowed to relax. I'm not running off."

"Really?"

"Well, maybe if you spit everywhere again, I will." Then he loses control and falls back, shaking with laughter again.

I decide to take the high road. "Not my fault you're immature."

"No way. If you'd witnessed that, you'd be in hysterics too."

"I'd never laugh at a date."

"Then you take them too seriously. Maybe that's part of your problem."

"Is it such a bad thing to want a first date with the possible love of my life to go smoothly?"

"Love of your life? What?" Seven rolls onto his side, finally back under control. "Do you go into every date thinking it's going to be forever?"

"How else would I approach it?"

"Ah, maybe for what it is. Meeting someone and finding out if you even like them as a human. Then going from there."

"Hmm ... maybe."

"If you're putting forever on a first date, no wonder you're cracking under the pressure."

"But it could be," I push. "You never know when you're going to be sitting across from your future husband. The future father of your kids."

"You want all that?"

"Absolutely."

He watches me for a moment. "What do you need before you can get to that point?"

"A boyfriend."

"And what do you need to do to get a boyfriend?"

I know where he's going with this. I sigh. "Nail the first date."

"Bingo. Now, I'm worried that you still haven't promised me not to slobber everywhere again."

I huff and place a hand over my heart. "I solemnly swear to keep all fluids inside of my body."

"Eh, I dunno that I'd go that far."

I break into giggles. "This isn't going well."

"Actually, I was just thinking it's one of the best dates I've had."

The fact I can pick up on sincerity in his tone makes me perk up. "It is?"

"Yep. I should probably tell you I can count the number of dates I've been on with two hands. But this is definitely top two. *Maybe* three."

"Well, my ego is safe with you around." I set the charms aside and start on some real food. And while Seven didn't know what I like, there isn't much here I'd pass up on. The tomatoes aren't for me, and there's one type of cheese that's a bit too strong, but I help out with everything else, and we make it through almost everything.

"You can put some food away," he comments as we pack up.

"I might be small, but it's not for a lack of trying. I take after my mom."

"Oh yeah?" He stacks the containers back into the bag. "You mentioned your dad before but not her …"

That's because I wouldn't know where to start. I give him a tight smile. "Not first-date conversation. Besides, I'm lucky to have an incredible dad, I know that."

"Sure, but one good parent doesn't halve the feelings of having a snot-face one too. I'd imagine."

"I'm sorry."

"Nah, don't be. I've got Z. And the rest of the Bertha guys.

You'll meet Aggy as soon as she's back from her trip, and trust me when I say she loves us more than any half-assed parent."

I've heard them mention their neighbor Agatha a few times. "That sounds nice."

"She'll love you too. And then you won't think it's so nice."

I laugh. "Why?"

"She's a cranky old bat." But even though his words might sound mean, there's clear affection behind them.

"A cranky old bat who you love?"

"Exactly. And when she's being especially batty, I wait until it's late and play my music right by her window."

"You don't react well to feelings, do you?"

"Nope," he says happily. "They're the worst."

My gaze flicks back to the bag again. "So … the activity?"

Seven pulls out a box, and when he gives it a shake, something rattles inside.

"Is that a puzzle?"

"Sure is."

"You want to do a puzzle on a date."

"Sure do. Now, get that judgment out of your tone." Seven lifts off the lid and dumps all the pieces on the ground.

"I can honestly say I've never had a date like this before."

He fist pumps. "Nailed it."

"Sure you did," I say, reaching over to pat his head.

He props the lid of the box against the tree trunk for us to use as a guide.

"One problem," I point out. "It'll be upside down for me."

Seven pats the place in front of him. "Come over here, then."

"And have you spoon me?"

"You'd love that." He winks. "But no, you're small enough to sit up."

Well, if he wants me closer, who am I to say no? I crawl to his side of the puzzle and sit in front of him. While we're not touching, there's something nice, something intimate, about having him curled around me like this. We work in silence.

"So why a puzzle?" I ask.

"No awkwardness."

"Except for the moment when you tell your date that you're doing a fucking puzzle."

His deep laugh fills my chest.

"This is the only time I've tried it, and I'd say we've gotten past the awkwardness well, wouldn't you?"

"True."

And when the silence falls again, I get what he means. We're concentrating, so there's none of that obsessive need to fill the silence. We work together, occasionally squabbling over where a piece goes. He talks a bit about Xander, and I tell him about Will, and for maybe the first date in a long time, I don't feel like my limbs are too big, like I can't control my body or my mouth. I'm actually able to enjoy myself.

And when I glance down at Seven, at his concentration lines and the way his tongue sticks out just a peek, I get the sneaking suspicion it's not the puzzle that's doing it.

Seven's an easy person to like.

Chapter 9

SEVEN

I wake up to Xander staring at me. At one point, it would have made me jump, but it happens so often now that I usually feel him before I open my eyes.

"Morning," I say, stretching my arms out.

"Morning."

"Are you dying?"

"Nope." He pops the *p*. "Except maybe over the idea that you went on a date. *You*."

I groan and cover my face with my arm. "Madden tell you?"

"Auntie Agatha, actually."

"How did she find out?"

"How did you think she wouldn't?"

I lower my arm again. "Some days, the whole living in each other's pockets thing wears thin."

"I like it."

"That's because you feel safe in there." A loud yawn rips through my body, and I stretch out over the bed. "It wasn't a date."

"Then what would you call it?"

"I'm helping him out."

"Uh-huh. Wink wink nudge nudge kind of helpful?"

"Do you make it your mission to be annoying?"

"Some days." Xander stares at me.

I stare back.

"Did you have sex?"

"Goose noose, what's with all the questions?"

"I'm *curious.*"

"No, you're nosy. There's nothing more to tell. He thinks he's bad at dating, so I'm helping out by telling him where he's going wrong."

Xander snuggles into my spare pillow. "That sounds oddly nice of you."

"Hey, I'm nice."

"To me."

"To lots of people."

He hums like he wants to disagree but can't be bothered. We know each other so well that he doesn't need to use words because I know what's going on in his head.

"I like him," Xander says.

"Who? Molly?"

"Yeah."

"Do you want to take over the dates with him, then?" I ask. But even when I say the words, I don't like them. If Xander has a thing for Molly, I'll back right the hell off, but … well, Molly's cool. He's easy. I don't see a lot of that in my life, and while this dumb date idea is a pain in the ass, it was nice to hang out with him a bit. Get to know someone new. Someone who doesn't already know every little thing about me.

Xander laughs. "And tell him what he's doing wrong? We both know I'd be hopeless at that."

"Well, the offer's there. Though, you should probably ask him on a real date."

Xander's frowning face pops up again. "What? Why?"

"You said you like him."

His pink lips form a little O. "Not like that. He's a sweetie though. I think he'd be good for *you*, actually."

"Please. You're enough of a handful."

"Yeah, but we're not dating." He chews on his lip for a moment. "You're allowed to do that, you know?"

"I know."

"So why don't you?"

"Why don't *you*?"

Xander snorts prettily. "We both know why. It's exhausting getting to know a guy and then scaring him off with my anxiety."

"They're all idiots if that's enough to scare them off."

"Agreed. But you don't have anxiety to scare people off."

"Just a crap attitude and terrible sense of humor." I'm a real catch. "Maybe I don't want to date. That's allowed too."

"Yeah …"

The unspoken conversation falls over us again though. Xander, feeling guilty that he's the reason I haven't found someone, and me, wanting to take that feeling away from him. He can't control anyone else's empathy. Anyone else's selfishness. I know dating me and getting him as a package deal would be hard to handle, but I make no apologies for that, and I don't want it any other way. If it means dying alone, I'll take it.

My perfect man would accept us both.

And I won't settle for anything less than perfect.

My phone dings with a message, and Xander grabs it before I can. He knows my passcode like I know his, and while I've never had secrets from him before, the second the image from Molly pops up, I wish we had a few more boundaries than we do.

"What … what is that?" Xander asks.

I chuckle and take the phone from him. "*That* is apparently a Sevipus."

"With your tattoos?"

"Yes."

"And a pun?"

"Uh-huh."

"And your dick?"

"Technically, I don't think it's my dick. Just the same piercings as mine."

Xander crawls over the top of me, wicked grin in place. "He's very obsessed with your cock."

"It's the piercings."

"I bet he'd suck it."

"Xander …"

"Do you think he's pretty?"

"No."

"Bullshit." Xander laughs. "He's very pretty. Very … *your type*."

"I'm not going to sleep with him."

"You should though."

"I know you're a big old virgin, but when it comes to sex, both people get a say."

"I bet he'd fuck you."

"You can't know that."

Xander crosses his arms over my chest. "If he asked you, would you?"

"That goes against Bertha rules."

"Fuck the rules. Fuck Molly. Fall in love. I want to be your best man."

"You already are my best man."

Xander huffs. "You know what I mean."

"I love you, but this conversation's gotta stop."

"Why?" He narrows his eyes. "You're thinking about it, aren't you?"

"I'm just trying to be nice to the guy. He's our family now. I want him to feel welcome."

"What's more welcoming than a rim job?"

I throw him off me before climbing out of bed. "How do I put up with you?"

"I'm extremely cute."

"And clingy … and needy …"

"Don't be mean."

I tilt my head. "Weren't we listing your good qualities?"

He preens. "For that, I'll get through a whole day without insulting Kill Diver."

"You know the way to my heart."

Xander chews on his painted thumbnail as he watches me hunt down clothes. He's wearing brightly colored thigh-high socks, a pink T-shirt, and short pajama bottoms with kittens on them. When Xander says he's cute, it's true. He makes sure of it. Always.

Considering he never knows when we're going to be rushing out the door with one of his medical anxiety attacks, he's always ready, even going so far as to get me to tattoo freckles on his nose last year.

I wanted to talk him out of it, but I didn't. When it comes to Xander, I can never say no.

"Seven …"

"Yeah?"

"If you *did* fall in love with Molly—"

"I already told you—"

"Yeah, yeah, not interested or whatever." He waves me away. "It's a hypothetical. Let's say you both fell in love and whatever …"

"You want to know where that leaves you?"

He hesitates for a second before he whispers, "Yes?"

I walk over and crouch in front of him. "Nothing changes."

Xander's aqua contacts study me. "How can you know?"

"Simple. I'm not capable of falling for someone who doesn't love you like I do."

"Yeah … that's what I worry about."

I press a kiss to his forehead. "You know it goes both ways."

He drops back onto the bed with a huff. "If the thought of sex with you didn't make me uncomfortable as hell, we'd be the perfect couple."

I snort. "We'd be the most dysfunctional couple."

"I guess we're destined to be bachelors for life."

And while I might not be dying to settle down or anything like that, I hope it isn't true. I want to have someone one day. I want that for Xander as well. He, out of everyone, deserves it.

"You know what?" he asks.

"Yeah?" I sling my clean clothes over my shoulder, ready to go shower.

"I think Molly loves me."

I almost roll my eyes. "You do, do you?"

"Yep. And if he doesn't, I'll annoy him until he does."

"I'm not sure that's how you get someone to love you, but what would I know?"

Xander's face screws up. "How else would you do it?"

"No clue." I shrug. "I don't think our way of escaping trauma together is for everyone."

"They don't know what they're missing."

I leave Xander in my room and head down the hall. I've got an early appointment today and then a back-to-back afternoon, so it's going to be a long morning of waiting around until things get busy.

I shoulder my way into the bathroom, immediately surrounded by a cloud of steam and then—

"Oh, shit," Molly gasps, foot on the side of the bath and razor poised over his smooth-as-glass balls.

Heat sweeps over me at the sight of his soft cock, his lean muscle, and small frame. Xander's right. Molly is *exactly* my type.

I tear my gaze from his light abs to focus on the way he's staring at me like Bambi.

"Ah, hey …" He very slowly lowers his foot and then clasps his hands in front of his junk.

"Watch that razor."

"Eeep." He tosses it in the sink, and I hand him a towel.

"Fun fact. That little knob on the back of the door handle? It's a lock. I tend to use it when I'm showering, jerking off, manscaping …"

"You're funny. I thought it *was* locked." But even when he wraps the towel around his narrow hips, it doesn't help. A trickle of water drips from his wet hair and slides over his left pec. I imagine following it with my tongue.

When I drag my gaze away, I find Molly's cheeks flushed and his teeth buried in his bottom lip.

"You didn't look at me like that on our date."

I stifle a groan. "You weren't standing in front of me naked, were you?"

"I didn't think nudity would bother you with Madden around."

"Yeah …" I can't stop myself from going back for another look. "Madden's not my type."

"But I am."

I groan, and not trusting myself to touch him, I grab the razor from the sink and poke him with the handle, nudging him toward the door. "Get out. I need to jerk off."

"But I didn't finish shaving my balls!"

"Don't need any more material, thank you."

He's laughing as I shove him into the hall and slam the door behind him. Then I turn the lock all the way like a normal human being.

Now I have to pray Xander never finds out about this.

Chapter 10

MOLLY

The house gets quiet during the day. Seven, Rush, and Madden are all at work, and Xander's either in his studio or sleeping or … I don't know. There are times when the house feels so alive and others when it's like this. Sleepy. Almost eerie.

I wonder what it was like when Christian and Gabe were here.

Footsteps come barreling down the stairs at the front of the house, and a moment later, Rush appears in the kitchen. He's a tall guy with a permanent five-o'clock shadow and the aura of someone completely fucking lost.

"Ah, hi," he says, blinking me into focus. Then he starts forward with his hand outstretched. "I'm Rush. Nice to meet you."

I shake his hand, trying not to laugh. "Molly. Nice to meet you. Again."

"Again, right … right … yes …" He looks around, knot between his eyebrows.

"Lost something?"

"Yeah, my phone. I slept through the alarm, and now I'm late for work."

"Your phone? Like … the one in your hand?"

Rush lifts the hand holding his phone and blinks at it. "Was I holding this the whole time I got dressed …" he mutters to himself.

"Want a coffee to go?" I offer.

"Please."

He sits down at the counter while I grab a to-go cup out of the cupboard and pour him a cup from the pot. "Sugar? Cream?"

"Just one sugar and some cold water. Thanks."

I follow his instructions, then give it a stir, pop on the lid, and hand it over.

Rush takes a long sip and lets his eyes fall closed. "Thanks, Molly, this is great."

"You're welcome."

He smiles at me, and I smile at him, and things get really awkward really quickly.

"Ah … you gonna go?" I ask.

"Oh. Did you need the kitchen?"

I swallow my laugh again. "I thought you were late for work?"

"Holy shit, *I am*. Thanks, Molly. I'll see you at Monopoly Monday later."

Rush runs from the room, and I don't have the heart to remind him it's Thursday.

I got most of my big jobs completed yesterday, and so I only have a couple of smaller ones going into the weekend. I'm just debating whether to put those off until Monday and to work on my graphic novel today when a voice comes from down the hall.

"Help … *Help!*"

I almost drop my coffee, setting it on the counter before I head toward Xander's voice.

"Molly!"

"Hey, hey, hey …" I call, pushing open the door. "I'm here. What's wrong?"

He blinks back tears. "Seven's not answering, and I've been bitten by something, and it *hurts*. My throat's closing up, Molly, I think I'm allergic."

When I first moved in, Madden warned me that Xander's delicate—his words—and that now and then, he'll have a medical anxiety attack where he thinks he's dying.

I'm ashamed to say that I blew the warning off, but as I watch, slack-jawed, as Xander gasps loudly, something deep in my gut twists.

Is this what he was talking about?

Did something actually bite Xander?

Fuck, *is* his throat swelling?

"It's okay, I'm here." I grab his shaking hand, scrambling to check him over with no clue what the hell I'm supposed to be looking for. He doesn't look like he's swelling or whatever, but what the hell would I know?

"Should I call an ambulance?" Holy hell, my voice is shrill.

Xander shakes his head, tears finally spilling over. "S-seven."

I scramble for Xander's phone and try Seven again.

Thankfully, this time he answers.

"Hey, Z, just with a client. Do you need me?"

"Xander's having a reaction to something and his throat's closing up and I think I should call an ambulance, but he said to call you."

There's a prolonged pause, which lasts way longer than any pause in an emergency should.

"*Hello?*" I shriek.

"I'm going to need you to calm down."

"Didn't you hear what I *said?*"

"I did. Now, I promise that he's in no immediate harm, but if you want to help, the only way you can do that is to breathe."

I suck down a shaky breath. "I'm breathing. Now what?"

The bastard actually laughs at me. "Another one."

"Seven!"

"Take another flipping breath, Molly."

He has no idea what he's asking me. Xander's gripping my hand tight, practically convulsing with the force of trying to get oxygen down, and my pulse is racing out of my goddamn ears, and he wants me to just breathe? Fucking *breathe?*

"Tell me what to do."

"I'm trying."

"No, you're not!"

"Look, I'll call Aggy to come over. She can help Xander until I'm there. I'll be ten minutes."

I force down a stubborn breath. "I can handle this."

"Don't sound like it to me."

"Goddamn it, he's going to pass out."

And the second the words are out of my mouth, Xander sways against me.

"For the love of goose pebbles, stop talking."

I huff and force down another breath.

"Listen carefully. Don't say anything alarmist or anything that'll give him ideas. He *knows* he's okay. Xander's perfectly aware of what's happening, but his brain is forcing these feelings onto him. The second he gets in a spiral like this, there's only one thing that will help."

"What?"

"He needs to go see Derek."

"Who the hell is that?"

"In Xander's phone, there's a contact 'for emergencies

GPD Pharmacy.' Call them and tell them Xander needs to come in and ask if Derek is available."

"And if he isn't?"

"He will be."

"But if he—"

"He *will* be. They know what to do."

"Okay. I'll call."

"Right. I'll meet you there."

"I *said* I can handle this, dammit. Stay with your client."

"Molly—"

"I'm serious."

Seven lets out a frustrated sound. "I … I can't."

"Don't make me blackmail you because I'll do it. Keep your ass at work. I've got this."

I hang up and find the number Seven mentioned, trying not to freak out when Xander slumps to the floor beside me. I'm shaking almost as much as him now, and while I *really, really fucking really* think the call I should be making is to a goddamn paramedic, I wait as patiently as I can until the line connects.

"George Park District Pharmacy."

"Umm, hi."

"Hi."

"I've got Xander here. Is, ah, Derek available?"

"Of course, sweetie. What are the symptoms?"

"He's been bitten by something and is having an allergic reaction."

"Not a problem. We'll be ready for him."

The line cuts out, and I stare at the phone for a second before turning back to Xander. He's on the floor, shivering uncontrollably.

His brain is forcing these feelings on him.

My heart sinks.

"Okay, up you get," I say.

I hook my arm around him and help him to his feet. He

can walk, thank god, and after strapping him into the front seat of my car, I jog around the hood to get behind the wheel, holding back the stress tears as best I can.

"Ah, where did you get bitten?"

"My ... ankle ..."

"Right. Umm." I cast my mind around for the limited first aid knowledge I have. "Pretty sure you're supposed to keep it elevated ... right?"

He lifts his foot onto the dash.

"Good."

Then I back out and follow the GPS directions to the pharmacy.

They'd been right in saying they'd be ready. As soon as we walk in, Xander's ushered away from the customers at the front of the store and into a back room. The woman's murmuring calming things as she helps him onto the bed, and then a man I'm assuming is Derek walks in the door.

He's tall with black hair, a scruffy jaw, and sharp brown eyes. Eyes that do a double take at the sight of me before he steps around me to get to Xander.

"Xander," he says in a smooth voice. "You've been bitten, and your body is simulating anaphylaxis, is that correct?"

Xander hurries to nod.

"I'm going to inspect the bite. Do you understand?"

Xander nods again.

"On his ankle," I say.

Derek throws me a quick smile before inspecting Xander's ankle. He shines a penlight on it before wiping over the site with an antibacterial wipe. The whole time, I'm expecting Derek to brush it off, to tell Xander he's fine and to go home, but he takes his time.

"I need you to open your mouth so I can look inside. Can you manage that?"

Xander's jaw drops open. Derek inspects from Xander's

tongue all the way to the back of his throat. Then he listens to Xander's pulse rate.

"Okay." Derek pulls a stool over to sit on. "After a thorough inspection, I've determined that you're not going into anaphylaxis shock. There's no closure of the throat, your tongue size hasn't increased, and the bite you've experienced looks to be that of a mosquito."

"A ... a mosquito?"

"Correct."

Xander's gasping takes a minute, but he manages to get it under control. He's pale and drawn as he wraps his arms around himself. "You're sure?"

"I am."

A shudder runs through him. "Why am I like this?" Xander's voice breaks, and he bows over, sobbing into his knees.

I'm about to start forward when Derek leans in closer and sets his hand on Xander's back. "You're in a safe space here. There's no judgment."

"*I'm* judging me."

"*Xander.*" Derek's tone hardens, and Xander finally looks up again. His eyes are red, and makeup is smeared under them.

"You are safe," Derek reminds him. "You are in control."

His voice is weak when he says, "Okay."

Derek drops his voice some more. "Have you done what we talked about? Did you call her?"

"I did, but I don't have the money. She's expensive."

"*All* psychologists are expensive."

Xander glances at Derek, face twisting into a dark expression I'm not used to seeing on him. "And that's why I'm still a headcase."

"What have I said about calling yourself that?"

Xander's empty gaze slides to me. "You agree with me, don't you, Molly?"

And while I think Xander's a lot of things—sweet, broken, confused, adorable—I don't think he's *that*.

I shake my head. "Actually, I think you're really brave."

Apparently, that's the right thing to say because Derek gives me a soft smile as Xander buries his face into his knees.

"Where's Seven?"

"At work."

Derek nods. "Good. Xander should have more than just him to rely on."

Chapter 11

SEVEN

It's killing me not to hear anything. My client knows something is up, but we don't talk about it. She just keeps throwing me concerned looks between flinching with pain. The way I'm fighting with myself to stop from running out of here is next-level, but Molly said he can handle it.

I don't believe him for a second, but I guess I'll find out soon enough.

Taking the gamble with Xander makes me feel like a failure. He needs me. If I could quit my job and make sure I'm always there for him, I would. But I need the money, and Suri pays well. Really gosh darn well.

So well that he expects bums in seats when we have a booking. The customers come first, and the few times I've had to ditch for Xander, he's been understanding but not impressed. He's never said a thing about me risking my job, but I also don't want to get to the point where he has to.

It's what stops me from leaving, no matter what Molly said.

And hey, by this point, we've got things down pat. Derek

will do his calming medical magic, and it'll get Xander back to himself. The day he had a panic attack while we waited for Gabe's antihistamines was probably the luckiest moment of our lives.

Those emergency visits were sending us both broke.

It's a pretty bleak day when the location of a panic attack is "lucky."

"There you go," I say, wiping off the woman's tattoo. She told me her name when she got here, but that information was lost the second I got the call from Molly—if only she'd had her own name tattooed on her instead of her kids'.

"Thank you. It looks amazing."

I manage a friendly smile and lead her to the front for payment. Once she's gone, I immediately grab my phone and almost break the screen hitting Xander's number. He answers after a few rings.

"I'm here and I hate myself," he says in his bored voice. It's the tone I hate most. I'd take our arguments and his petty insults over this tone.

Because when Xander sounds bored, he's disassociating from himself. I have no idea if that's the exact medical term or whatever because he still hasn't been to see a damn psychologist, so I've had to do my own research. And since I'm a bit of an idiot, my research doesn't always go well.

But after an attack that really gets to him, sometimes he just … checks out. Empties of feeling.

"That bad, huh?"

"Well, I almost made myself pass out, and Molly saw it all, so yeah, good times."

"It's been a while since something hit you this hard."

"I'm fine. I just love being messed up in the head. It's my favorite thing about myself."

I clench my jaw. Yeah, I definitely prefer when Xander is mad at me over this. Petty insults directed my way, I can take. When he directs them toward himself, I want to shake him.

"How was Molly?"

"A complete peach. Did everything you said. It was very subby of him."

I ignore that last part. "Good to hear."

"Makes me hate myself even more."

"What?" It's a mission to keep my frustration under control. "Why?"

"Because I've probably freaked him the fuck out and ruined any chance of you two being together."

"Can we not go there again?"

"Well, there's no point now, is there?"

"You haven't ruined anything." There'd have to be something there to ruin, which there isn't. We're barely friends, and sure, Molly's cute, and thinking of that naked, lean body following my every order in the bedroom is a total turn-on, but there's nothing else there. A bit of physical attraction, a baby friendship, that's it.

Xander still is, and always will be, more important than any of that.

He gives a disinterested hum, which is his way of calling bullshit without having to say the word.

"I'm serious." I can't help my frustration this time. "Stop being so hard on yourself. I don't care. All I care about is that you're okay."

"I'm never okay."

"*Physically.*"

"Oh, well, that makes such a difference."

I can't talk to him like this. I press my fist into my eye socket, not wanting to draw him into an argument. "I'm going to call my boss and tell him I need to cancel my appointments this afternoon. I've got a few free hours now, and then I'll be here late, so—"

"Don't bother."

"I didn't ask your permission."

He snorts. "Then do what you like, but my door is locked, and I won't be unlocking it until nine when you finish work."

"Would you be reasonable for one second?"

"Oh, please. I don't need you doing your pappa bear thing. So don't. I'm not being the reason you leave work and lose a day's pay."

"I don't care about the money."

"Well, maybe you should."

"This again? Really?"

"If you cared about something other than me once in a while, your life wouldn't be so fucked-up."

I let out a frustrated laugh. "You're so lucky I don't curse because there are a lot of names I want to call you right now."

"Bet none of them are anything I haven't already called myself."

"I *like* my life. If you're judging me for it, that's a you problem."

"How can you not judge you? You're basically a wet nurse looking after the little baby who can't look after himself."

Ooh, yeah. He's *so* lucky I don't swear. "You look after yourself every day. What are you even talking about?"

"The big baby who needs Seven or Derek or Molly to make it through the day. Derek was right. I shouldn't be putting all this on you."

"He *said* that?" My molars almost snap. I'm ready to hang up on Xander and call through to the pharmacy to give that guy a talking-to when Xander lets out a hollow laugh.

"He told Molly I should have more than just you to depend on, but I knew what he was saying. You need a life."

Okay, that sounds more like it. Derek genuinely cares about Xander. He's always there when we need him and doesn't hesitate to drop everything in order to help. He's never made us feel like an inconvenience; he's never made Xander feel bad or belittled. Him wanting more people to help Xander sounds right in character.

And so does Xander willfully misinterpreting him.

"Here's an idea," I snap. "Maybe if you stop acting like such a big baby, you'll stop feeling that way."

"See? Even you're bored with me."

"This attitude, I am. But we're stuck with each other, so if you won't stop sulking for yourself, why don't you do it for me?"

"That's not fair."

"Sue me."

I don't even feel guilty for exploiting his weak spot. I'll do anything for him, but that feeling goes both ways.

"You know, you're a real dick sometimes," he sneers, more life coming back into his voice.

"I'm sorry, were you somehow unaware of that?" I'd never get frustrated with him over his attacks because that's not something he can help. This attitude is though, and using his attacks as an excuse to lash out at people doesn't fly with me. I'll call him out on that all day long. The thing is, Xander's safe with me. He knows that no matter what, I'm here. He can treat me like a dog turd, and I'll still be there, and the thing about Xander is that when he gets shirty, he has no limits. There's nothing he won't say to make someone hurt, and given what we've both been through, I don't blame him.

My coping mechanism is to make my trauma into a joke.

Xander's is to turn his into a shield.

His voice is softer when he speaks again. "I'm serious. Nine o'clock."

"Fine. But I'll be home to the minute."

We hang up, and this feeling of being out of control claws over me. I hate not being able to leave. I know I can't fix things, I know that's not my job, but I *can* be there, physically, so he knows he's supported, even when he doesn't want to acknowledge it.

It's the one thing I *can* do, so the fact he won't let me is making me restless. I pace around the shop, Tia and Ross both throwing me filthy looks while they're trying to work.

I could go home anyway and check in on Molly. But I'm a frog's belly coward because I'm scared to face him. I will, but if I wait until later, until after I've spoken to Z, I'll know exactly what happened and how he handled it, and if Molly's the one who needs a little extra support, I'll be able to give it.

The last thing I want is to head home, ask him how he feels, and then be all, "Hold that thought for another eight hours."

I pick up my phone and text him a quick *thank you* and smile as I see the Sevipus he sent this morning. It's so damn cool. He even got my tattoos right.

I narrow my eyes as an idea takes hold.

I think I've found a way to kill the next few hours.

Chapter 12

MOLLY

I'm sitting on the back step, staring at the Japanese maple in the dark yard, when I hear him come outside.

I've been waiting. Seven got home an hour ago and went straight to check on Xander, who hasn't left his room since we got home. I'm still not sure what to think about this morning, and I've been so distracted all day that I haven't gotten anything done. The frustration is eating at me, but I feel like I *need* to talk to Seven before I can move on from it all. Maybe I should have told him to come home. Maybe I shouldn't have tried to handle all that myself.

"Hey." His deep voice already feels familiar.

"Hi."

"Big day." He drops down beside me, smile flashing white teeth in the dark. "How are you holding up?"

While I knew he was going to come down here eventually, that question catches me off guard. I'd thought for sure he would have started making excuses for Xander and trying to explain, but when I meet his eyes, there's genuine concern there.

"I'm …" I stop myself from saying "good" because I'm actually not at all sure how I am. "Frazzled" is what I land on.

"Understandable."

"Is it?"

"Of course. I've had years to learn what Xander needs and how to help him. That all just kind of fell into your lap. So, I'm sorry."

"It's not your fault."

"Technically, what happened isn't anyone's fault, but I could have prepared you better."

I wrinkle my nose. "Yeah, I don't think anything could have prepared me for that. Madden mentioned it. Said sometimes Xander thinks he's dying, and I thought it'd be like those hypochondriacs in movies. Where they're all drastically self-diagnosing and—"

"First, it's not hypochondria."

"It's not?"

Seven's lips pinch. "No. He has medical anxiety. Usually he can keep it under control, but there are times the invasive thoughts take over to the point you saw today. When that happens, he needs help, kinda like we all do at times. His panic attacks go deep, and then when he can't breathe, he fears the worst. Lung cancer. Anaphylaxis. Whatever else pops into his head."

"Shit."

"Yeah, but don't feel sorry for him. He hates that." Seven nudges me, the heat from his elbow traveling the whole way up his arm. "He said you told him he was brave."

"He was."

Seven's quiet for a second. "Thank you."

And as sweet as it is that he cares about Xander, I need him to know I meant it. "I didn't do it for you. Or even for him. It's just … fact."

"Agreed."

I hesitate for a second, almost sick with nerves as I reach over and squeeze his forearm. Seven's confused gaze lands on my hand, but I don't keep it there for long. "I'm glad he has you."

"Nah, I'm the one who's lucky to have him."

I know I shouldn't ask, but I can't help myself. "You, uh … there's really nothing between you?"

He jostles me lightly. "Every time you ask me that, a twink somewhere ruins their makeup."

I laugh. "A twink?"

"I have a type."

"Oh, really?" I prop my chin in my hand and look up at him. "Xander's a twink who wears makeup."

"Argh, no! There goes another one." He covers his face dramatically, and I chuckle, wondering whether I should point something else out. And … why not? We've already been on one date.

"You know, *I'm* a twink. I don't wear makeup, but it still counts."

The smile he sends me is wicked. "I've noticed."

"You didn't answer me last time, but I am your type, aren't I?"

"If you weren't my roommate, you'd be exactly my type."

My stomach swoops at that knowledge.

"But don't worry, I know old dudes are your thing, and I know my place."

I huff, blowing a chunk of hair off my forehead. I'd thought the same about older guys myself, but it's not an attraction thing. It's about wanting to be respected and valued as a partner. Which Seven does. Well, as a friend. When it comes to attraction, there's definitely something drawing me to him.

"Umm ... so are we going on another date?"

"Of course." Seven shrugs. "Though I have to say, our first one was fulloping easy. You sure you're a mess on these things?"

"Please don't make me remind you of the spit."

Seven tries to hide his amusement, but it shines in his eyes. "Oh, yeah. Good times."

"Maybe we should do a restaurant next. It's where I'm most likely going to end up, so it makes sense to see my complete meltdown in one of those settings."

"Fine. I guess I can't avoid it forever."

"Wow, calm down. I know a date with me is exciting, but—"

He hooks an arm around my neck and ruffles my hair with his free hand. "Relax, Tiny. I told you, I hate restaurants, nothing to do with you."

"Why though?" I ask, pulling away, cheeks suspiciously hot.

"Never went to them growing up. The bill confuses me, I don't understand what half the things on the menu are, and then I always get weird looks because of my tattoos and piercings. They're not enjoyable places for me."

His answer opens up a world of questions for me that I'm dying to get out, but since he's helping me with all this, the least I can do is not pry. Even if it's killing me. "Then we'll skip that idea."

"No, I agree we should try one out."

"Listen, I might want to get over my disastrous dating history, but I'm not going to do it at the expense of your comfort. We'll plan something else."

"Okay, but—"

A voice comes from behind us. "If you're flirting now, does that mean you've stopped talking about me?"

I laugh, cheeks burning even hotter, and glance back at Xander. His blue hair looks fluffy and freshly washed, but his face is still pale, and he's not wearing makeup for the first time since I've met him. I slide over and pat the place between us.

"You okay?"

"No asking that question, thank you," he says, wriggling in next to me. He's forcing a happy tone, and my heart actually hurts for him. Seven said not to do the pity thing, but that's easier said than done.

Seven wraps an arm around his shoulders. "You eat dinner?"

"Yes, Dad," Xander says, rolling his eyes at me.

"Did you drink lots of water?" I add. It was the last thing Derek said to us as we left.

Xander huffs and plants his elbows on his knees, resting his head in his hands. "I've been a good boy, now both of you leave me alone."

Seven and I grin at each other over his back.

"Your daddies just care about you," I tease.

"Great. And now you're making me hard."

Seven whacks the back of Xander's head. "We have company."

"I wasn't talking to *you*."

"Yeah, but I'm still within earshot, Z. I don't wanna hear that."

"Then tell Molly not to call himself Daddy."

Watching the two of them clears up any niggles I might have had about interest between them. They're … like brothers. Maybe closer than most brothers, but I'm not detecting anything more than love between them.

"You started it," I point out to Xander.

He sits up suddenly, staring at me like I've said something revolutionary. "If you're my Daddy, does that mean you love me?"

"Umm ..." I glance at Seven like he might be able to help me out, but he's too busy giving a long-suffering stare to the back of Xander's head. "As a friend ... yes?"

Xander squeals and pulls me into a crushing hug. "I knew it. I *knew* it. See, Seven? See?"

"Stop it."

"I told you."

"I'm serious. Cut it the croc out."

"But now you can—"

Seven's hand comes down over Xander's mouth, and Xander tries to shove him off. They jostle back and forth for a minute, me leaning away from them to avoid being collateral damage, when Xander slaps Seven so hard across the chest the *twack* echoes through the yard.

"Ah, mother-turkey-duck!" Seven cries, letting go, and Xander immediately jolts back.

"It wasn't even that hard."

Seven's teeth are gritted, and he's pinching his shirt, holding it away from his chest.

"Wait." Xander points, eyes wide. "You got a new tat."

"Nope." Seven releases his shirt and straightens. "No tat. Nothing to see here."

"You did." Xander pulls at his shirt. "Why are you hiding it?"

"I'm not *hiding* anything. I just—"

"Then show us."

The look Seven throws Xander would have made me recoil, but Xander bats his eyelashes and says, "I was *very* sick today."

"Z ..."

"I almost died! What if you don't show me and then I don't wake up tomorrow? How would you feel then, huh? *Huh*?"

Seven closes his eyes, head tilted back, like he's begging for strength. Then his eyes snap open, and he throws Xander a glare as he yanks down the neck of his shirt. There's so much ink there that I don't know what I'm looking at to begin with, but then my gaze focuses on the slightly red, slightly darker design right in the middle of his chest.

"Oh my god!" I yelp, practically climbing over Xander for a closer look. "Se-sevipus!"

Seven chuckles, but it sounds forced. "Told you I liked it."

"It's *tattooed* on you."

"Yep."

"Forever."

"Basically, yeah."

"But I was just fucking around."

"And like I said, that doesn't mean it's not incredible."

I'm sort of in shock that something *I* created now makes up the art on his *fucking body*. My design. On another man's body. "Wow."

"You drew dicks for me. It was love at first sight."

I cross my arms over Xander's thigh, still taking in the sight. It doesn't hurt that Seven's body is as eye-catching as the ink on his skin.

"Done yet?" he asks.

"Maybe another minute."

Xander runs his hands through my hair before starting on a braid. I lean into his touch, kinda blown away by how much I love this, and it makes me realize that, yeah, I *do* love him as a friend. The both of them. It hasn't been long, but when you're around two people like them, who open their hearts without question, who don't hold back and play games, it's hard not to feel connected to them.

I lean into Xander's touch like a cat, and he kisses my hair.

Seven sighs, letting his shirt fall back into place. "I'm in a world of trouble with the two of you, aren't I?"

Chapter 13

SEVEN

"We're going to have to do a family dinner. Think you can get everyone together?" Elle asks.

"Sure. I'll have to tie Rush to something so we don't lose him, but it's doable."

Her brother, Émile, and my roommate Christian are flying home for one night this week. I swear that guy's been gone forever, but each time I chat with him, he sounds happy. Which, for Christian, is a big turken deal.

It also happens to be when I'd booked a surprise restaurant date for Molly, but that mess is gonna have to wait. This weekend, Molly is going to be initiated into what it really looks like to be a Big-Boned Bertha boy. He hasn't met Christian yet, and Émile and Elle are both honorary members. Molly usually only has to deal with one or two of us at a time, so it'll be a shock for him to see us all together.

"So, there'll be the six of you and two of us—"

I cut Elle off. "Seven."

"Yes, I know your name."

"No, I mean there'll be seven of us."

Her forehead wrinkles for a second. "Oh, the new guy. He's coming?"

"Obviously."

"Okay, snappy …"

"I'm not snappy. I just don't understand why that was even a question."

"Yeah, sure, right, totally believe you." She widens her pretty blue eyes at me.

"He's family now, so he's automatically included, okay?"

"Okay. I get it. Calm down, Rambo."

"Duck off."

"It's super cute how defensive you're getting over him."

"I'm not—"

"Do you like *like* him?"

"You in high school?"

Elle hums prettily. "I could ship it."

"And I could ship you out to sea."

"Ohh, quaint joke for the shipping heiress."

I snort. "Except you're not the heiress of anything, spare."

Elle's family has some messed-up worldviews where the family business—and we're talking an international shipping company that's been around basically forever—stays with the males in the family. It's why she's such a hard-core feminist … toward everyone but them. So while she's loaded now, she's focused on building her own life outside of them because once they kick the bucket, other than her trust, the cash flow will be gone.

From what I can tell, Émile walked away from it all, so it goes to their cousin instead.

"Can't help but notice how you've changed the subject," she muses.

"If you mention Molly—"

"Can I just say how much I adore that his name is Molly?

His parents must be fucking awesome, and I want you to get married so I can meet them one day."

"Sure, I'll get right on that," I deadpan. From what Molly's said, his dad is awesome and his mom isn't, but I've never thought to ask which of them actually named him. Not that it matters. Molly is just Molly. He'd be weird with another name.

"I'm so excited to meet him," Elle says. "I've heard so much that I feel like I already have."

"Let me guess, Xander?"

"He might have mentioned it."

A groan rumbles through me. "What matchmaking plans do you two have in play?"

"What? Us? No. Nothing. Not a thing."

There is no way I'm believing that. Xander's always overstepped in every part of my life, but apparently, now he has an accomplice. "Don't."

"You don't even know what we have planned."

"I don't give a shot what you have planned. Just don't. There's nothing there."

"Well, I guess I'll see for myself on Saturday. Ooh, maybe I should bring Darcy? From what he's said, he prefers big bulky guys like you, but I've known him to go for a twink or two. *Oh my god*! A Molly/Seven sandwich. He'd be in heaven."

I'm not even going to respond. I know what she's doing. The second I tell her he can't come, she'll assume I'm jealous, and I'll never hear the end of it. I won't fall into her trap.

"Molly and Darcy could be like a Cinderella story," she continues.

I grunt.

"The handsome, insanely rich prince, sweeping the newbie off his feet—"

My jaw tightens.

"Taking him back to his castle on the hill, to make the newbie squeal all—"

"It's *family only*."

She smiles, taping her stylus against her digital notepad. "Random, but okay."

"Oh, the levels of hate you bring out in me …"

"Who knew you had such strong feelings?"

"Only for you, babe."

"It's honestly atrocious you haven't introduced me to Molly yet. I think I should be offended."

"Yeah, after Saturday, I'll be able to gesture at you and be like *this, this is why*."

"Well, just for that, I'm going to be on my best behavior."

"Right."

"I'll be the most demure flower you've ever seen."

"Don't threaten me with a good time."

She cocks an eyebrow, her silent tell when she accepts a challenge, and now I'm looking forward to Saturday even more.

ME:

You working?

MOLLY:

I was. And now you've distracted me. Bad, Seven.

ME:

Should I leave you to it?

MOLLY:

Fuck no, where are you?

ME:

Right outside.

ALMOST AS SOON AS I hear his message tone go off, Molly throws open the office door. He's got all the windows in the corner room open, flooding it with more sunlight than I usually let in here, and the beams highlight the dust stirring behind his head. The guy looks like a flipping angel.

Until his eyes drop to my torso.

"Some days, I wonder if you're purposely trying to turn me on."

I bite back a laugh. "Yeah, until you catch me shaving my balls, you don't get to claim that."

He leans against the doorframe and crosses one ankle over the other, his short athletic shorts showing off nicely sculpted, tan thighs.

Molly grunts. "And now you're checking me out. That's not fair."

"You were shamelessly ogling me."

"You're shirtless and a foot taller than me. It was right there in my face."

"Didn't try to look away though, did you?"

"I mean …" His teeth bury into his bottom lip as his gaze drops back down. "I just really love that tattoo."

My lips twitch as I mirror him, leaning against the opposite jamb. "When I agreed to date you, I thought you'd be more high-maintenance than you have been."

"Really?"

"Just from what you said. But so far, I've only had thirty-six texts and two random calls, one about a bee you saw outside the window and one about how the knighting system in England works."

"I was curious."

"You also have Google."

He drags his bottom lip between his teeth. "Too much?"

That's a hard question to answer. Molly texts like he talks. Every sentence is a new message, all short sporadic bursts, bouncing around in a way that's impossible to follow but fun to try. So instead of giving him the full answer, I hedge. "Maybe if I was at work, yeah. Or had, I dunno, a corporate job."

"Okay …" He very obviously catalogs that information, and I'm hit with a stab of something. Something that doesn't sit right.

"But, hey. If I'm texting back, go wild. As many as you want."

"Really?"

"Well, with me, at least. You can usually pick up on tone when people are trying to blow you off."

"Yeah, I'm not the best at that."

"Then ask. Communication is important in any relationship, and it's better that you know that stuff up front and avoid an easy problem later."

"And … with you? I can text you if you're not working?"

"Well, I can't write back when I'm working, but as long as you're okay with waiting for a reply, I'm happy to read them all when I'm done. Just don't be texting me things like *hey, where are you* or *why aren't you texting me back* because that'll get old fast."

He laughs softly and holds out his hand, pinky extended. "Promise."

"There's no horse-drawn way I'm pinky swearing with you."

"Aww, come on?"

And because I'm worried that Molly has the kind of power to make me do just about anything, I cross my arms. Be strong, Seven. "Hard line for me."

Molly huffs. "Fine. But tomorrow, I'm going to send you a hundred texts to go through once you've finished work."

"Oooh, that'll show me." I don't tell him that I'd like it.

It takes me a moment to realize we're both standing there, smiling at each other.

I clear my throat and step away. "Don't forget it's your turn to set up the next date."

"Already working on it."

"Oh, and the reason I came up here before you started drooling over me and distracting me—this Saturday. Bertha thing. You're in, right?"

"When you say thing, do you mean like Monopoly Monday or an orgy? Because while the second isn't a deal breaker, I'd probably need some time to think it over."

"Huh. Never thought you'd be interested in sleeping with Madden."

Molly shrugs. "It's been a while for me. But okay, no. Not him." His eyes flick to me and away again.

I grin and step forward. "If I didn't know any better, I'd think you're angling for another look at my cock."

"Good thing you know better, then."

"Pity for you. It's a *great* cock."

Molly smirks. "I know. I've seen it."

I search his eyes for a second, wondering how far to push this thing. We're date training and becoming friends, and I'm apparently not his type. But *lawd* Molly's pretty. He makes me want to break the rules. I've never been so tempted by one person before.

"Saturday's dinner," I tell him. "And then Elle's booked out the VIP section in one of the clubs downtown."

"Fancy."

"Friends in high places. Never thought I'd have one of those."

Somehow, we've gotten really close, and when Molly's face lights up with mischief, it's only too easy for him to press onto his toes and rub the tip of his nose against mine.

"What—"

"No pinky swears for you. We'll do nose kisses instead."

I take a huge step back. "I'll do nose kisses when I'm dead."

"Too late," he sings.

I shake my head as I walk off. "Saturday."

"I'll be there. And I'll wear something extra slutty. Just for you."

Chapter 14

MOLLY

"Here kitty, kitty …" I call to the ugly ginger thing sitting on the boundary between Big-Boned Bertha and the house next door.

As expected, he stares at me and lets out a low-level *mewww*.

I scowl right back. "I just want to love you." Giving up, I toss the kibble I'd been baiting him with into the center of the yard and watch him creep forward, one eye on me and the other on the bird that lands nearby. He doesn't stop watching me the whole time he eats.

Stupid cat. He's my one roommate who hasn't been overly welcoming.

Just thinking about my roommates brings a trickle of nerves with it.

This Saturday, I get to meet them all. The whole gang. And try to contain my flirting with Seven while I do it. The thing is, Christian is super important to these guys, and I'm worried about what will happen if he doesn't like me.

I stretch out my back and then prop my elbows on the stair behind me. Cars drive past on the street beyond our stone front fence, mostly hidden by the large trees and overgrown shrubs. We might be right in the heart of the George Park District of Seattle, but it's like our own little oasis.

The whole time I've been here, I've been waiting for home-sickness to kick in. For that deep longing to head back to Kilborough to take over, but either it's a delayed reaction, or it's not coming. There's a sense of rightness to being here, and while I miss my dad and Will, I know they're only a flight away.

Here, I get to start fresh, and I like that more than I should. It's one of the reasons I haven't spoken much to Dad and Will since getting here, always making an excuse for why I can't catch up properly. I don't want them to think I'm happier being away from them—it's not that, but trying to explain the freedom my new life gives me is hard. It would mean admitting how much I was hating myself before I left.

I can't put it off forever though, and when I thumb through my contacts and land on Dad's number, I figure now is as good a time as any. I'm in a sleepy, content mood and emotionally ready to handle a conversation with the both of them on the off chance Will's home too. I'd pushed him to move in with Dad when I left because he had nowhere else to go, and even though I'm jealous of their … what would I even call it? Friendship? Substitute dadship? That doesn't mean I wanted Will going home to his homophobic family.

At least they can look after each other while I'm not there, and maybe neither of them will notice I'm gone.

Ope, there's that bitterness.

Shake it off, Molly.

Dad answers almost immediately.

"About time, kid. I was getting ready to jump on a flight and make sure you were still alive."

I chuckle. "Sorry," I say, and hearing his voice has me instantly feeling guilty. He's been the best dad I could ever ask for; I know Will can't replace me, but feeling rejected is my default. "I-I've missed you." And it's truer than I even realized until I say the words.

"Yeah, I bet, but some time away will be good for you."

"Do you ... miss me?"

Dad laughs. "Doesn't that go without saying? I've always told you I'm happy to have you live with me until I kick the bucket. You're my whole world, Mols, but I can miss you like crazy and still be proud of you for looking out for yourself."

I smile down at my knees, hating that I ever doubted him. We argue and butt heads, but he loves me.

"Tell me about Seattle," he says. "Oh, wait. Will wants me to put you on speaker."

A tiny piece of jealousy niggles at me, but I ignore it as soon as I hear Will's warm voice.

"Molly! I've missed you. Where have you been? Are you okay?"

"It's fine. I'm fine. I was just settling in." I'm trying to hold my next question in, but it doesn't work. "What are you both doing?"

"Your Dad's being an old man and doing a crossword."

"And who keeps asking to help?"

"Because someone was grumbling under his breath about four down."

My eyes flutter closed for a second, trying not to let their bickering get to me. "So, Seattle's *great*."

They immediately cut off.

"Sorry, Mols," Dad says, softening his voice. "Tell us."

And even though I love them and miss them, I'm not as eager to share it all as I was a minute ago. I'd been ready to tell Dad all about my roommates and tell Will about my shitty date and fill them both in on Seven's fake date and how he got one of my artworks *literally* inked on his *fucking* skin.

But in the space of a second, those things suddenly feel too personal.

"I'm enjoying it here," I answer truthfully. "The house is nice, and the guys I live with are fun. Madden's changed *a lot.*"

Will laughs.

"But I feel settled here."

"That's great to hear."

"Yeah … how are things back home?"

And unlike me, they both have plenty to fill me in on, which is shocking, considering small-town life feels like it never changes.

"How are Ford and Orson?" I finally ask. I don't think I'll ever not feel regret when I think about how I treated them.

"Good. Orson asked about you."

I roll my eyes. "Of course he did." That man is a freaking saint. When I kissed his boyfriend, instead of getting angry at me, he made sure my drunken ass got home safe.

Movement by the front path catches my attention as I'm expecting to see Kismet make a reappearance, but an older lady with a cane and a cunning look on her face steps into view.

"Ah, I've gotta go," I tell them as she approaches. For someone using a cane, she's damn fast.

"Okay," Dad says, not sounding happy about it. "But call again soon?"

"Yeah. Of course." I'm not sure if I'm lying when I say it though. "Love you both."

"Love you too."

I hang up and turn my attention on the woman. "Auntie Agatha?"

She eyes me. "Molly?"

"The one and only."

"Why don't you invite a kindly old lady inside for a tea?"

"Kindly?" I pin her with a look. "The others have warned me about you."

She sighs dramatically. "Another smart-ass brat to live next door to. However will I manage?"

I've heard stories about Aggy, and while I don't know her and don't want to push our first meeting, from everything they've said, she seems fun. Loving. But far from innocent.

"Maybe with some tea," I suggest, trying not to laugh.

"Excellent idea."

"Need help up the stairs?"

"I'm seventy-nine. I'm not dead."

"Noted." I open the front door for her because while she's capable, it's too ingrained in me not to. Dad taught me how to be polite, which was a skill he had to learn early on as a cash-strapped teen dad. "What tea do you like?" I ask as I follow her down the hall.

"My lost boys usually keep some Twinings on hand for me."

I rummage around in the pantry while Agatha *plonks* a heavy bag on the counter.

"What's all that?"

"Thought we could get to know each other while we whip up some dinner for the others."

"You do that often?"

She shrugs and rounds the island to get the water ready. "Usually, I'll batch up some things at home and drop them in the freezer a few times a week. My boys have got to eat."

"That's kind of you."

"Well, the lads in this house could use some kindness. It doesn't cost me anything."

"That's a nice way to put it."

I make her tea while Agatha unloads her cloth bag onto the

counter. I'm trying to pick what we'll be cooking based on the ingredients, but I'm stumped.

"Any guesses?" she asks.

I hand her cup over. "None."

"Creamy vegetarian pot pie."

"That actually sounds delicious."

"That's because it is."

"That you, Aggy?" Xander calls a second before he steps into the kitchen. "Oh, and Molly?"

Movement catches the corner of my eye, but before I can turn to her fully, Agatha drops her hand.

"Yes, sweet boy. Just me. And your new roommate. I'm interrogating him."

Xander's smile trembles across his lips. "Be nice. We like him."

"I *am*, I am. In fact, we're cooking together, aren't we, sweet pea?"

It takes me a beat to realize that *I'm* sweet pea. "Ah, yep, sure are."

"Vegetarian pot pie." The pointed way she says it, and the way it makes Xander's eyes light up, puts me on guard. They share a look before Xander turns away.

"You two have fun, then."

He leaves, and I turn slowly to the old lady fussing beside me. "What was that?"

"Don't know what you mean. Chop those mushrooms, would you?"

I move toward the chopping board she's slid onto the counter. "Sure, but so long as you know I caught that weirdness."

"Weirdness?"

"Is this pie an inside joke?"

Her gasp is dramatic. "The cruel things you'd accuse an old lady of."

"That innocent card doesn't work on me." I bite back a laugh. "I bet you keep things interesting around here."

"Nonsense. I make sure my boys are fed and healthy. Never make much of a fuss, myself."

"Right."

"Except when Seven insists on blasting his damn music all night."

I think about how he told me that he only does it when she annoys him. "He's a good guy."

"He is. Beautiful soul, that one. Deserves a beautiful soul of his own."

I'm not about to disagree with her there, but I don't like the idea of Seven settling down with someone. "Maybe ..."

Almost as soon as I'm done with the mushrooms, celery and cauliflower are dropped in front of me.

"Xander said you've been spending a lot of time with Seven," Agatha says.

"Yeah, but I've been spending a lot of time with Xander too. And Madden. I'd spend more time with Rush if he was ever home."

"Works himself to the bone, that one. And he's a simple fellow. Sometimes I wonder about him ..."

"I think he said he has a boyfriend."

"*Did* he now? Well, there's something I didn't know."

I side-eye her. "You know most things that go on around here?"

"Sure do."

My teeth trap my bottom lip for a second. "How much do you know about Seven and Xander?"

"Everything."

"Like ... how they grew up?"

"Every. Damn. Thing. They both deserve better."

"I don't even know what happened, and I can easily agree with that."

She hums, and I get the feeling she's side-eyeing me too. "They're both very special people."

"I know."

"A package deal, as well."

That makes me laugh. "I kind of figured. They're super close."

"But not in that way." She turns suddenly, brandishing her knife. "Don't misunderstand me, those two are platonic and brotherly. Nothing else there."

"Also picked up on that."

"Right. Well." She turns back to cutting the leek.

"The thing is, I'm curious about how it all started. But it feels weird to ask them."

"And it doesn't feel weird to ask someone you've literally just met."

I nudge her with my elbow. "You're practically family."

"And you're a sweet-talking little shit, aren't you?"

"If it gets me what I want."

She laughs, and it's rough, gravelly, and warms me to her instantly. "Don't think too hard about it. It's a story they tell when they're comfortable with you."

"Okay."

"*Or* if they're rip-roaring drunk."

I snigger. "You're not what I expected."

"Right back at you. So, how long are you planning on staying?"

"No plan, actually. A while. I like it here though."

"Not hard to do."

I smile, thinking of my roommates. "It's definitely not." So far, I feel more welcome and appreciated here than I have at home for the last few years.

By the time we've finished making the pie and topped it off with pastry, Agatha looks me directly in the eye. "I like you, Molly."

"You too."

"Good. Now, I'll like you even more if you keep the others away from that pie until Seven gets home." She winks at me. "It's his favorite."

And like that, I'm pretty sure I've just been played by Agatha and Xander.

"Nothing's going on between us," I assure her.

"Uh-huh. Better tell that to your smile, then, sweet pea."

I slap my hand over my mouth.

She heads for the hallway. "Keep an eye on that pie. Twenty minutes. Seven will be home not long after that." She pauses right before she disappears. "I'll see you soon."

"Yeah. Sounds good."

At this point, it's not like I have any choice. My gaze strays back to the pie, and I laugh. At least I know where she stands on my interest in Seven.

Even though the wait isn't long, I can't stop myself from pacing, from checking the pie and making sure it's still warm and hasn't miraculously evaporated from the dish. And when I hear the front door open not long after Seven's due home, I shoot out into the hall to intercept him before he heads upstairs.

"Hey, Mol—"

"Yeah. Hi. Come with me." I grab his hand and all but drag him into the kitchen. "I made dinner. With Agatha's help, but it still counts."

He sniffs, concentration playing over his pierced brow. "Is that ..."

"Pie! Yes. It's pie. Your favorite. At least, that's what she told me." I clench my hands together behind my back, trying to drown the nerves going haywire in my gut.

He uncovers the dish and breathes deeply. "Hot damn, that's good."

All the air rushes from me. "You like?"

There's something in his gaze as he looks me over, and then he smiles, one of the rare ones that meet his eyes. "Think we can smuggle this up to my room before the others catch us?"

"I'll grab the forks and cups, you take that and something to drink?"

"Good plan." He slaps my ass on the way past to the fridge. "Go, team."

I need to remember to thank Agatha next time I see her.

Chapter 15

SEVEN

Having the lost boys together again feels like coming home. Christian and Émile are here, curled up together on one side of the table, Gabe fills out the opposite end to me, Xander is between Christian and Rush, with Molly, Madden, Elle, and Elle's friend Darcy all down the other side.

As I look around at my band of misfits, I'm filled with a deep kind of warmth. The type of family vibes I never thought I'd get in my life. Bouncing between foster homes until I hit the one Xander was living in, alienating myself from our parental figures because of the abuse I'd already seen. The disdain thrown my way, the way some of these so-called parents would section off a portion of their house for the *other* kids. We'd eat separately. Sleep separately. Basically, all they gave us was a roof over our heads. No connection. Definitely no love. Xander's issues developed due to his need for attention and blitzed his brain up royally. There are a lot of great foster families out there—apparently—but until my final placement, none of them wanted someone with my issues.

I've seen a lot of dark stuff. For a while, I didn't think I deserved love. Or family. I hated that Xander attached himself to me and wouldn't let go because he deserves someone better. Someone who doesn't struggle to emote.

I didn't know that I was simply waiting for my real family to find me.

Elle's true to her word and has shown up dressed like something out of a period drama. Dress down to her ankles and hugging her neck. Flower crown resting over her shaved head.

I send her a silent look of "what the hell do you think you're doing?" and she throws back an evil smile before turning to Molly.

"Hello, my dear child," she says in a breathy voice. "It's so wonderful you've joined my lost lambs today and they've welcomed you into the fold. I hold you *all* in my bosom and wish you nothing but the sincerest—"

Émile breaks out in laughter. "What, pray tell, dear sister, is this shite?"

Elle fakes a gasp. "The audacity of you, *dear brother*, to curse in the presence of a lady."

"A lady? Biggest load of bullocks I've ever heard."

I snort. "Yeah, you're acting like I didn't tattoo a PSA on your butt cheek."

"Come again?" Émile asks, on the verge of more laughter.

"I have a small, professional artwork," she answers, still in that weird-ass voice. "On my buttocks. But can we return to the heart of the matter, which is our dearest friend Molly?"

I lean forward and hit my head on the table. "This isn't happening. This is *not* happening."

"Promise it is," Xander sings. "No idea why, but I'm enjoying myself."

"Me too," stuffy Darcy says.

So much for family only. At least she hasn't tried to set him up with Molly yet though. The man is fucking fine.

Not that I care about him being set up with Molly. Obviously. I just know he's not Molly's type, is all.

And Molly's still learning how to date. It's too early for him to get back out there.

But almost as soon as I'm finished that internal battle, Elle leans back slightly, resting one hand on Molly's shoulder and the other on Darcy's.

"I don't believe you two have met."

"Actually, I don't think I've met most of the people at this table," Darcy points out.

"Irrelevant, dear one. This sweet face is Molly. And Molly, my love, Darcy is one of my oldest, dearest friends, and I'm told he has an incredibly big cock."

Molly chokes so hard he actually sprays his drink over the table.

At the look of sheer mortification on his face and the shock of everyone around us, I lose my crap laughing. I'm dying for him as I hand over a napkin and say, "We covered this on our first date. No covering people with spit, Tiny."

The embarrassment drains quickly, and his eyes light up. "Clearly, you're not a very good teacher." He wipes the liquid dripping from his chin.

"Hold up," Christian says, leaning forward. "What do you mean, date?"

"Relax." I hold off rolling my eyes. "It wasn't a real date."

"Seven's helping teach me to be a normal person when I go out with other normal people."

Émile lightly taps Molly's hand. "Normal is overrated. The first time I met Christian, he single-handedly ruined a wedding. If the men you're dating can't handle messy, they don't deserve you."

Molly lights up, and damn, he's pretty when he smiles. "You think?"

"I tried to walk through the window out front instead of

the door," Christian says. "There's no turning that shit off. I used to be really hard on myself about it, but Émile helped me see there's nothing wrong with being a bit …"

"Chaotic?" Émile supplies.

"That. Chaos is fun."

And this is what I mean about family. They're all incredible, different, but big-hearted people.

"I'm so glad there were no further issues for you," Darcy says to Émile. And everything about his plummy accent makes me stabby.

To distract myself, I glance over at where Rush is rapidly texting.

"You good?" I ask.

He glances up and looks around as he locks his phone. "Yep. Totally fine. Just the boyfriend. He's away for the weekend. We're making plans. Hopefully for next week, but—"

His phone lights up again, and he all but dives for it.

Well, at least two of us lost boys are happy and in love.

I can't stop my gaze from straying back to Molly, and he's already looking at me. He gives me one of those enormous smiles of his, the kind that reaches right down into my gut. The guy has me softening to him tenfold every day, and if I'm not careful, Xander's won't be the only fingers I'm wrapped around. All I know is I'm regretting taking the seat at the head of the table when I want to be sitting where Elle is instead. Well, maybe not next to Darcy.

The server comes around, and we place our orders, and as she leaves, Gabe gives me a little upnod. I send a questioning look his way, and he subtly waves a finger between me and Molly, then makes a heart with his hands.

I flip the butthead off.

What was I saying about family again?

I hate them. The lot of them. Everything from Gabe's smirk

to Elle's over-the-top angelic expression to where Émile's groping Christian under the table. Madden keeps tugging at the collar of his button-up and seems as distracted by his clothes as Rush is by his phone, and Darcy's just sitting there awkwardly, staring at his plate and looking like he'd rather be anywhere but here.

Poor guy was probably told he was coming to meet a hottie. Too bad for him.

Xander's folding his napkin into a swan.

"What are you going to use to wipe your face with?"

"Yours?" He flutters his lashes at me.

"Not a chance."

He pouts his pink lips. "It's like you don't love me anymore."

"I'm sorry," Darcy interrupts. "Are you two …"

"*No*," we answer as one.

"My mistake."

"It's okay, darling," Elle says. "You're not the first to make that assumption. But their love is as beautiful as the purest flower—"

And lucky for me, my plate is set down at that exact moment, allowing me to pick up one of my fries to throw at her.

She blinks in shock as it bounces off her nose. "The fuck was that?"

"Oh good, you're back."

"And you're still an asshole." She bats her lashes at me in perfect imitation of Xander.

"Okay, what the hell? How do I keep getting stuck with you people?"

"Whatever do you mean?"

"You three manipulative little shirt faces." I point from Xander to her to Molly.

Molly gapes. "What did I do?"

"*You know*. Sitting there and smiling at me all cutely. Quit it with that."

And like he's found what I've said funny, he physically has to hold back a smile. "I'm so sorry for being cute."

"You should be."

"You two are *so* adorable," Elle gushes.

"And hot," Xander adds.

I look over at Christian. "You *had* to come home, didn't you? There's a reason we don't do family dinners. You all suck."

"What did *I* do?" Madden asks this time.

"Dude, your *pants* aren't even done up."

He glances down to where I can make out the button popped and his fly open.

"Ha. Ooops. Didn't think you noticed."

"We *all* noticed," Gabe says. "Hard not to pay attention to your bro when he looks like he's about to pull his cock out."

Elle lifts the tablecloth and leans over Molly. "Nope. It's away."

"Well, that's a relief," I mutter.

"Why didn't we just have this dinner at home?" Molly asks, still struggling not to smile. The effect is even cuter than before, damn him.

"Because my sister is somehow under the delusion we're appropriate to exist in public." Émile leans back and wraps his arm around Christian's shoulders. "While the rest of us are simply waiting for Christian to upend the table."

Christian slaps his hand over his boyfriend's mouth. "Well, now you've said that, it won't happen. Which means it's going to be something much, much worse."

Chapter 16

MOLLY

Seven thinks I'm cute. And he actually admitted that in front of the whole table of his friends. Sure, the house has rules. And sure, Seven's said he won't cross those lines, and I'd never try to pressure him to, but ... he *thinks I'm cute*.

Technically I'm supposed to be acting like I would with any other man I'm dating, and if he was my actual, real-life boyfriend, oh, *swooooon*.

I send heart eyes across the tiny drinks table to him, but he doesn't even notice. He's too busy gazing out at the crowded dance floor of the club Elle has brought us to. It's dark, with neon flashing lights and music that pounds a steady rhythm in my ears. The VIP section is above the dance floor, with a full view of the club, and has waiters in assless chaps bringing us our drinks. I try not to ogle the men, but some of those butts are delicious.

I could only imagine how Seven would look in those pants. Instead of keeping that thought to myself, I pull out my phone and text him.

ME:

> Exactly how much money would I have to bribe you with to get you into a pair of those pants?

SEVEN:

> Nothing, actually. I have a pair at home.

My eyes almost fly from my skull. I glance over at him again, mouth hanging open, and Seven laughs.

SEVEN:

> Your expression is hilarious right now.

ME:

> Mean! I was already picturing how to get you into them once we're home.

SEVEN:

> First time a man's ever wanted to get me INTO pants. Normally the aim is to get me out of them.

ME:

> Are you saying that's a possibility?

Seven stamps down a smile at that message, but instead of replying, he locks his phone and tucks it back into his pocket.

My jaw drops, and I send through a steady stream of messages.

ME:

> Rude!

> First of all, how very dare you?

> Second, why you gotta be so mean?

> Don't you love me?

> Pay me attention, dammit!

I know his phone is going off, but he ignores it, and the expression he's wearing makes me wonder if he's challenging me to call him on it.

Well, he doesn't know Molly Gibson.

I huff and turn toward Darcy. "Hey, person I've never met before tonight."

"Perhaps I misread the dinner, but that could be a few of us, right?"

"Yeah, sure, but I've heard of Elle, Émile, and Christian before. Hard not to with the way they all live in each other's pockets."

"That's true. But it's kind of nice, isn't it?"

"I'll have to get back to you on that one."

Darcy chuckles. He's a traditionally handsome man with kind eyes, but there's no spark there. No jolt of awareness like when I look at Seven.

"I have exactly one close friend, and my family is ..." He sighs. "Well, my father isn't well. So everything feels a little disjointed right now."

"Wow, I bet." The pain in his voice makes me hurt too. If something happened to my dad ... fuck no. I wouldn't be okay. We only had each other for a very long time, and trying to imagine life without him is painful. "I'm really sorry. Think he'll get better?"

"Unfortunately, no. But that doesn't mean I'm not still hoping."

I reach over and squeeze his arm, and he covers my hand with his to squeeze back. "Is that why you came out tonight?"

"That and I believe Elle's words were *you have five minutes to get dressed, otherwise, I'm dragging you out in whatever you're wearing,* and considering it was a pair of pajama pants and I knew she was serious, it was easier to play along."

I glance over at Elle, who's changed out of the old-lady

dress she was wearing earlier and looks jaw-dropping—and terrifying—in a skintight jumpsuit with her boobs spilling out.

"She scares me," I admit.

"Oh, me too. I learned early on that once she gets an idea in her head, it's easier to go along."

I laugh. "What's the wildest thing she's ever—"

"This looks fun," Seven says, stepping between Darcy's and my legs and wriggling his body down between us. "What are we talking about?"

Darcy audibly swallows, eyes going wide, and I'd recognize that reaction anywhere—he's attracted to Seven. And suddenly, like history repeating itself, I see Darcy and Seven starting a conversation, getting closer, maybe making plans to meet up after tonight, again and again and again, until *it* happens.

Darcy gets Seven.

And I get no one.

Sheer panic grips me, and I'm ashamed to say that I know, without a doubt, that I can't let that happen. I'm not strong enough to see another man, someone who actually knows me, throw me away like that.

"Wanna show me to the bathroom?" I ask Darcy in one long rush. Maybe if I can get him alone, I can beg him to take his hot, rich ass to literally *anyone* else in this club. Sad and pathetic? Me? Guilty!

"Oh, but it's just—" Darcy goes to point toward where the bathrooms are very obviously indicated when Seven jumps up instead.

"I got you, Tiny."

Well, I can't exactly beg *him* not to hook up with Darcy, but at least I've succeeded in separating them.

"Lead the way!"

Seven wraps his arm around my shoulders, directing me toward the short hallway that has signs for the bathroom and emergency exit. Only when we step inside, I realize I'm going to have to actually *go* now, and I've got nothing waiting.

"So. Darcy," he says.

"He seems nice."

"Yeah, rich too."

"Good to know."

"He's basically a bazillionaire." Seven crosses his arms and leans against the sinks.

"You're just, umm, gonna listen to me pee, huh?"

"He's not old, you know?"

I stare at Seven for a second, wondering what's happening here. "I do have eyes."

"So he's not your type."

"I've been over this; I don't know what my type is."

"Well, then by all means, go back out there and hook up with the super-wealthy Abercrombie model. I hear his daddy's supposed to be dying soon, so think of all that money he'll inherit."

"What the fuck is wrong with you?"

Seven scowls. "Nothing. What's wrong with *you?*"

"I literally just needed to piss."

"Then do it." The challenge in Seven's tone makes me think he knew that I never actually needed the bathroom. But like hell am I going to confirm that.

"Well, maybe I don't want to now."

He snorts. "Sure, because what you really wanted was to drag him back here and hook up. You couldn't have been more obvious."

"Are you kidding? If anything, he's clearly into you."

"What?" Seven looks like I've whacked him.

"Yeah, the bazillionaire wants your dick. You're welcome."

"Good. You can do better."

"Better than a hot, nice, rich guy?"

"Exactly."

"Right … well, you enjoy." My voice barely stays level.

Seven shrugs. "Maybe I will."

"Good."

"*Good.*" He goes to turn, and that irrational panic from earlier surges through me again.

"You *can't.*"

He stops halfway to the door and glances back at me. "What's that?"

"You can't hook up with him."

"Why?"

"Because …" *I don't want you to* and *you're mine* don't feel like the right answers here. "You're not allowed." Yeah, like that's so much better.

"Allowed?"

"You're *my* fake boyfriend."

"We're not fake anything."

"But we *are* dating."

"We're going on dates. That aren't real."

"Well, while we're dating, I don't want you hooking up with anyone else. It's not fair."

"*Fair?* You could hook up with anyone in the club you wanted."

"We both know that's not true, hence the whole dating thing in the first place. Which means you can't go out there, and I won't let you."

Seven smirks and draws himself up to his full six-three height. And he doesn't even need to say a word to prove his point. *Just try and stop me, Tiny.*

"I know he wants you and you were all jealous that I was the one talking to him, but please, *please* don't do it. I'm the one you're supposed to be paying attention to, not him." I both want the words to stop and need to get them all out there.

"Tell me this is a joke."

I grunt. "I get that this is probably one of those things

you're not supposed to say on dates or to boyfriends and that I'm being all desperate and needy or whatever, but I don't fucking care. Sometimes *my* feelings get to matter, and right now, my feelings will be really, really hurt if you hook up with him."

"Molly, come on! You think I'm jealous over *him*? You think I wanted to trade places with *you*? Wake up you tiny, needy little man. I was jealous over *you*. I was jealous he was talking to *you*."

"W-what?"

"Did you somehow not get that?"

"I'm going to need you to slow down for a minute."

"Really? Because I'm not going very fast here. You've annoyingly got a hold on me, and the thought of you and *him* makes me want to tear this place up. I will gladly promise not to hook up with anyone else while we go on dates as long as you can promise the same."

My smile fills my face. "I'm ... I ... Huh. Struggling to follow."

"Then let me make it easy for you." Seven closes the distance between us, pushes me up against the sink, and cups my face. Then his lips close over mine.

My mouth immediately opens for him, and I melt as his tongue brushes mine. All that raw, passionate power that he keeps in check pours into the kiss, making my head fuzzy as little zaps go off in my chest.

I clutch his shirt, head tipped back, as I try to kiss him with everything I have. I'm eager to show him how good I can be, how *perfect*. And maybe I'm scarred from past experience, but patterns don't repeat themselves for nothing. As soon as I hook up with a guy, it's all downhill from there. No callbacks, no second dates. I mean, hell, sometimes I don't even make it that far.

It's all these thoughts and more that are taking over what

should be a mind-blowing moment and making me want to cry. I push the urge down and try to relax, to enjoy it. Because even though I've never cried on a guy before, even I'm aware enough to know that turning into a sobbing, snotty mess isn't the way to win a man over.

And I don't think I've ever been as determined to win a man over as I am with Seven.

He's kissing me.

On purpose.

Now I need to figure out how to make him never want to stop.

Chapter 17

SEVEN

I should probably stop.

And I will.

Any second now ...

The problem with that thought is every time a second passes, I promise myself just one more, and then it's over with and on to the next. So I keep promising infinite seconds and never stop kissing Molly.

Is it *my* fault he feels incredible in my hands? That his small face rests perfectly in my palms and his strong tongue skims mine again and again and again.

I grunt, releasing his cheeks and wrapping my arms around him, crushing his lithe body against mine. Molly's dick is firm and insistent against my thigh, and the feel of it has me absolutely feral.

This is the last thing we should be doing. I'd been more than happy to uphold the rules of the house that we'd all agreed to, right up until Molly showed up with his big eyes and mop of hair. He's so goddamn tempting. Big personality in a small package. Complete sweetness undercut by that steadfast determination to find his person.

Which is another reason why we really, really shouldn't be doing this.

I yank apart from him with a gasp. "I'm sorry." It's a reflex because, if I'm honest, I'm not sorry at all. Well, apart from the whole screwing with his feelings thing.

"Don't be sorry." He moves closer automatically, like he's magnetized, and he curls fists into my shirt. "I'm not sorry. I will be if you stop kissing me, but this feels like one of the most perfect moments of my life."

"In the seedy men's room of a nightclub?"

"I've sucked dick in worse places."

My pulse rate surges. "You wanna suck my dick?"

Molly's swollen lips twitch, and the flirty thing flutters his lashes at me. In so short a time, he already knows exactly how to play me. "I'll even ask very, very nicely."

"How so?"

He presses closer, arms trapped between us, and pushes up onto his toes. His voice is syrupy sweet and makes my cock kick at the sound. "Pretty please take pity on me, Seven. I want to be good for you. To lick and suck until I make you feel so, so good and you reward me with the taste of your cum."

Ohhhhhh no.

I swear my brain checks out for a second.

It's almost impossible to say no to him. "It wouldn't be right. I wouldn't—I don't want things to get mixed up. I don't want to hurt you."

He drops the innocence. "I'm not an idiot. You told me straight up that relationships aren't in the cards for you, and I get it. But on the other hand, you're so fucking hot that it's becoming impossible to concentrate around you. Just this once?" A wicked glint hits his eyes as he flutters them again. "*Please.*"

"You're dangerous."

"What if I like being dangerous?"

"Then I'm goddamn screwed."

Molly laughs, then takes my hand and leads me out of the bathroom, down the hall, and to a door marked "emergency exit."

"What if it's alar—"

Molly ignores me as he shoulders it open and pulls me through. We're in a narrow, dimly lit stairwell. The stairs and walls are painted black, narrow strip lights at our feet and over-head. Molly grins, shadows playing across his face, and backs me into the wall.

"We're all alone out here."

"I see that."

"And tomorrow, we can both pretend like we were very, very drunk and can't remember anything."

My nostrils flare at his offer. Having him with absolutely zero strings? No commitments?

"Just this once?" I check.

Molly's smile spreads, hits me deep in the chest. "Onetime offer."

"Well, in that case …" I stoop to grab my hands around his thighs, heft him into the air, and then turn and press his back against the wall. He's a featherweight, and it takes almost no effort to hold him up.

"Fuck, that's hot."

I wrap his legs around my waist, then palm his needy dick. "So's this."

Molly hums. "Do that again."

So I do, shamelessly, enjoying the way his hard shaft fits perfectly in my hand. His breathing deepens, latching onto something deep in my gut and tightening the need drawing us together.

His arms and legs are octopused around me, and it makes me chuckle. "I've got my own personal Sevipus," I note.

"Open your shirt, and let me see it."

I shift so my knee is under him, hips taking his weight, and undo my shirt with my free hand while my other continues to explore. The second my tattoo is revealed, Molly moans and buries his face in my neck.

"Still can't believe you did that," he murmurs.

"I like good art." Sure, that's the reason. It has nothing to do with his stupid octopus reminding me of him every time I catch a glimpse of it. Nothing to do with how it makes me smile stupidly and want to seek him out.

The desperation I'm feeling for him is sizzling under my skin. Making me reckless, like I can do anything. And if we're doing this, we're doing it. One time, leaving no regrets on the table.

I draw him into a filthy, open-mouthed kiss. My tongue fights with his, lips hard and demanding, needing to pour all my want and lust into this moment together.

Molly's arms tighten around my neck as his hips rut forward, subconsciously seeking friction that I'm desperate to give him.

It's a challenge to get his shorts open with one hand, but the second his fly is down, his cock springs out. *Urg, he's commando.*

The heat from his shaft fills my palm as I wrap my hand around him. He's leaking and already desperate, hips giving a sexy little shudder when I touch him.

"Seven …" he gasps. "Keep going. Keep touching me."

My mouth finds his again, tongue exploring as I jerk him off. I rub his tip with my thumb as I stroke and squeeze from base to tip, alternating between palming his smooth balls and trying to milk him for everything he's got.

The breathy little noises, the way his hips thrust into my

hand, it's all doing it for me. My cock is rock hard and begging for release, but it doesn't get to play until Molly is satisfied. He's gripping my shoulder with one hand, the other clasped over the back of my head, deepening the kiss, trembling in my hold.

His mouth breaks from mine suddenly, and Molly grunts, head dropping back against the wall as he looks down at where I'm gripping him.

"I'm ... Oh, fuck ..." He spills into my hand, cock twitching with the pressure of his release, and I wait him out, milking each drop of pleasure from his body. When he finally relaxes against me, I let him go, lift my hand to my mouth, and lick up every drop of cum he spilled. Molly's eyes are sharp as he watches me, and he doesn't fight when I close my hand over his throat. My thumb finds the underside of his jaw, and I tilt his head back, getting the perfect angle to bring my mouth back down over his.

Molly hums into the kiss, his cum sliding from my tongue onto his and back again. Sharing his taste between us has me craving release, needing to let go. Kissing Molly isn't like kissing anyone else, though, because every time we start, I never want it to end.

His legs slide from my grip and find the floor, pulling him from me.

"I need to taste you now."

I glance toward the door, less scared someone will catch us and more wanting to bar the door and make sure no one can stop this. Ever.

"Get on your knees," I croak.

But Molly sidesteps me and turns us so it's my back against the wall this time. His hands slide down my arms as he folds delicately to his knees, and when he looks up through his lashes, I already know I'm a dead man.

Molly's sweet smile has turned wicked, and he guides my hands behind my back and clasps both wrists together. There's no human way he'd be able to keep me restrained like this, but the illusion of it is enough for me to tilt my hips forward, inviting him for more.

He holds both wrists in one hand as the other tugs down my fly, then pulls the front of my briefs down and hooks them under my balls. As soon as my cock is free, he leans in, running his face down my length and inhaling deeply.

"You smell incredible."

"Uh-huh. Great. Kinda in pain here though."

Molly's chuckle is cool against my overheated skin. "Pain? Whatever for?"

I whine, thrusting forward to encourage him. I'm tempted to free my hands and grip his hair, but Molly taking control really does it for me. "Don't tease me."

"Now, where's the fun in that?"

"Fun? There's lots of fun. So much fun in coming, and I'd really like to get to that part."

He flicks his tongue over my crown, making me hiss. "Tell me you don't like it."

"Molly …"

"Tell me."

"I hate—"

He lifts an eyebrow, and I slump.

"How much I like it."

"That's better." Molly hums, then drags his tongue along my piercings. "These are even sexier up close."

"Sexy enough to suck on?"

"Do they hurt?"

"Nope. Not unless you get super rough with them, but mostly—"

I cut off as Molly closes his teeth around one of the barbells and gives a gentle tug. With how steely hard I am, it sends shivers along my dick and into my balls. I groan and drop my head back against the wall behind me.

"Cruel. So pretty, but so cruel."

His soft laugh brushes my shaft again, and I cant my hips forward. I need to feel his mouth, to see it stretched around me, those big eyes gazing upward and sending shivers right through to my bones.

"Come on …" I complain. "Stop being so mean to me."

His tongue is wet as he strokes it along the underside of my cock, slowly running over me again and again until I'm aching for him. I'm so desperate I'm ready to beg when he finally closes his mouth around me.

His lips are soft, breath warm, mouth wet and intoxicating. I want to use his face until he can't breathe, but I give Molly the time to set the pace, to take me deeper and deeper until my cockhead nudges his throat. Molly swallows, and the pressure almost makes me blow before he pulls back again. Over and over, he bobs up and down, licks me with his wicked tongue, sucks me tight enough my dick feels like it's in a vacuum, wrapped in pleasure.

"So good," I praise. "Take me deep."

He does exactly that.

The stairwell around us echoes with the sounds of his slurps and heavy inhales while my moans and grunts bounce off the walls. Anyone could walk out and find us, anyone could break this up. We could be kicked out of the club, the rest of our roommates could find out, and I don't even care. Molly's mouth is ruining me for anything else, and I'd rather die than stop what we're doing.

I'm acutely aware that we're pushing it though. Expecting this much privacy isn't smart, especially not with how close to the edge I'm getting. I need to come. I need to relieve my balls. I need to let loose all this built-up desire that I'm brimming with. My skin tightens, pleasure shivering into my limbs.

"I wanna grip your hair," I tell him, and his eyes flutter. "Hold tighter. Don't let me."

His grip on my wrists increases, and my hips start to move faster. My cock pistons in and out of that sexy mouth, Molly's eyes are rimmed with tears, and his mouth is puffy, but he grips the base of my shaft with one hand and is going to town on me like he can't get enough.

The sounds he's making are incredible. So sexy. Tingling through to the base of my spine.

"Yes. Yes, I'm … I'm gonna …"

My dick throbs through my release, orgasm rolling over me in waves as I unload into his mouth. Molly's quick to catch it all, swallowing like he's desperate for it, and seeing him like that only draws my pleasure right out.

He sucks on my tip until my orgasm eases and I have nothing left for him, and then he slides his lips back until I pop from his mouth.

"Wow."

He lifts one shoulder, the confidence from a moment before gone. "I'm good at what I do. It's the only thing that gets me a callback." The light laugh he gives me is forced, and where a second before I felt amazing, dread knocks me down again.

"Tell me I didn't mess up," I say.

His eyes shoot up to meet mine. "You didn't. I promise."

Yet that doesn't do a whole lot to make me feel better about things. I offer Molly my hand and pull him to his feet.

"We both know this was fun, right? We established it wasn't the start of a relationship."

"I know."

"Then why are you looking at me like that?"

The softness in his big eyes is making me uneasy. "No reason."

"Molly …"

"I'm cum-drunk, okay? Simmer down."

"Right." I eye him, not sure whether to push. "We're still good for our next date?"

He rolls his eyes and gives my nipple a quick pinch. "Yes, of course. The more dates you take me on, the faster you can teach me, the sooner I'll find my future husband and be out of your hair."

And even though I can tell he means it, I don't feel any better.

"Sounds good."

"It does." He leans up and presses one more slow, soft kiss to my lips. "My future boyfriend will thank you."

"Yeah." I shift out of his grip. "And so he sure as hell should."

Chapter 18

MOLLY

This is nothing. Not a relationship. Not more than a friend helping out a friend. I'm gazing across at Seven, and he's steadfastly avoiding my eye by looking over the menu. This place so isn't what I would have expected him to choose, but hey, we're here. I'm going to enjoy it. And try to work out how to be a normal human in a restaurant setting.

"Stop it." He huffs, still not looking up.

"Stop what?"

He waves a hand across the table. "Stop … *that*."

I bite my lip to stop from laughing. "I'm just sitting here."

"And being cute. And looking at me with that cute, dumb look on your face. It isn't happening again."

"Psht. Anyone would think *you* want it to happen again you keep bringing it up so much. I was good, wasn't I?"

Seven hurries to glance around. "Your voice is loud."

"You're ignoring the question."

"Of course I'm ignoring the question. We're in a busy restaurant, spending more than anyone should ever spend on food, and …" He grabs the front of his button-up and fans it out a bit.

For the first time, I notice the sweat prickling at his hairline. "Are you nervous?"

"I don't like these places."

"Then why did you pick it?"

Seven's eyes finally fly up to meet mine. "I didn't pick it."

"Yes you did."

"*You* picked it. It was your turn to choose the date."

My mouth falls open as I stare at him for a second, and then I grab my phone and open my messages.

SEVEN:

Meet at Kygaros at seven?

I hold it up and show him, and he gets the most adorable scrunched look on his face.

"I didn't send that."

"It's from your phone."

He smirks and grabs his, then shows me the exact same message … from me.

"What?"

"I think we've been played."

"But … *what?*"

Seven chuckles, deep and warm. "If I'm going to guess … Xander."

"Xander? But why?"

"He thinks he's Cupid."

"But how did he get my phone? And your phone? And why? We were already planning another date."

"If you haven't worked it out by now, Xander is a nosy little bug head who will do what he wants, when he wants, and literally nothing we say will deter him."

"Deter him from what?"

"Setting us up, obviously."

My face twitches as I struggle to keep it straight. "I guess you didn't tell him about last week?"

"*No one* needs to know about last week."

"Agreed." Because *I* know about last week, and I don't want people to know how heart-eyed I've gotten over him since then. Not until it happens again. Hopefully again.

"That little turd ..." Seven mutters.

And while I'd love to keep sitting here and playing date night, Seven looks about as comfortable in this restaurant as I'd feel watching ... like ... my dad and *Will* getting it on.

Urg. No, thank you.

I shove to my feet and round the table, then pull Seven out of his chair.

"Ahh ... what are you doing?"

"We're going to have some fun."

"I'm scared."

"Of *this* innocent face?" I tilt my hands under my chin, and he exhales loudly.

"Now I'm doubly scared."

I wave down the waiter and give him my card to cover our drinks. My mind is whirling while we wait for him to get back, but the second the card is in my hand, I'm all but rushing out of there.

"Gotta say, you're being weird again," Seven calls, trailing after me.

"I didn't offer to blow you in the bathrooms in front of all the guests, so I figure we're a step up on my last restaurant date."

Seven laughs and lifts his hand. "High fives for improvements."

I high-five him, then link our fingers together as his hand drops. "So, you'll do high fives but no pinky swears?"

Seven's gaze is locked on where we're touching. "Something like that." He holds our hands up between us. "What's this?"

"I'm holding your hand."

"Yeah, that much I can see. But … why?"

"Because I wanna?"

He looks at me like I'm speaking another language. Then he huffs and starts along the footpath, tightening his hold to stop me from falling behind. My chest lights up with little *I win* fireworks.

"You're such a grump."

"And?"

"I like it."

"Yes, it's so much fun having my innocence stripped away as a kid, so now I assume everyone and everything is as screwy as me." He says it so flatly anyone would think he was making shit up.

"Can … can I ask about it?"

"Nah. It's a mood killer."

"I can handle it."

He turns those kind eyes on me and watches me for a moment. "Yeah, you're probably right. But I don't think I could. At least not tonight."

I respect that. If he wasn't telling me because he wanted to spare my feelings, you can bet your ass I'd push, but if it's because it's too much for him? I'm more than happy to let it go.

"So what fun are we going to have?" he asks.

A wicked grin crosses my face. "We're going to mess with Xander."

"We are?"

I nod. "You two know everything about each other, so I'm assuming he knows you don't like places like that."

"Ah, yeah …"

"And he made you go there anyway. Not cool."

Seven shakes his head. "It's really okay. We probably should have stayed and practiced."

"Nope. You're helping me, but I never want you to do something you're not comfortable with. And so now we're going to mess with Xander for putting you in that position and making me cranky with him."

"You're cranky with him?"

"Very."

"We don't even know it was him."

I tug Seven to a stop. "Know of anyone else sneaky enough to go into our phones, message the other, then delete the message that was sent?"

Seven gives me a dry look. "Yeah, it was definitely him."

"Then let's show him how his meddling could have ended up."

"On one condition: don't stay cranky with him for long?" The pleading in Seven's voice catches me off guard.

If anything, his worry makes me fall for him all that much deeper. "I'll be over it as soon as we're done. Maybe even sooner." I relent. "Maybe I'm not all that cranky with him, even though I really, really want to be because you didn't deserve that."

"It's kinda nice having someone stand up for me. Are you going to be like my little attack dog?"

"If you need me to be."

"How nice." Then he gives me his teasing smile. "Like having my own personal Chihuahua on hand."

I go to stomp away from him, but he refuses to let me go. "Oh, look at that, now I'm cranky with you."

"Awww, did I hurt your feelings?"

"Chihuahuas are ugly, little demons."

"You match two out of three of those things."

"Ugly and little?" I pretend to hold my heart with offense.

"You *know* what two." He ducks his lips near my ear. "The things you can do with your tongue are drop-dead demonic."

"And just like that, you're back on my good side." Because hearing Seven talk about what happened, reminding me he *enjoyed* what happened, lights me up in a way nothing else does.

It also makes me frustrated as all hell because I am desperate, *desperate* for it to happen again.

I drive us back to the house, filling Seven in on my plans for Xander.

"You ready to make him think he broke us up?" I ask.

"There's that demon side to you again."

"You can say no …"

"Nah, I'm way too curious about seeing someone actually call him on his overstepping. Duck knows I can't do it."

"You're both a mess, and that's fine by me. And so you know, it goes both ways; I'll call you out on your shit if you screw with him as well."

"I have no doubt."

"Okay, now … *pinch* me or something."

"Come again?" His eyebrows almost hit his hairline.

"I need to cry."

"I'm not pinching you."

"Just a little one."

"No fulloping way."

I huff. "You big baby." So I pinch myself. It doesn't work.

"You know, if you had years of trauma behind you, this wouldn't be an issue."

I give him a dry look. "Is that why you're always walking around crying?"

"Nah, because I keep my trauma in a locked box under my bed. Can't get to me from there."

"Except the nights it keeps you awake."

"Good point. Maybe I should move it."

And now I don't know whether he's serious or not. I'm tabling that for another day.

"Can we focus on Xander, please?"

He cocks his head. "Were we not?"

"How good are you at acting?"

"Ehh."

"That doesn't fill me with confidence. Why don't you just scowl a lot—exactly like that—and I'll do the rest?"

"I'm not scowling."

I pat his hand. "It's cute you think that."

Still, when I jump out of my car, Seven follows me along the driveway and up the stairs to the house. I pause at the front door, taking a *biiiig* breath, and whisper, "Showtime."

I throw the door open with so much force it hits the wall inside.

"I can't believe you did that to me!" I shout, storming into the house. "You're a complete asshole, and I hate you."

"The hell ..." he says under his breath, and his confused tone alone almost sets me off laughing. *Don't look don't look don't look ...*

"You're not going to say anything?" I demand.

"I thought I just had to scowl?"

Good lord, he's terrible at this.

Footsteps rush along the hall upstairs, so I raise my voice even louder. "Of course you don't have anything to say. You never have anything to say unless you're insulting me!" And ... fuck, what else? Luckily, I'm saved by Madden.

"What the fuck's up?"

"Are you guys okay?" Xander gasps, bolting down the stairs. He's going so fast I'm worried he won't pull up in time.

"No! That was the worst date I have ever, *ever* been on."

Seven doesn't do much more than study me for a moment. "I'm starting to feel the same."

"What happened?" Xander rounds on him. "What did you do?"

Ah, ooops? *Get it together, Gibson. This is supposed to make Xander feel bad, not Seven.*

"He's not in love with me!" I shout, then cover my face and pretend to sob.

Unfortunately, the room goes really fucking silent, which only increases the pressure to make this believable.

I hear Seven clear his throat. "Yeah. Umm. Maybe ... maybe if it wasn't ..."

"You took me to a beautiful restaurant ... held my hand ... gazed into my eyes ..."

I make the mistake of looking at Seven, who's about a second away from rolling his eyes.

Oh no ...

"Why'd you pick ..." *Don't laugh don't laugh don't laugh.* "Pick such a ... a ..."

Seven loses it first, and seeing him double over sets me off. Well, damn double shit fuck.

"You know what," Madden says. "I don't want to know."

He leaves us with a stunned Xander, and it's only the confusion on his pretty face that makes me pull it together.

"Are you guys in a fight or not in a fight?"

I sigh. "Not."

"Then ..."

"I wanted you to think we were."

His eyes flick between us as he tucks a chunk of his blue hair behind his ear. "Umm ... why?"

"Because you meddled. But not only that, I had to sit across from Seven and watch him stressing out over being somewhere he didn't feel comfortable. Not cool."

Xander drops his head. "Sorry, Seven."

"I know you didn't mean anything by it."

I shoot Seven a look.

"But, uh … yeah. It wasn't cool."

Xander glances up at him, and then his eyes slowly slide to me again. "Are you angry with me?"

I cross my arms. "Now I know why Seven hates when I act all cute with him."

"It's an act?" he echoes.

I wave him off, attention still on Xander. "You're supposed to love Seven. Don't do that to him again."

"I promise."

"Thank you."

Xander turns and jogs halfway up the stairs before pausing. "Just saying though … it was super cute of you to stand up for him like that. I hope one day I'll have a boyfriend who'll do the same for me."

"He's not my—" But Xander's gone before Seven can finish his sentence.

Probably just as well, though, because Xander's reminded me of everything I'm supposed to be aiming for. The only reason Seven and I were on a dumb date tonight is so that I *can* find my forever man. The person who'll stick by my side. Yet here I am trying to force it again.

"He's got a point," I admit.

"We're not boyfriends."

I shake my head. "Not about that. Just that it would be nice. To have a boyfriend one day who'll stand up for me." I give Seven a soft smile. "See you tomorrow."

I leave him in the foyer, wondering what it would feel like for *Seven* to be that boyfriend.

And knowing I'm getting it all wrong again.

Chapter 19

SEVEN

There are a few things that the Bertha Boys have always done that mean a lot to me. Our Monopoly Mondays. The monthly taco hunt. And how, once summer is about to hit, we take a trip to Ocean Shores and spend the day getting fried by the sun and cooling off in the ocean. Only this year, Elle has invited herself along and booked us a beachfront cabin for the weekend.

I'm not about to complain about that kind of luxury.

I stretch out on one of the sun loungers on the deck, marveling at the view of the wide, blue ocean. Rush is inside, on the phone, and Xander, Madden, Gabe, and Elle all headed down for a swim an hour ago. Between that and relaxing by myself with a cocktail full of fruit that Molly made me, it was an easy choice.

Only he disappeared right after that, and I haven't seen him since.

Considering I'd planned to relax, that shouldn't be something I'm even thinking about, but not knowing where he is doesn't sit right with me. I'm not someone who gets attached easily, but Molly and me, we have that something. That something that makes our conversations flow and the comfort I feel around him deep. I miss Gabe not living with us, I miss Christian now he's been away for most of the year, but while I consider them my brothers, just like I do Rush and Madden, the connection I have with them is nothing like the fast one I've built with Molly.

I turn in the chair and strain my eyes to see inside, but the only person I can make out is the back of Rush's head from where he's sitting on the couch. Molly isn't in there. And I'm pretty sure he didn't go to the beach with the others. I'm hit with the unsettling thought that he's sitting in his room by himself. That won't do at all.

I jump up and head inside, then veer off down the hall. The house is enormous, but Molly's room is two down from mine, and when I knock on the door, he immediately calls out for me to come in.

I push open the door and stare at where he's sitting on his bed, knees hugged to his chest.

"What are you doing?"

"Sitting."

"Yeah, I see that. Why are you sitting alone inside?"

He hesitates for a second before shrugging. "I didn't want to go to the beach."

"And you're too cool for my company?"

He laughs. "Actually, I didn't want you to think I was smothering you."

And even though he says it lightly, it strangles my heart. "You think I wouldn't tell you if that was the case?" I mean for it to come out supportive, but this off feeling tells me I've missed the mark. I'm not sure what else to say to that though. Giving people comfort isn't something I'm great at, but even though he relaxes, I want my words to do more than that.

"True. I can always count on you for honesty."

I frown and cross to where his swim trunks are on the floor, then pick them up and toss them at him. "Get changed and come sit with me."

"Okay, but do you want me to sit with you because you miss my company or you feel sorry for me?"

"Miss your company? I saw you an hour ago." The way his face falls makes me cringe, and I hurry to fix it. "I don't have to miss you to want to spend time together."

And apparently, I've finally hit the mark because Molly gosh darn beams. His smile is so bright it lights me up inside.

"Yeah, yeah," I say, brushing his reaction off. "Just get changed and get your butt out here."

Before I can walk away, he strips off his shirt, then jumps up from the bed, turns his back, and drops his shorts.

My gut flips over itself at the sight of all of Molly's bare skin. I forget the fact I should probably look away. I forget the fact I told myself one and done. I forget the fact I'm not supposed to be thinking of him in all the ways he's currently filling my head.

Molly glances back over his shoulder as he leans forward and pulls on his swim shorts. "I knew you'd be checking me out."

I quickly look away. "Sorry."

"I wouldn't have taken my clothes off in front of you if I didn't want you to enjoy the view."

"You're going to get me into trouble."

Molly sighs, long and wistful. "If only."

I lead him back out onto the safety of the very public deck, where I know for a fact I'll keep my hands to myself. He picks up two more cocktails from the kitchen on the way and hands one over as he slides onto the sun lounger beside me.

"Comfortable there?" I ask him dryly.

"Very." He wriggles, warm skin moving deliciously against mine. "Only don't look down and see how much."

So of course, I glance down and am greeted by the incredible sight of tight material over a hard shaft.

I inhale deeply, but that doesn't stop me from ending up with the same problem. "I hate you."

"I know." He slides his sunglasses on, turning his attention to the water. "But I also know you really, really don't."

"Eat glass," I grumble.

Which, apparently, he finds hilarious. "Is that Seven speak for fuck off?"

"You know it."

"So why don't you just tell me to fuck off?"

I open my mouth to answer him, but it occurs to me that while people know I don't like to swear, no one has specifically asked why. Xander's never known me to, and even when I met my friends, they respected my choice and went with it. Molly though, he's not asking to be nosy but to get to know me better, and that's weird on a whole other level.

"It … makes me uncomfortable."

"Really?" He spins around, looking shocked. "Would you prefer if I didn't swear?"

"No, nothing like that. It's …" How to make this make sense? "I'm a big guy. My tattoos and piercings make me feel good, but I know that when people look at them, they see a certain type of person. Society sucks for that, by the way. But I know what it's like to be intimated by someone. I know what it's like to be scared. And while swearing is common from just about everyone these days, it doesn't take much for an f-bomb to sound aggressive. Coming from someone like me, it takes even less. So I make words up or use dumb phrases. Even when I'm mad, those things usually don't bother people. If someone cut me off in traffic and I dropped all the swears under the sun, it would be a whole lot of a different scenario to if I called them a frog-faced duck head, right?"

Fingers, cool from his icy drink, slip between mine. "Tell me something else about you."

"Like what?"

"Like … Seven's your real name, right? Is there a reason for it, or your parents just liked it?"

"First of all, they're not my parents. They're two people who I wish I could scrub from my memory forever." I let out a bitter laugh. "I'm named Seven because it's the most powerful number, and my dumb witch of a birther wanted me to always feel powerful … which is ironic when you consider how powerless I've been so many different times in my life. Sometimes while she was right there."

"I'm sorry," he whispers.

"Eh. Not important. But yeah, Seven's a real name. Rush is the only one of us who goes by his nickname."

"It suits him."

"It sure does, Tiny."

Molly rolls his eyes. "Careful, or I'll give you one."

"Oh, yeah, like what?"

"Like … saint. Or angel. Or red."

"Literally all of those options suck."

"You're right. Besides, Seven suits you. You know why?"

"Because it's as inaccurate as Rush's name?"

Molly shakes his head. "I looked up what Seven as a name means. It means loving. Blessed perfection. You don't see it, but you're all of those things and more."

Those three things are so far from how I see myself they barely make sense. "And Molly means deluded," I say with no real conviction behind it. But I struggle to take a compliment. Who knew?

Chapter 20

MOLLY

I love seeing Seven go such a bright shade of red. Behind all those tattoos, his skin is pale and gives away all of his secrets. I wriggle against him again, loving the way his breathing hitches for a moment, and the bulge in his swim trunks grows again.

While he might not want more with me, he'll never be able to deny that the attraction is there. And *boy*, is it there. Sipping this drink, body pressed up against his big one, sneaking glimpses of his tattoos and pierced dick print, and those strong thighs that make my mouth water ... whoever invented swimsuits was a goddamn genius, and I want to kiss Elle for renting this house out for the weekend.

I grin and stretch my arm out across his body. "Look at how bare I am compared to you."

Seven snatches up my wrist and runs his other fingers down the inside of my arm, uncovering goose bumps in his wake. "You have no idea how much I'd love to get my needle into this skin."

"Things creepy stalkers say for five hundred!"

He chuckles, and I love bringing the rare sound out in him. "For real. Would you ever let me tattoo you?"

The thought of that is nowhere near appealing, even with Seven being the one to ask. "It looks painful."

"It is." He releases my wrist, but before I can pull my arm away, he grabs my hand again and rests it between us.

I fucking melt.

"Pain isn't my friend," I say breathlessly.

"I'd be gentle."

"Now why, when you say that, do I picture you meaning it in a very, very different way?"

"Because you have a filthy mind."

I snap the fingers on my free hand. "That must be it."

"Seriously though. If it wasn't for the pain, would you get one?"

"Maybe. I think it's one of those things where I'm kinda nervous about committing too? Like, it's permanent. What would I get? What if I don't like it in ten years?"

"Remove it? Get it tattooed over?"

"Is that what you're going to do with Sevipus when you eventually get sick of me?"

He squeezes my hand so hard it almost hurts. "Don't say that bull dirt."

"There's more chance of it happening than not."

Seven bites his thumbnail that's already been bitten back as far as it can go. All his nails are like that, a raggedy mess, and I can only imagine the anxiety that runs through him for them to end up like that. "You're really hard on yourself, you know that?" he asks.

"Maybe I'm just honest."

"Nah. I'm honest. You're … it's like … never mind."

"Never mind? You did not just never mind me. How am I supposed to go about my day when all I'll be thinking about is what the hell you were going to say?"

"My opinion isn't all that important."

"I'd argue it's very important, given our deal is you literally giving me your opinion on how I'm screwing up on dates."

"True."

"So what was the never mind?"

"I dunno …" He picks up his drink and has a long gulp. "I guess, it almost feels like you put the worst in your head so you're prepared for when it happens."

"You think I'm doomsdaying?"

"Well, have I ever given you the impression I'll get tired of our friendship?"

"I'm drawing from past experience."

"Well, why don't you let me speak for myself, huh? Instead of comparing me to other people, let me be me, and understand when I tell you that I like you being a bit clingy and overeager that I mean it."

I'm sure I'm giving him puppy dog eyes. It's confirmed a moment later when he glances at me and does a double take.

"Nuh-uh. Stop looking at me like that. I didn't say anything special."

"You said so many special things all in a row."

"I'll also never get tired of you thinking I'm so much better than I am." His laugh is so quiet I almost miss it. "It's a nice change."

"Xander thinks you're amazing."

"Xander also isn't the most reliable source for healthy relationships."

"And I am?"

"From where I'm sitting, you're doing a thousand percent better than either of us."

"I'll take it. Even if the bar is very, very low."

"I don't know how to set it much higher, if I'm honest." He turns and suddenly meets my eye. "But you're making me see that I should try."

It takes everything in me not to throw myself at him. The urge to hug him, kiss him, grind up all over his body is so overwhelmingly strong I want to cry. It kills me every day that this brave, strong, incredible man doesn't know that he deserves the world. I wish he'd let me show him. I wish he'd let me try to smother him in all the good feelings I could muster up.

His lips twitch as he tears his gaze away. "I've gotta stop saying nice things to you."

Even though he says that, I know he won't. I pick up my drink again and cuddle into his side, head resting on his shoulder. He doesn't say anything, just like I'd assumed he wouldn't. I know I'm only setting myself up for the kind of pain I've never felt before, but being near Seven, physically and emotionally, is becoming addictive. Keeping my distance isn't something I even want to try.

Rush wanders outside a moment later and drops down onto the lounger next to us. I hurry to put as much distance between me and Seven as I can, but the gorgeous man doesn't release my hand.

"Everything okay?" I ask Rush.

"Yeah, yeah, fine." He rubs his scruffy jaw. "Tried to get the boyfriend to meet us down here, but he must be at work. He works a lot. Not his fault, obviously, but I do want him to meet you all at some point."

"Could invite him over on a Monday?" Seven suggests.

"Why a Monday?"

Rush sounds so earnestly confused it's hard not to laugh. "Family Monopoly," I remind him.

"Oh. That. Maybe."

"I didn't even know you had a boyfriend," Seven says. "How long have you been dating?"

"Really?" Rush blinks over at us. "But I talk about him all the time."

"I've heard about him," I say before Seven can argue the

point. It might have only been once, but it still counts.

Rush nods and falls silent.

"So …" Seven prompts.

"So what?"

I bite my cheek. "How long have you been dating?"

"Oh! Six months. Or … almost six months? We met on Christmas Eve last year. Big party."

"What's he like?"

"Busy. Hot. Great in bed. Messages me poetry sometimes."

"Poetry?" Seven asks.

I slap him before he can say anything negative. "That sounds so romantic."

Rush gets this dopey look over his face. "Yeah, I guess it is. I might go call him."

"Weren't you just talking to him?" Seven asks.

"When?"

"When you were on the phone inside?"

"No, that was Mom. Ian hasn't answered. Which makes sense. He turns his phone off when he's in meetings and forgets to turn it back on some nights." Rush laughs. "He's as forgetful as I am."

Then Rush stands and disappears back inside.

I'm debating whether to say something when Seven beats me to it.

"I don't like."

"Rush's boyfriend?"

"Yep."

I sigh. "I was hoping it was just my general skepticism, but … it's the weekend. Who has meetings and needs to turn their phone off on a Saturday?"

"Exactly."

"Rush is right though. It's exactly something he'd do."

"It is, but …"

"Yeah." I shake it off. "We just have to hope for the best.

I'm sure it's all fine, and honestly, I wouldn't put it past Rush to end up dating someone as chaotic as he is."

"I hope so."

"Besides," I snuggle into him again. "Should we be worrying about Rush's love life when mine is such a hot mess? I want someone I can do this with always."

"And by *this*, I'm going to assume you mean use as a human pillow."

"Well, duh. What else?"

He doesn't say anything for a long time. "You'll find your guy, Tiny."

"How can you know that?"

"Because any guy who doesn't want to date you is a frog-mouthed duck face."

I snort into his shoulder. "Does that include you? Because last I checked, you don't want to date me either."

"Yeah, but as we've already established tonight, I'm not the standard to base anything off of."

"Whatever you say, *Seven*."

"Don't say it like that."

"Like what?"

"Like … it has meaning."

"Maybe if I say it like that enough, you'll finally believe it."

"I can promise you that will never, ever be the case. But thanks for trying."

Little does he know that I'm never going to give up on him.

The others come back not long after, and we spend the night playing drinking games and getting way too sloppy and hungover for the swim Elle drags us to the next morning. It's not until we're driving home the next afternoon, my head heavy with dehydration, that I realize for the first time since moving into the house I haven't felt like the odd one out. I'm not sure if it will last, but I'll hold on to that feeling for as long as I can.

Chapter 21

SEVEN

My least favorite time is night. When it's dark. The house is silent. My thoughts get too loud. Some people say they can't remember their childhood, or only parts of it, and I wish I was that lucky.

For me, those memories are a constant. The haunting faces, the brutal hands. The tightening in my stomach deepens, twists, making my body feel like I might lose control. I roll onto my front, face buried in the pillow I'm clutching onto, but it doesn't help. I'll take a monster in my closet any day over the ones that exist in my head.

Times like this, I wish I could reach out to Xander. Text him to come here and let me hold him like I used to when we were younger, but I hate putting that on him because then the memories will get him too. Xander has way too many other things going on in his head to fit all the things in mine as well.

Xander's issues come from his neglect.

Mine come from having way too much attention.

I draw my knee up to my chest, fingers finding the Medusa

tattoo on my foot. It's easy enough to remind myself I'm safe now; I'm bigger, stronger, the protector. But that damned kid inside me won't stop pressing his feelings on me, won't stop trying to drag me under with him.

Everything feels so … hopeless. Dark. What's the point of even fighting when it's not like my situation is uncommon? I'm just another washed-up statistic.

The isolation, the loneliness, the rampant thoughts sweeping me under are so hard to fight against. Xander helps, he always does, but I will never, ever ask for it, and unless he comes to me while I'm already like this, I'm good at hiding.

Fighting the depression in my chest, I throw off my blankets, force myself out of bed, and pull on some sleep shorts, then head for the home office.

The stillness of the house presses against me as I walk, but when I drop down into my desk chair, hear the familiar purr of my computers waking up, some of the panicky feelings lessen. I still feel like shirtsleeves, still want to bow forward and let myself cry, but I resist the urge.

The click of the keys is loud as I log in to my fan site.

Kill Diver is a retro video game turned blockbuster movie turned universe. There are books, a TV series, spin-offs, all along with the conspiracy theories, and I'm deep in it all. One of the short-term foster homes I stayed in after I was beaten so badly that child services stepped in had the video game, and from there, I was hooked. I started my site at the local library, before Kill Diver was much of anything. It was a place I could hide, could build up an obsession about this world I loved, and lose myself in it for hours.

I never expected a community. I never expected the fan fiction options to explode or the fan art to be shared there constantly. We've got chat threads and topics about every part of the universe, and it's growing more popular and active every day.

I have no idea what I'd do without this community. I'm protective of it. Even Xander doesn't know how deep it all goes.

Is Omron actually Diver?

That theory always makes me smile because it's a common one, and everyone who posts about it thinks they're the first to have figured it out. It would be a mind melt if it was true—the whole objective of the game is for Omron to hunt down and kill the character called Diver. The problem is, no one knows if Diver actually exists.

Making your audience question everything sure is one way to build a franchise, and at this point, I think I'll be disappointed if Diver is ever revealed. That'll mean things are all over.

I write back to the comment thread and then answer a few more. Unlike how blunt I can be in real life, I'm gentle with my replies, wanting to make sure that the forums are a safe space for anyone like me. I'm quick to boot out troublemakers, but it doesn't mean I enjoy it.

Slowly, the panic and wildfire thoughts dry up, and I'm engulfed by the fictional world. Fully immersed, to the point reality ceases to exist and the world of Kill Diver is the only one.

"Seven?"

I jolt so hard my chair jumps, and I whirl around to find Molly standing there. He's in tiny sleep shorts and a tank top, hands cupped around a steaming mug, big eyes reflecting the glow from my screens.

"You almost gave me a heart attack."

He grins. "Now you sound like Xander. I knocked."

"I didn't hear you."

"Clearly. For you." Molly sets the mug down on my desk and grabs his desk chair, sliding it across the space until it's beside mine.

"What is it?"

"Tea. To help you sleep."

"I won't be sleeping tonight."

And while I'm hoping he'll get up and leave, it's also a complete relief when he curls up on the chair beside me. "Want to talk about it?"

I automatically tuck my foot with the medusa tattoo under the other one. "No. Literally never."

"I talk to you, you know."

"And that's your choice."

"And not talking is your choice." Molly props his chin in his hand. "That's not healthy."

"Like you can talk. *Healthy*. You have so many guy issues, and all you do is talk about that. It doesn't seem to have helped."

"I'll have you know I'm feeling very optimistic about the future. Bet you can't say the same."

"I'm very optimist about my future."

"Really?" he asks skeptically.

"Yep. It's getting me away from my past."

"I'm no shrink, but that doesn't sound like a well-adjusted outlook."

"Then you don't know what you're talking about." I pick up the mug and take a cautious sip. Tea isn't something I usually drink, and this one smells sweeter than *anything* I normally drink, but it's not horrible. "Thanks."

"You're very welcome."

"How did you know I was here?"

"Tracking device." Molly's face is so deadpan, and he's so obsessively needy in general, that I can't be sure he's joking.

I lift an eyebrow, and he sags.

"Thought I heard you come in here, and when I poked my head in, you were hard at work. So I went and made you a tea."

"Thoughtful of you."

"I'm very thoughtful." He leans forward so both elbows are planted on the armrest of my chair. "And *giving*."

I brush him off. "Be sure to mention that on your next proper date. I bet it'll go down a treat."

"I told you, I don't hook up on a first date."

And I can't resist teasing him. "Technically, we only had the one date before getting nasty."

"Yes, but it wasn't a real date, so it doesn't count. But I've already got plans for our second, so start thinking about the third. I want to power through them and learn everything I can because I was lust-drunk when I agreed not to hook up with anyone while you were training me." Molly rests his face on my shoulder. "I'm going to be so horny by the end of it."

My jaw clenches at the idea of him going on his first date, so boned up from all the celibacy, that he jumps straight into bed with the guy. His choice though. Nothing I can do about it. I was an idiot for sleeping with Molly the first time, and it's not going to happen again.

"And your needs are my main priority," I say, snappier than I mean to.

"Good. Now, are you sure you don't want to talk?"

"Positive." Until he'd come in here, I'd successfully distracted myself. If anything, Molly went and ruined all that progress I'd been making. That said, it's not like I'm any worse off now. Well, other than the whole picturing him sleeping around thing, but that's a completely separate issue.

"What are you working on?" he asks.

"Nothing."

"Urg … you are so boring. I got up in the middle of the night for you, and you're all *nothing, no, leave me alone*." He picks up the tea and has a sip before setting it down in front of me. "Well, fine. If you won't let me talk, and you won't spill your deepest secrets, and you won't even let me blow you—"

Say what, now?

He stands up and sets his hands on my shoulders. "You asked for this."

"For what?"

But Molly straddles my lap, slim thighs slotting on either side of my hips, and then ... he wraps his arms around me.

"What the hell are you doing?"

"Hugging you. And don't fight me on it—you need this. I'm not afraid to bite."

I almost laugh but rein it in. "And what if I don't like hugs?"

"You do."

"How do you know that?"

"Because I might not know much about you, but I still pay attention. Don't tell me your secrets. I don't care. But I'm going to help with whatever had you awake anyway. I'm stubborn like that."

I sigh as Molly rests his head against my shoulder and makes himself comfortable. He's right though. I do like hugs. Thanks to Xander.

He was the only person I ever willingly let touch me once I was old and big enough to have control over that, and then when we moved in here, these guys became like my brothers. Madden has no personal-space issues, Christian used to need a literal pile-on to stop his spirals, Gabe was always friendly with a shoulder squeeze or a tap to the head, and Rush will sometimes grab you out of nowhere while he's trying to manage his thoughts into a coherent stream. Learning the difference between good touch and bad was a real lesson, but everything about Molly's touch is good.

So good.

And surprisingly, strictly platonic.

I don't feel taken advantage of or pressured, just ... safe. Protected.

When usually that's all me.

"You can keep working," comes his muffled voice. "I'm facing the other way. I promise."

I believe him. But I don't need to keep working now because Molly's giving me everything I needed from Xander, but instead of feeling like I'm piling more crap on Xander, who's already overloaded, it feels like Molly's taking it from me, offloading it from my shoulders and burning the darkness with his sunshine.

I'm not thinking when I wrap my arms around him. Crush him against my chest. Bury my face in his neck and squeeze my eyes closed against the tears. I refuse to let any of them fall, but it's a struggle. Made even harder when Molly's fingers dip into my hair and massage my scalp.

"It's okay," he soothes. "You're always here for me, and now it's my turn."

I don't say anything back, just hold him. Bathed in relief and letting myself be weak, to need him. Because I really, really need this.

Molly falls asleep at some point, steady, deep breaths loud by my ear. I flick the lever on the side of the chair to release the backrest, our combined weight making it bend right back.

Then I keep my nose near his hair, one hand resting on his back to anchor him there, and go back to my forum. I type one-handed, feeling secure, warm, wanted. Surrounded by my obsession, and with Molly pressed against me, it almost gives the illusion of being invincible.

None of the bad in the world can touch me like this.

Chapter 22

MOLLY

"Does Xander know we're in here?" Seven asks, looking around Xander's paint studio. It's one of the darkest rooms in the house and looks like a chaos dungeon. There are canvases stacked against almost every wall, then more still on easels, but those ones are wrapped in plastic. There are forgotten frescos and sculptures abandoned mid-creation. Paint covers the floor and walls in a built-up design of half-finished thoughts, and while I don't understand how Xander can work in this disarray, there's something comforting about being in here.

"Of course he knows." He's the one who helped with this date idea.

"Look, I know my date was technically at home too, but at least we actually stepped foot outside of the place."

I laugh and tug him further into the room, closing the door behind us. "Dude, you bought a fucking puzzle. I gave that a chance, the least you can do is show me a *little* trust."

Seven huffs and crosses his tattooed arms. "Liked it though, didn't you?"

"That's my point. Now, shut up and act like you're enjoying yourself."

Seven forces a broad smile that shows off all his teeth.

Close enough!

I walk over to the corner and switch on the cheesy colored disco light I bought online and watch the disgust cross Seven's face as it flashes red, then green, then purple.

"Tell me we're not dancing."

"It's for *ambience!*"

"Thank fookies for that."

"I know you better than to make you dance. Though it would be incredibly romantic."

"Hard pass on that, Tiny."

"That's okay." I give Seven my most innocent smile. "I have other things we can do together."

I step closer and lace my fingers through his before leading him over to where there's a large canvas sheet laid over the floor.

"I've decided there are too many questions to ask," he deadpans. "So, I'm gonna go with it and hope I don't end up dead."

"Perfect attitude!" I sit down and pat the place right beside me, amused by his hesitance.

"I can smell pie," he says as he sits, strong, tattooed legs stretched out in front of him.

"Good nose." I uncover the food I've spent today making with Auntie Agatha. I'm lucky that when I showed up on her doorstep with ingredients today, she was more than happy to jump in and help me. Creamy vegetarian pot pie again, rocky road, and sourdough garlic bread.

He moans and absently rubs his stomach. "That looks good."

"All your favorites."

"They are." He side-eyes me. "You called in reinforcements."

"Nothing wrong with doing a little prior research."

And like our one-and-a-half dates before this one, it's *easy*. Seven's as blunt and un-sweary as ever, I'm a complete dork, and somehow, it works. Feels right. I'm trying not to trust the feeling. Every time something deep inside me tells me I've found the one, it all turns out to be horseshit, and I end up discarded and alone. Some days, it feels like I'm not supposed to find my person, and then others ... My eyes catch with Seven's, and he chuckles.

"How are you such a mess?" His big hand crosses the small distance between us, and his thumb swipes over my chin. I'm all melty at his touch, and then he goes and sucks that same thumb into his mouth. Lips around skin ... Hollowed-out cheeks ...

Hot. Fucking. Damn.

My whimper is completely unintentional.

"Molly ..." Seven groans. "No more of that."

"Am I being cute again?" I ask, and my dumb voice comes out kinda breathless.

"You don't know how to turn it off, do you?"

His indulgent tone goes a long way toward fanning those feelings of rightness. I shake my head, heart feeling almost too big for me to answer. Seven's a gorgeous man, but that's not what's gotten me all starry-eyed over him. Everything about him is *good*. And flashing back to when he held me the other night, when those kind eyes turned stormy and he couldn't fight his frown, only makes my chest feel floatier than before.

I'd bet all the money in my bank account that Seven wouldn't have let just anyone see him like that. He chose to let me in.

Well, he chose to let me squirrel my way pushily into his life, but that still counts.

"Dessert time!" I say, all but diving for the rocky road. When he goes to grab a piece, I slap his hand away. "I want to feed you."

"What?"

"And you can feed me. Since I'm a complete mess who can't feed himself, it's the perfect solution. Obviously." I'm definitely not staring at his lips.

His lips that pull into a sexy fucking half smile. "Deal."

I break off a chunk of chocolate and marshmallow, then raise it to his lips. My gut is in knots as he parts them and I slip the treat inside, and then Seven closes his mouth around it, tongue skimming the tip of my finger before I pull it away.

"M-my turn."

He lifts the chocolate, and I immediately open, which makes Seven chuckle. "There you go being eager again."

"Of course I'm eager. It's … chocolate. I really, really like chocolate."

He shifts closer until we're side by side, hips touching, his torso all but curved around mine.

"When you're on a date, make him work for it," Seven says by my ear. The chocolate runs along the length of my bottom lip. "Make him see that you're worth it. Make him desperate for you. Make sure he knows that being with you is a mother-trucking gift."

I'm silent, not wanting to say anything and break the moment.

He leans forward, watching himself drag the chocolate over my top lip. "These lips kill me," he rasps. "They looked so at home wrapped around me. They were greedy for it, weren't they?"

"So greedy."

He smirks. "Open."

My mouth drops, and Seven pushes the food inside, his

index finger following it. He strokes over my tongue, and I'm so turned on that I close my mouth over his digit and suck.

His pupils flare to life, and he slowly withdraws his finger and pushes inside again, over and over, until he works out what he's doing and pulls it away completely.

"So," he croaks. "I don't think you brought me in here just for dinner?"

"Nope." But given that my cock is hard as ice, I'm kinda second-guessing the rest of our date. My gaze flicks to the basket Xander has set up for us and back to Seven, wondering whether to back out now.

Only he catches my look and reaches for the basket before I can. "Body paint?"

"Ah, funny story ..."

"I'm listening."

"Well, you know how you asked if you can tattoo me? And I'm too scared?"

"Yes ..."

"I was looking up date ideas, and I saw couples painting and thought—"

"Were you looking up dating or sex?" he asks. "Because body painting your partner isn't usually second-date level. Just so you know."

"Ah, right. Maybe we'll forget about—"

"Nope." Seven shifts back closer again and tilts my head up until I meet his eye. "What did you think, Molly?"

I swallow. "That you could paint me. Instead."

"What, like your face? Arms—"

"All of me."

I expect him to be shocked or to turn me down. To remind me that we agreed no more sleeping together, and with the tension in the room right now, if I get naked, I'm going to be hard as fuck. He's going to know exactly what I'm thinking. *Will he act on it?*

Seven's a no-bullshit kind of guy—maybe he thinks naked body painting is a totally innocent thing that can happen between friends.

"All of you could take a while," he says.

"I don't care."

His grip on my jaw tightens. "Better get comfortable, then."

Excitement surges through me, and I scramble to pull off my shirt. Seven busies himself with the paints, and the fact he didn't argue or second-guess has me full of relief because if he'd said no, if he'd been even the slightest bit unsure, this wouldn't be happening. I want him in all the ways you can possibly want someone, but I'm not going to chase him. If he's already running from me, that's not a sign of a great start to the relationship.

It's taken me this long to figure it out.

I kick my pants to the side and then lie down, front to the canvas. Apparently, when it comes to the floors, Xander can make a mess on them, but nobody else can. Given the type of mess I'm hoping to make tonight, Xander's forethought is probably spot-on.

"What are you doing?"

I freeze at the confusion in Seven's voice.

Oh, fuck, this is what we agreed to, isn't it?

"Umm ... getting conformable."

His chuckle is dark, and I jump when his fingers slide down my sides and beneath the band of my briefs. "You're still wearing these."

"Ah, right. Do you ... do you want them off?"

"You promised me everywhere." He leans in, face brushing mine as he pushes down the material. "Were you lying?"

"Nuh-uh. No. Nope. No lies."

"Good. Then hold still and let me get you ready for me."

Hold still? Way to set me an impossible task, Seven. Does

this guy not know what he's doing to me? I'm almost vibrating out of my skin at his touch, and when he slides my briefs off my ass and down my legs, leaving my hard cock trapped under me, a chill of being naked and exposed sends goose bumps over my skin.

"You ready?"

"So ready." I'll beg if he asks me to. I'll do anything. In fact, I'd be more than happy to skip the painting and just have Seven's hands on me. He has other ideas though.

I turn my head slightly so I can watch him pick up a paint-brush and dip it into the paint. It's a tiny brush, giving me the very clear sign that Seven isn't in any kind of hurry.

And when he gets started, neither am I. Kind of. The brushstrokes glide over my sensitive skin, making every feeling heightened. The way it tickles along my neck and over my shoulder, brushes the curve of my spine. It'd probably be relaxing if I wasn't so turned on, but the lust pumping through my blood is making it burn, a complete contrast to the cool paint coating my skin.

And he isn't in a hurry. He paints down my back, my arms, and then up my legs. It tickles and feels weird as the paint dries, but every time my eyes flutter open and I glimpse Seven's concentration mixed with the same intense want that's flooding me, lust surges into my system again.

I'm almost sure he's going to skip my ass, when the backs of his fingers skim up my inner thighs. He gently nudges them open, and I part them willingly, heartbeat hard and fast as he drags a slightly larger paintbrush along my taint. The bristles are soft, the paint smooth, but my breathing kicks up a notch as I clench against how good it feels.

Seven chuckles. "You like that."

"Honestly … I'm trying not to come."

He slaps my ass, and I jolt, hard cock scraping the rough canvas.

"*Ouch.*"

"No coming. I still have your front to go."

"You're so mean."

"You wanted this."

"I've changed my mind. Tattoo me instead. Anything you want, just let me come."

"Nope. But if you're really, really good for me, I might get you off when we're done."

Holy shit, yes. Yes, yes, yes, please.

All I can do is hope to fucking heaven that he does because while I want to say fuck it and jerk myself off, I also never, never want this to end. The two feelings are so strong and overpowering they're driving me out of my mind.

Seven is a sadistic bastard because he takes even longer to paint my ass, making sure to drag the paintbrush over my taint when I least expect it. My whole body is a live wire, in tune with every movement from him, desperate for more of his touch. His skin. His mouth.

"Shoot me, you look incredible," he says at last.

The compliment shivers through me. "I want to see."

"Not until I'm done. Turn over."

"Won't the paint smudge?"

"I only did a thin layer, so most of it's dry."

And if I felt exposed before, it's nothing to how I feel now. I roll onto my back, hard cock resting against my lower abs, leaking a pool of precum against my skin. His gaze sweeps over me, and I'm so sensitive I swear I feel that too.

The paintbrush tickles over my collarbones, dips into my belly button, sweeps over my nipples until they're hardened and tight. He does my torso, my arms, my legs, thankfully faster on this side, and when I peek at his sweats, he's as hard as I am. Big cock held in place by his underwear, spot of precum staining the material and the telltale bumps of his piercings taunting me.

I'm so distracted by his dick print that when the paintbrush sweeps over my balls, I gasp, hands clutching the canvas sheet.

"Oh my fucking god."

He does it again. And again. Brush circling my sac, flicking gently over the skin. I want to sob at how good it feels, how sensitive I am, but then Seven sets down the brush.

"What are you doing?" I pant.

"Admiring my work."

And in that moment, with his dark eyes looking intently, really seeing me, I know I want him to look at me like that forever. I reach for his phone and slide it to him.

"Take a photo."

"What?"

"Do it." I want him to know I'm sure. "Then I can see too."

"I promise I'll delete it right after."

"No." I cover his big hand with mine. "I want you to have this."

"Naked photos of you?"

"Maybe I'm an idiot, and maybe it'll bite me in the ass one day, but I trust you."

"When you helped me. On my bed …"

"This isn't the same thing. You didn't consent to that. I'm giving you my complete permission for this."

Seven leans down, hulky body hovering over me, and his lips brush mine gently. "I will protect your trust with my life."

His gentle hands move me into position, and he takes a series of full-body and close-up shots. I roll over when he tells me to, head rested on my crossed arms, and let him move my legs open to where he wants them.

I'm nervous. Almost afraid to see something so intimate, but I meant it when I said complete permission. There isn't anyone in the entire world who I'd trust to take care of those shots like he would.

Chapter 23

SEVEN

I can't concentrate on the sight in front of me, I'm so incredibly turned on. Molly is … complete temptation. His long, lean body. That mouthwatering bubble butt. His smooth calves and lightly toned thighs. I want to run my hands over every inch of him, but I also don't want to ruin the things I've painted. I will, because it's inevitable, and admiring them isn't enough to hold me back from what I really want to do.

"Finished?" he asks, sounding dazed. The way he doesn't try to hide how much he wants me is both hot as hell and a worry. We know this is just us messing around, and he's safe with me. I'd never take advantage of him, but some guys would, and it's becoming clear to me that Molly doesn't hold back his interest. He'd do anything for the guy he cares about, and that almost makes me wish it was me. Almost.

As much as I'm starting to feel things for him, there's no way I'm going to drag someone this amazing into a relationship with someone as damaged as me. If people think I'm protective of Xander, that's nothing to how I'd be with someone like Molly. Someone so sweet, and pure, and inno-cent. I'd suffocate him.

And yet, I'm not putting an end to this like I should be.

"Wanna see?"

"Yes, I'm dying over here."

I swipe back through the gallery to the images of his front, my stare tracing his long, red cock. It's the only part of him I haven't painted because I've got plans for that thing. I sit down close and hand the phone over.

"Wow," he mutters, zooming in on random parts of his body. "You're really good. Like, *really*. Maybe you should sell some pieces like Xander."

"Nah, paint isn't my thing."

"Have me fooled." He pauses and pouts over his shoulder at me. "You didn't do my dick."

I smirk and lean in. "It might be nontoxic, Tiny, but paint doesn't taste great."

"T-taste ..."

I grab him by the hips and flip him over, then yank my T-shirt over my head.

Molly's gorgeous lips have fallen open, and I make eye contact with him before leaning down and sliding the tip of his cock into my mouth.

"Oh, fuck, it's happening," he rambles. "Your mouth is on my dick. My dick is in your mouth. Shit. Fuck. Holy mother of sex toys ..."

I pull off him and chuckle. "Kinda sounds like you want me to stop."

"I will *end* you."

He's adorable when he's all turned on and ragey.

"You know what I *really* want to do?" I ask, running my tongue over his slit.

He grunts, cock twitching. "What?"

"Swipe across to the end."

Molly hurries to pick my phone back up and does as I've said. There, on either side of his gorgeous ass, I've painted my handprints, and right before I took this shot, I pulled down the front of my sweats and got my dick in the frame. The tip is hovering right in line with his ass.

"I want a copy of this," falls out of his mouth.

I chuckle and lick him again. "Gladly."

"Also yes. Sex. I want that. Right now."

"Do you have a condom?"

"There's, like, five in the basket. And lube."

Of course there is. "You're an eternal optimist, aren't you?"

He nods, but as I move to collect the supplies, his hand grabs mine. "I know I brought those things and planned all this, but I don't ever want you to feel pressured, okay? I'm so fucking attracted to you that if I get the chance, my answer is always yes, but if yours is a no, I'll respect that."

Molly has no idea how much those words get me in the chest. "Thank you."

"Are you going to say no?"

Like that's even possible. "I think my dick would murder me if I did."

He smiles wickedly and spreads his legs. "Good. Then hurry up and get inside me."

His enthusiasm is such a turn-on. The way he so brazenly says what he wants, and the way I fall for it every damn time. He has my dick aching for him, and every second I'm not touching him is driving me out of my mind.

I find the condoms and lube hidden in the side pocket of the basket and set them out on the floor. Part of me is trying to warn that this is the last thing I should be doing, but I can't help myself, not when Molly has offered himself up for me like this. If I was a better person, I'd have something to offer him other than a mind-blowing orgasm, but I'm not, so we only have this.

"You're taking too long," he rasps, and when I glance back up, the teasing is gone, and his bright eyes are pure fire. "After all this edging, I'll probably come the second you're inside me."

I chuckle darkly, pushing off my sweats and briefs before tearing open a condom and rolling it carefully down my shaft. "It's been … what? An hour?"

Molly shakes his head. "All week. I've been hard up to make this happen again."

Damn, I both love and hate hearing that. To stop from having to answer him, I lean in and kiss him, but I know it's a mistake the second I do. Somehow, I'd forgotten how addictive his kisses are, and second after second of promises to stop disappear like last time. I can't even break away to find the lube, just feel around blindly until my hand brushes the small bottle.

Molly's clinging to me, kissing me back with as much force as I'm using, and it feels nice to be wanted like this. To know that it's not all physical, not all about getting off as soon as possible. We're friends, something more brewing dangerously between us that I'm set on ignoring while I enjoy this moment.

I give in to the urge to move closer and crush Molly to the floor with my body weight. His legs immediately curl around my waist, octopusing himself to me like last time, and I give him what he wants; I bring our cocks together as I pop the lid on the lube.

My thrusts against him are slow, softer than I'd usually use, but with how much I want to be inside him, I don't want to risk tearing the condom and having to deal with putting another one on when I could be inside him already.

Molly's hands are exploring my shoulders, my arms, my back, his touch lighting up parts of me I'd thought had long since died. I deepen the kiss, one hand holding the back of his neck while the other manages to squeeze lube into my palm.

Then I reach between his legs.

Molly whimpers, knees drawing back to give me more room to work, and I revel in how trusting and open he is. He's not afraid to be vulnerable, and while opening myself up like that makes me want to crawl into a hole and die, it's something I admire about him.

The kind of brave I'll never be.

He moans into my mouth as I work him open, finger pressing deeper with every stroke. He's wrapped around me with warm suction, and if this is how good he feels on one digit, I can't imagine how it'll feel when I fill him with my cock.

"You like me playing with your pretty little hole?"

He whines. "Say more stuff like that."

"Like what? Like how sexy you look while I finger you open for me? Or how mad you're driving me wanting to be inside you?"

Molly's head falls back, painted ribs expanding and contracting rapidly with his breaths. Even covered in paint, I admire the way his light muscles ripple every time I pass over his prostate, the way his abs clench and release when I work a second finger into his hole. He opens for me beautifully, willingly, so ready to be filled.

I shouldn't be as in awe of him as I am, so I put it down to the horniness overriding my ability to brain properly.

His ass grips my fingers tight, and though I know I should probably give him another one, I'm dying to sink inside his body, to feel what it's like to own Molly's body.

"Please fuck me," he begs.

I widen my fingers, making sure he's as stretched as I can get him. "Are you ready?"

"I don't care."

"I'm not going to hurt you."

"You won't. It'll feel good. So good."

I snort but pull my fingers out anyway and slick up my cock. "If it hurts, you need to tell me to stop."

He smiles wickedly up at me. "I will. Promise. Now, give me what I want."

I chuckle and position myself over him, the sweat on his thighs immediately smearing paint over mine. "I hope you're ready," I say, pressing my tip to his hole. It's a tight fit as I push forward, and Molly's breathing catches for a moment before returning to normal, but he doesn't tell me to stop.

His hole stretches deliciously around me, yielding to the intrusion, and I take it slowly to make sure there are no issues with the condom or my piercings, but once Molly's good and relaxed, that won't be necessary anymore.

"Ohh …" He breathes. "Y-your piercings …" His back arches briefly off the canvas. "Wow. Umm. They're …"

My hips meet his ass as he's rambling. He's stretched perfectly around me, sucking my cock in nice and deep, the warm pressure like the most cosmically incredible hug. I have to take a minute to make sure I'm not going to set off too soon.

"I'm never, ever having sex with someone who's not pierced again," he says, cupping my face. "Are you okay? They don't hurt?"

I chuckle. "They're fully healed. As long as you don't go tearing them out, they just make everything more sensitive."

His legs wrap around me, pulling me down closer. "Then what are you waiting for? Fuck me."

I give a slight thrust, loving the way he shivers under me, and before I do any more, I duck my head and drag him into a kiss. My mouth melts into his as I thrust harder this time, testing the movements, testing what he can take, and I build up the pace, gradually getting faster, getting harder, deeper.

My forearms are cramping under my weight, but I ignore them, knees digging into the floor as I drive in and out of

Molly's body. He's clutching me close, paint slick between our torsos, and I have a brief moment of picturing dragging him to the shower to wash my work back off again when his mouth breaks from mine.

"My cock, please. Please touch me."

I shift my weight to one side and reach between us with my free hand. He's leaking everywhere, and I love the feel of his stiff, slick cock slotting in my hand. Like it was made to be there. Made just for me.

"You gonna come?" I breathe against his mouth. "Come while you're being split open by my cock?"

"Yes, yes, yes. Make me come, Seven." His thighs twitch. "I need it, please, I need it."

His begging does it for me. Molly might talk about men playing games all the time, but he's not one of them. He wears his emotions and wants right out there on his sleeve, and it both stokes my curiosity and makes me terrified of him. I find it hard to believe someone could be this good and pure, but he's done nothing for me to think otherwise.

My dick is getting sensitive, racing with more pleasure than I've felt in too long. The piercings are tugging gently, pressing against my shaft in the way that makes my incoming orgasm crackle. I can already feel it's going to be a big one, and I'm aching for it. Wanting release like I've never wanted anything while at the same time desperate to hold on to how this feels for as long as humanly possible.

He tugs my mouth back to his as he stiffens in my hold. Molly's mouth claims me as he releases, cock pulsing in my hand as I stroke him through his orgasm. When he's finished, I straighten, grip his hips, and don't hold back.

His hooded eyes, the mess of paint over his skin, the puddle of cum splashed across his abs … he's an erotic artwork for my eyes only, and I never thought a moment could be made for me and me alone until this moment right here.

"You look so beautiful," I grit out. "Feel so good. I wanna come. Wanna fill your ass. Press my cum so deep inside you until I've painted you inside and out."

"Do it. Come."

My fingers bite into his hips as I pound once, twice more, and finally let go. Sheer relief crashes over me, and I grunt, cock throbbing inside him as I empty into the condom. I'm covered in sweat and paint, and Molly is the same. My images are all but unrecognizable, and I'm suddenly really heffing grateful he asked me to take those photos.

And told me I could keep them.

He lets out the most adorable, satisfied sigh, and I collapse forward on top of him. My hands are kinda stiff from holding him, but I wrap my arms around his back, crushing Molly's frame to mine.

My dick slips out of him, and I regret that it's all over already. That we can't just bone all night and not worry about any of the other stuff.

"So, I guess we're both big old liars," Molly says, kissing my neck. "We've now doubled our agreed sexy times limit. Think we can triple it?"

I lower my weight so Molly's trapped beneath me. "Twice. That's it. That's us done." But even I don't believe my words.

He rakes his fingers through my hair. "Uh-huh."

"I'm serious, Tiny."

"Whatever you say."

His teasing eyes and gorgeous face hit something deep in my gut. Something that makes me say, "Well, *maybe* once more. Then that's it. Third-date celebration and all that."

"Ooh, I better make our third date a good one, then."

"I dunno, I think you'll struggle to top this."

"I'm confident."

"Well, in that case, I can't wait to see what you come up with."

Chapter 24

MOLLY

"What's all this?" Rush asks, wandering into the room like he isn't sure how he got here.

"Family dinner. Well, kind of. I know Monday is when you all make sure you're home, but I thought for whoever is here, we could do family fun Fridays or something like that ..."

"Awesome idea." He claps me on the shoulder on his way into the kitchen, where he pulls down a cup that he fills at the sink. "Who'll be here?"

"I still have to check with—"

He lifts the glass for a sip, and a pair of googly eyes look back at me.

I laugh. "What's that?"

"Hmm, what ..." Rush turns the glass and blinks at them. "Huh. No idea."

"Weird."

"Is it?"

Considering Rush isn't exactly on the conventional scale himself, I'm not surprised that's his response.

"So are you home tonight? Seven and Xander should be here, and Madden mentioned maybe going out with Penn, but he wasn't sure yet."

"Yeah, my boyfriend's out of town. I think." He looks upward, finger bouncing like he's counting. "Or was that next week … If today's Friday … and we spoke yesterday—the day before? Was it …" He wanders right back out again, empty glass still clutched in his hand.

I'll put him down as a maybe.

While Monopoly Mondays are good fun, they're a bit too competitive for me. Gabe stops by for them occasionally, and whenever he's here, I get that feeling of being the outsider again. He's friendly, and the others don't treat me any differently, so I know the feeling is solely on me, but they all have a connection I couldn't hope to build. Most of the time, I get out first and end up sitting with Xander while Madden and Seven battle it out for the win.

This should be more my speed. I have food Auntie Agatha helped me cook and one giant-ass puzzle that should keep us going all night. I like the calm connection I built with Seven the night we did one together, so I'm hoping for the same vibes here.

No smack-talking, just love.

Unfortunately, I overestimated my roommates.

"Dude, no, you start with the edges first," Seven says, smacking Madden's hand away.

"You're wrong. You've gotta color match."

"You're both cheating," Rush says, shouldering his way between them and flipping the box lid facedown. "If you have the picture, it's a guide. It doesn't matter where you start because you can just follow that."

"You want us to do this thing *blind?*" Seven snaps. "It's five thousand pieces."

"His idea is about as dumb as yours," Madden sings.

I bite my lip, equal parts frustrated and amused. So much for peace and love. I thought Monopoly was the culprit, but turns out it's all them.

Xander drags his chair over next to mine and curls up in the seat. "It was a good idea, in theory."

"You know, I thought there'd be less ..." I wave my hand over them. "*That.*"

"Madden might not play sports anymore, but he's still a jock at heart. Competitive as fuck. And while Seven likes to pretend that he enjoys challenging him, that's not why he's like this."

"Why is he?"

Xander shrugs. "He just never learned how to stop fighting, I guess."

"Fighting ... what?"

He's quiet for a moment, rubbing his thumb back and forth over his knuckles. "Everything."

I think back to how Seven was that night I found him last week. He and Xander have a story, I get that, but they've clearly been through some things I'd never be able to imagine. While I'm curious as hell about it, it's also something that I know not to push on, and honestly, I'm probably better off not knowing. I already feel a lot for Seven, and Xander is someone I felt close to instantly; thinking of anything bad happening to either of them makes me want to throw something.

Since I found Seven in his office that night, I've been checking up on him. He doesn't know, and I'd never tell him, but I set my alarm for just after midnight every night, tiptoe down the hall, and press my ear to his door to see if I can hear him breathing inside. Then I tiptoe back to bed.

I'm not even sure *why* I feel like it's on me to do it; I just know that I never want him to feel alone again.

"What's Seven's favorite thing?" I ask Xander.

"Me."

Of course that's his answer. "Well, since I can't take you on our date, what's his *second* favorite thing?"

"Well, that's easy. Kill Diver."

"The *movie*? Seriously?"

"It's not just a movie. It's a video game too. And there's this whole online—you know what? You should ask *him* about it."

"But then it won't be a date surprise."

"Dress up as Pilot Markie, and he'll nut in his pants."

"Who the fuck is Pilot Markie?"

"The guy Seven's been boy-band-level obsessed with since he was a kid."

I cross my arms and huff. "Fuck Pilot Markie."

Xander laughs. "He's the sweet, kinda nerdy sidekick, who's dumb as fuck but in a golden retriever way. Other than the dumb-as-fuck thing, you remind me of him. A little."

"I'm not *nerdy*."

"No, it's ... the vibe. This wholesome, cheery, boost-every-one-up thing. Seven likes that, I think."

"I see myself *very* different to you."

"How do you see yourself?"

"Like ... a blister. Painful, popping up in unwanted places, and no one wants to deal with me."

"Whoa. No. Rejected."

I give him a perplexed look. "What is?"

"You can't be as broken as the rest of us. I won't let you. You're my *who I wanna be when I grow up*."

"I'm a year older than you."

"Exactly. This time next year, I want to be happy and positive and shit rainbows toooo."

"I think you're setting yourself up to fail. Shitting rainbows is something I was born with."

He sighs dramatically. "Well, there goes that idea. Though, you should probably see a doctor about that condition."

"Maybe I'll book in with your nurse."

Xander almost swoons. "You should. He's amazing."

"Cute too."

"Yup. Makes having to see him so much more embarrassing." He plays with one of his gold-painted nails.

"What do you do if he's not working?"

"Haven't had to deal with that yet, thank fuck."

Considering they've been going there for a while and Xander's attacks can be frequent, that's a huge fucking coincidence. I can only hope that his luck holds. And that if Derek isn't there, it's not one of the times I'm with him because I'd have no goddamn clue how to handle that.

"Speaking of dates …" Xander says. "How did the painting with Seven go?"

My lips twitch, but I'm determined to keep what happened to myself. Not because I give a shit about the house rules on not hooking up with each other but because it's up to Seven to tell Xander. I don't want to overstep in their friendship.

"It was good."

"The messy canvas you left behind says otherwise. All I could smell was sweat and cum when I picked it up. The hormones were practically airborne. I could have *caught* something."

I cringe. "No idea what you're talking about, but I went back the next morning to clean it all up, and you'd already been there. So. Umm. Sorry."

"Don't be." Xander tugs his glossy bottom lip between his teeth. "I *wanted* to do it."

I roll my eyes. "You're such a perve."

"Did he fuck you?"

"Nothing happened."

"You're *such* a liar." He drapes himself over my lap. "Why don't you love me? Why won't you share all the sordid details with me?"

"Because there were no details. And I thought you didn't think of Seven that way?"

"It's complicated. The thought of him fucking *you*, hot. Like …" He shivers.

"Why do you assume he'd fuck me?"

"Because he's a strict top."

Interesting … and a better answer than him stereotyping us.

"But Seven touching *me*?" Xander continues. "Actually sickening. Like, it makes my skin crawl."

"You guys hug all the time."

"Yep, but it really is platonic. He's my safety. And I know that even when we're snuggling or whatever that there's nothing sexual going on in his head, and it's the same for me."

"Eh, well, it's not my business, is it?"

He sits up, pinning me in his stare. "I think it is. I want you to know, and I want you to ask me things if you're not sure. Or tell me if you ever think I'm overstepping. I won't let Seven go. I can't. But I can share. And … I want to share him with you."

Something about that gets me. Hits me right in the chest. Maybe I should feel threatened by Xander or uncomfortable about him saying that Seven will always be his, but given he feels that strongly and he wants to share his person with *me*? It's oddly sweet.

I reach for his hand. "You have a big heart, you know?"

"Nope. This is where we disagree again. I'm actually a bit of a selfish asshole."

"There's no way that's true."

"I just really like attention. Sometimes I do things I don't even *want* to be doing to get it."

"Unfortunately, I know a little bit about that feeling."

He gives me a sad smile. "The world is kinda fucked-up, isn't it?"

"That's something we can agree on."

"If it wasn't, you and Seven would probably be together by now."

"While you're sweet, and I love that you're shipping us, there's one problem: Seven doesn't want to be with anyone."

"But you had sex."

"Sex doesn't mean anything."

His face falls. "It does to me."

"And that's okay too," I hurry to assure him. "But for Seven, it's just a casual thing. It doesn't have to have any emotions behind it."

"I don't believe it. I bet the emotions are there, but he's fighting them. It's what he does."

As much as I wish I could believe Xander, I'm also not going to get my hopes up. Seven's been clear with me, and while he's admitted that he's not opposed to more sex, that doesn't mean anything in the scheme of things. I've had sex with plenty of guys because I was horny. It doesn't mean I wanted more.

Even though I usually did.

I think I'm more like Xander. A bit of a romantic, looking for my forever person. Seven is too logical for that.

"Does it mean something to you?" Xander asks.

I know I should probably lie, but I can't bring myself to do it. "With Seven … I think it might."

Chapter 25

SEVEN

"You *had* to pick a puzzle," I mutter, sorting through the pieces in front of me, unable to believe that a week later, we're still working on the dumb thing.

"You like puzzles! It was fun when we did it."

"Yeah, but the one we did was a couple of hundred pieces. Five thousand? Really?"

"There were more of us," Molly explains. "So I thought it would need to be bigger."

"Well, you've done it now." Ever since our family fun night, where we barely made a dent in the puzzle, it's sat on the table and been worked on bit by bit by whoever's around. We're still only a quarter of the way through, and it's frustrating me every day to know that it's sitting here unfinished.

"I think it's more fun this way," Molly says in his usual peppy way. "That it brings us together even when we're not together."

"You *would* think that." I try to make it sound like an insult, but it doesn't come out that way. Probably because it's one of the things I like most about him. How sincere and sweet he is. It also doesn't surprise me that he'd want to feel a connection to the people in the house when they're not here because Molly seems starved for it. I've heard him talk to his dad and best friend a few times, and I can't help but think he holds back with them both. I know he said he felt like the third wheel between them—and *that* isn't at all weird—but it almost feels like he *wants* to be.

"Question for you," I say. "What were you like in college?"

He chuckles. "Hello, random."

"Yeah, yeah, go with it."

His nose scrunches up as he tries a piece that doesn't fit and sets it back down again. "I was good. Roomed with Will from when I was a freshman until senior year when—"

"The douchebag boyfriend?"

"Yeah." He sighs. "Until him. Otherwise, I did well in classes, got reallyyyy messy on the weekends, and worked part-time making coffees."

"Nice. Other than Will, how many friends did you have?"

He throws me a look. "That's a weird question."

"Well, there was Madden …"

Molly thinks for a moment. "I knew Madden, but he was more Will's friend."

"Okay, then, who else?"

"Well … the ex-boyfriend, obviously. There was a girl I used to sit with in one of my typography classes. Oh! And the twins I'd eat with sometimes."

I bite my lip, putting together more of the Molly puzzle than ever. "What about at the cafe?"

"Yeah, there were a few nice people there."

"Anyone you were friends with?"

"Not really." Molly glances up at me. "That actually sounds kind of depressing. Four years at college, and I only walked away with one friend."

"I don't know about Will, but I do know that Madden considers you a friend."

"Yeah, he does *now*."

"Well, that's something."

"Is it?" Molly's mouth hangs open as he stares at the table. "It's worse than I thought. I really am a people repellent."

"You're gonna blame yourself for that, huh?" I ask dryly.

"Who else's fault would it be?"

And I get what he means, but this isn't coming out right. "Obviously if you don't talk to people, they can't get to know you, but you're a talker. I'd be shocked if you weren't like this in college."

"Ah. Yes. I guess I was."

I look him over. "Can I say something without you getting mad?"

"I'm not going to promise that." He snorts. "If you say something worth getting mad over, of course I will be."

"Fine. But I'm gonna say it anyway. I think you want people to keep their distance."

Surprise falls over his features. "That's ridiculous."

"Is it? Your dad asks how it is here, and you tell him it's good. That you like it. Nothing else. Will asks if you've met any guys, and you didn't bring me up once."

"Did you want me to bring you up?"

I wave my hand because it's not important. "All I'm saying is that when you're close to people, you talk about important things. You don't talk about anything."

"What do you call this?"

"More coaching."

He purses his lips. "I talk to people plenty."

"Look, do what you like, I'm just saying that while people say Xander and I are too close, and I probably agree with them sometimes, we talk about everything. I've always got his support, and he's always got mine because we don't hold back."

"I wouldn't hold back if people actually wanted me around."

"And who says they don't?" I keep going before he can cut me off. "You know I won't bull crap you, so pay attention. You're amazing. All of you. The kinda person I wish I had a chance to be, and you shouldn't keep all that to yourself. Madden was already talking you up before you even moved in here, and Xander and I think the world of you. You know why? Because for some wild reason, you wanted to let us in."

"And Rush?" he whispers.

"I'm half-convinced he doesn't even know you've moved in yet, so we won't think too deeply about what's going on in his head."

"I'll give you that. But also, you and Xander make it so easy." His hand covers mine, and he whispers, "I think you're amazing too, Seven."

I look over at him, sitting close, big eyes sweet and hopeful and looking at me in a way I don't deserve to be looked at. He tugs at my heart like I've never felt before. I don't want to lead him on. I don't want to pretend like I'm available to give him anything more than bad dreams and a broken soul, but sometimes I look at him and think I can try. Sometimes Molly makes me believe that I can be the type of guy he needs.

And then I remember I'm me.

And I'd only end up dragging him down to my level.

I pull my hand out from under his. "We said third date, remember?"

"You're no fun."

"Oh yeah?" I cock my head. "What would make me fun in your eyes?"

"We'd be naked for a start."

"Of course."

"And I'd be bouncing on your cock."

I facepalm to hide how much I like that idea. "Do you think about anything else?"

"Anything other than having sex with you? Not really."

"Well, there's the next part of your training. Raise your standards."

"Maybe I like dumpster diving," he says innocently, turning back to the puzzle.

There's no way I'm letting him get away with that. "Ex-muffin-cuse me? You did not just call me a dumpster!" I hook my arm around him and drag him backward into my lap.

Molly cries out as I tickle him. "Technically ... technically no," he gasps. "I said you were what's inside the dumpster."

"*Trash!*" I wrestle him to the floor, Molly still struggling to breathe around his laughter and me still trying to keep my smile under control. "I'll give you trash."

"Y-yeah. This is totally ... t-totally changing my mind."

I grab his thin wrists and pin them above his head, and finally, his laughter dies. His pink tongue flicks over his bottom lip.

"Up your standards from me and my trashy cock."

Molly squirms under me. "Don't tease me with that thing."

"But why? I'm just reminding you how far you've fallen."

"I'm sorry." He struggles against my hold. "So sorry. I've been so bad, Seven. You should definitely punish me."

"Should I?" An evil idea forms in my brain. And even though it's going to torture me too, it won't be half as bad as it'll be for Molly.

I reach down, undo my pants, then pull my half-hard cock out through the fly.

His jaw drops as he stares at it, his own bulge growing beneath my thigh. "I've been so, *so* bad."

"You have," I agree, giving myself a firm stroke. I gently tug one of my piercings before rolling my palm over the crown of my cock. The attention and Molly's lust-filled gaze help get me all the way hard in seconds. It'd be so easy to shift up and press my tip to his lips. To hold him down and fill his mouth. To watch the way his face goes all sexily dazed when he's turned on.

But instead of doing all the many, many things I want to him, I tuck myself back away and give him a quick peck on the lips.

"H-hey!" he protests, but I'm already pushing off him. "That wasn't fair."

"Maybe. But it was fun for me."

"You sure about that?" He scrambles to his feet. "You're hard. You don't want my mouth to help you?"

Another flash of pushing him to his knees, those big eyes gazing up from under his lashes at me. He's way too hard to resist.

"I'm good," I tell him with a wink. "Enjoy the puzzle."

Then I turn and leave the room, bounding up the stairs before Molly can follow. I close my bedroom door behind me and lock it for good measure, because if he walks in here right now, I can't be held responsible for throwing him on my bed and using those pretty lips.

I'm trying to ignore my raging hard-on when my phone dings.

I wish I was surprised to find a message from Molly, and I can't even exercise the slightest bit of self-control to stop myself from opening it.

It's a picture. Of him in one of my T-shirts that he's clearly snatched from the laundry. A long breath rushes from me at how sexy he looks in my clothes. He's sitting with no pants on, legs open, and my oversized shirt just covering the good bits. His mop of hair is a sexy mess, and he's sucking one finger into his mouth.

Holy forking hell.

MOLLY:

Sure you don't want a hand?

I'm not a saint. I'm not even a strong-willed person. It takes every last scrap of willpower to grab my lube instead of barreling down the hall to his room. I jerk off hard and fast, photo right in front of my face, imagining giving it to Molly while he's wearing my things.

When I finally spill over my hand, I take a photo of the sticky mess and send the picture back to him.

ME:

Mine work just fine on their own.

Then I collapse onto my bed, knowing it's only a matter of time before Molly gets what he wants.

Again.

Chapter 26

MOLLY

I spend the next few days turning over what Seven said in my mind. I don't *want* to let people in. I'd call him on his bullshit, but the more I think about it, the more I'm worried he's onto something. How many times have I gone to tell Dad something and shied away because keeping it close to the chest is easier? How many times would I be hanging out with him and Will and then slowly slink away into the background because I didn't feel like the center of their attention?

I take a deep breath and walk outside to where Madden is doing his morning yoga, Kismet half-hidden under one of the bushes, watching him like a little perve.

"Gonna join me?" Madden asks, glancing over.

"Nah, not today."

"Starting the day with exercise is good for you. Especially when you're holed up in that office at a desk for hours."

"Yeah, yeah, I've been told."

"What's going on?"

And I should have known Madden would pick up on something. He's oddly intuitive.

"What was I like in college?"

Madden thinks for a second, stretching his arms out slowly to the side. "Quiet," he answers.

"Quiet?"

"Not as in you didn't talk or whatever. You did. But … how do I put it? I didn't know much about you. When we went out, you were fun, but otherwise, through the week, you'd just stick with Will, always either working or studying."

"Seven thinks I shut people out."

"And do you?"

"I … don't know."

"It's an interesting theory. I feel like I know you a lot better since you've moved in than in the years we had in college."

"Right." I huff. "I don't know how to feel about that."

"Do you have to feel any way about it?"

I frown at Madden stretching out his hamstrings. "What do you mean?"

"Well, you're aware of it now. Can't you … move forward?"

It sounds so simple when Madden puts it that way, but he should know as well as anyone that it isn't that easy. When he was injured in college, it took him all year to come to terms with the fact that he'd never play professional ball. He could have rejoined the team, maybe even had a great season, but his shoulder was fucked, and after the operation, he was more of a liability than anything.

"I could try to let people in more …" I think out loud.

"It kinda sounds like you don't want to."

He's right. Letting people in and talking about myself should be simple, but there's a big wall holding me back. Because if I take the chance and let people in, there's every possibility they won't like what they see.

"I'm a bit confused."

"Well, it seems like you're already letting them in, whether you're meaning to or not."

My eyebrows fall. "How?"

"Xander and Seven. You're always with them."

"Yeah, but they don't give people a chance," I say, smiling as I think of them. Xander especially isn't good at keeping his distance. "Where are they anyway? Seven's normally up by now."

"Xander had an attack an hour ago, and Seven took him to see that nurse at the pharmacy."

"At six in the morning?"

"He can't time when they happen."

I wave Madden's comment away. "I mean, the nurse was available at that time?"

"Maybe it's a twenty-four-hour one."

I didn't pay a lot of attention when I was there to know for sure, but even if it is an all-night pharmacy, what's the chance that Derek was on duty this morning? I almost wish they'd woken me up to go with them because while Xander is the one who needed the help, Seven also needs support in those moments. It can't be easy to see someone you love struggling like that and knowing you can't be the one to fix it.

"Hey, so I've found another guy you might like," Madden says.

"What do you mean?"

"You know … my mission to find your forever guy? I know the last one was a bust, but Damien's cool. His high school sweetheart left him a year ago, and now he's ready to find someone again. He's an architect. Gets paid the big dollars but isn't a dick about it. You'll like him. I vetted the fuck out of him and had him drooling over your photo."

My gut turns over at the sound of that, but … this is what I wanted. A forever guy. It's what Seven is literally training me for. The excitement I should be feeling is dulled by every single memory I have with Seven. The whole not falling for him thing was bullshit because I've gone and fallen hard.

"That ... thanks. Can I check with Seven first?"

Madden stops stretching and drops down to sit on his mat. "Seven? Why?"

"You know, because he's been training me. How to date people and not make a dick of myself. I just ... I want to make sure he thinks I'm ready."

My answer must satisfy Madden because he nods. "Probably a good idea."

"Yeah."

And I don't know how Madden is somehow unaware of the sexual tension between me and Seven, but it's probably a good thing. It's bad enough that Xander has squished his cute nose into our business; the fewer people who know, the fewer people there are to see me end up heartbroken.

I would say *again*, but the more I get to know Seven, the more convinced I am that I've never felt for someone what I feel for him. If I thought I'd been heartbroken before, I'm about to be ruined.

The thing is, I *want* to talk to someone about it, but the words feel too big to get out.

I wander back inside to make breakfast, turning everything over in my head. I can keep going on acting like everything is fine and that I'm happy with how things are, but am I really? When it comes to the distance between Dad and me over the last year or so, the answer is a solid no. When it comes to growing apart from Will? I'm not happy about that either.

All I want is to be loved and have people think I'm worthy of their time, but if Seven's right, I'm not giving them much reason to think that's the case.

I swallow thickly and call Dad.

He answers immediately. "Mols, hey."

"Hi."

There's a second pause. "You okay?"

"Maybe."

"What is it? Need me to come over there?"

I smile at him jumping immediately into dad mode, because even if I have been pulling away, it's nice to know that he's still as protective as ever. "No, I'm *okay* okay, I'm just … have I been distant?"

"Where's this coming from?"

"Someone pointed out to me recently that I don't talk much when you call."

Dad hums, all gravelly and warm like he used to do when I was a kid with my head on his chest. It's calming. "Honestly, I've been worried about you for a while now. You've been … unhappy."

That's news to me. "But I'm super happy."

"Are you? Because you weren't when you left here, and I haven't been able to get much out of you since you moved."

I sigh because that basically confirms it. Dad has no idea where I'm at.

"I'm worried about you, bub."

"Sorry. I …" I let out a frustrated growl. "I'm doing good here. The move was the smartest thing I've done in a long time, and I miss you and Will obviously, but it's been good for me."

"How so?"

"I get to start over for one. All that mess with Ford kinda knocked some perspective into me."

Dad laughs. "Yeah, I should hope so. My friends weren't all that thrilled with me either."

Considering Dad is friends with Ford's boyfriend, I'm not surprised. "I'm sorry."

"You were hurting. I get it, and Orson forgave you immediately."

"Not Ford though."

"Ford wants you to be happy. We all do."

That's kind of nice to hear. That maybe I haven't completely ruined everything back home. "Then you'll be happy to know I am here. My roommates are a weird bunch, but I love them."

"Tell me about them."

"Well, you already know about Madden. I didn't tell you that apparently he's a *nudist* now though, so I have to deal with seeing his dick every day. Surprisingly, it didn't take as long to get used to as I thought it would. Then there's Christian, who I don't really know because he's traveling, but he was cool when I met him. Rush is ... different. I *think* in a good way. It's hard to tell, though, because he's in and out all the time and super scattered."

"I dunno, he sounds like an interesting guy to me."

"Yeah, he's nice, at least."

"Who else? You live with five guys, don't you?"

"Yep! Xander and Seven are the other two. They're a package deal and who I've gotten closest to." And as I tell Dad about them, it's like the floodgates have opened. There's no weirdness, no holding back. I want to fill him in on all the interesting and wild things my roommates do, and he sounds starved for the connection.

"Sounds like they've been through some heavy things together," he says.

"Yeah, it does. I don't know the details, but it can't have been good. Oh! And Seven's been helping me."

"How so?"

"Well, you know how I've had rotten luck with guys? He pointed out that maybe *I'm* the problem—"

"He *what?*"

I chuckle. "Calm down, papa bear. He wasn't being mean —he's just super up-front, and I like that. Anyway, we worked out this thing where we'd go on pretend dates and I'd act like I normally do on them, and he'd point out all the ways I was going wrong so I could get better for real dates."

"Oh, did he?" Dad asks dryly, clearly not impressed.

"I promise, he's super sweet about it. He's been keeping up his end of the deal, and it doesn't make me feel bad. In fact, it's kinda funny, some of the things he's pointed out to me, like *duh*. And also, I like spending time with him. Even though he's been through a lot, he's special. Deep. I wish I could wrap him up in cotton wool and protect him from mean things."

Dad doesn't comment at first, but when he does— "Molly … you like this guy."

How is that what he's focused on after everything I've told him? "And?"

"And I don't want you getting yourself into another mess."

"A *mess*?"

"This guy obviously has a thing for Xander, and you're developing feelings for him anyway."

"You don't understand."

"Don't I?" His voice hitches. "You did this with Ford as well. Convinced yourself there was something there when there wasn't. I love you. So much. I don't want to see you get hurt again."

My insides turn to lead as I try not to cry. "So glad we had this chat."

"Come on, Mols, that's not fair."

"Uh-huh. I have to go."

"Molly—"

I hang up, anger tearing through me.

Not necessarily because Dad is wrong—except about Xander—but because I think he might be painfully, painfully right.

Chapter 27

SEVEN

MOLLY:

Hello.

I'm working.

What are you doing?

Heard about Xander.

:(:(:(

I hope he's okay.

Message me when you get this.

Wanna date this weekend?

I'm bored.

Xander still isn't home, sad face.

I miss you guys.

Oh my god, I saw a squirrel carrying a nut! F;gkjadgj It was the cutest effing thing. I used to see them all the time back home and it's just occurred to me that was the first one I've seen since I got here. We might need to set up a feeder.

... is it okay if I set up a feeder?

If that's overstepping, I don't have to.

Ooooh I think Xander's home!

My mouth is hanging open as I read through the stream-of-consciousness thoughts Molly's sent my way. And not for the first time. He's ... different. How is it that even through message he's so golden? So happy?

I close out of his texts and call Xander instead.

"What?" he moans, clearly feeling sorry for himself.

"We spent the morning on you. Can I have the floor for a second?"

"Is it gossip?"

"Might be."

"Then you have my full attention." Of course I do. Gossip gremlin.

"Molly just sent me thirty-seven texts." And I know it was thirty-seven, thanks to the super helpful little red dot.

"Okay ..."

"*Thirty-seven*, Z."

"Right."

"Is that weird?"

"Weird or cute?"

I snort, clearing off my workstation before my first client shows up for their appointment. "If you need to ask, then it's definitely weird. He's done it a few times, and I'm just ... Who does that?"

"Ah, *Molly* does that."

"But ... why?" If I didn't write back after one text, why the heck would he send thirty-six more?

"Because he likes you, dummy. He wants to talk to you. He wants your attention. How are you not getting that?"

"Well, fluff a duck. That's what I was worried about."

Xander lets out a long, drawn-out groan. "What do you mean worried?"

"I told him I'd help him, but it meant nothing. I don't want him getting all ... feelings and things."

"Unlike you, most people have a heart. I'm told it's a good thing. But also, what did you think would happen when you stuck your dick in him?"

"I didn't—"

"Don't lie. I saw my paint room when you were done. I'm thinking of hanging that canvas up in there, by the way. It's got a great Molly-shaped butt print."

"How are you so messed up?"

"Trauma," he says simply.

I huff and rake my fingers through my hair. "What do I do?"

"Well, first, after thirty-seven messages, I think he deserves at least one back. Though I'm sure if you push yourself, you could make it two or three."

"I don't want to lead him on."

"Too late for that."

"You're not helping."

"Oh, I am, but you want me to encourage you to end things with him, and I'm not going to do that."

"You're supposed to be on my side."

"Says you." Xander lowers his voice to a hiss. "You hurt that little angel, and I will gut you. *Gut you.*"

"Pfft. No one is going to let you near sharp instruments."

"If you think I can't use my eyeliner, you'd be sorely mistaken."

"Well, this conversation was fun," I say flatly.

"What did you expect? I'm obsessed with Molly."

"Then why don't *you* write back to him thirty-seven times?"

"Because I'm drained from almost dying this morning."

"And now we're back on you."

He ignores me. "If you love me, you'll sweep him off his feet. I want to see you happy and in love. You never know when it's too late."

"Ah. I forgot my entire existence revolves around you." And while I say it like a joke, we both know it does, and we both know I don't actually care about that.

"I obviously need to up the near-death experiences if you're getting that forgetful."

"I have to go. My client will be here soon."

"Fine. But you need to message him back. Seriously. Just the thought of his poor heart breaking makes me want to cry. You'd be lucky to have him."

I pinch the bridge of my nose. "I know. That's the problem. *I'd* be lucky to have *him*. And what would he get out of it? A grumpy, broken shirt-for-brains with no future."

"Don't talk about my best friend like that," he pouts.

"It's true."

"Fuck you and fuck the filthy horse you rode in on. If you're broken and have no future, it means *I* have no future, and I'd actually like to maintain a tiny bit of hope in this shitty existence. So why don't you pull your balls out of your ass and ask Molly on a date? A proper date. And stop being a fucking dick to him and pushing him away when you two are the most beautiful, amazing people I have ever met, and if you try to tell me otherwise, I will dump condiments all through your bed while you're sleeping."

"Ouch."

"You'd deserve it."

"I love you."

"I love you too. And you're allowed to be happy. So stop being a dumbass about it."

Xander hangs up, and when I look back at my phone, it's still open to Molly's messages. And he's sent more.

The first is a photo of him, and he's drawn all over it to turn himself into a squirrel.

> Aren't I cute?
>
> I think I'd suit a tail.
>
> Have you ever done that? Like dress up, or furries, or animal play or whatever? I can picture you as a horse, and I'll give you three guesses why.
>
> It's your dick. Just in case you didn't get that.
>
> Sorry, you're probably working. I'll stop now.
>
> One more thing first!
>
> You're cute.
>
> Bye.

When I look up from my phone, it occurs to me I have a smile stretched over my face and a pleasant ache in my chest. Molly is ... *phew*. I scroll back to the photo he's sent, and how one man can be so fridging cute is beyond me. I know I need to write back *something*, but I'm not good at this. At being friendly and texting cute things and sending through every thought that's in my head.

My own emotions have never mattered, and talking about them has always been useless anyway, so why start now?

I tap my fingers on the side of my phone as I try to figure out what to say.

ME:

> I think this is one of those times you're red-flagging again. Over forty messages? Dude, be cool.

I hit Send, then reread what I wrote, cringing when it doesn't sound as playful as I meant it to. Okay, try again.

ME:

> I just mean for some people, it might look needy.

> Not me!

> I'm okay with it. Because it's not like we're dating anyway.

> Like, as friends, that's okay. You can message.

> For other people though, they might not like it.

> But I do.

> To be clear.

I'm horrified as I read back over every message that I can't stop myself from sending.

> And now I sound like a trash monster. Sorry.

> It's really okay.

> Gaahhhh what's wrong with me?

> Is this what it's like for you? Panic-texting? Why can't I stop?

MOLLY:

> Like I said, you're cute. I'm gonna attack you with snuggles when you get home.

ME:

Siiiigh. I guess I asked for that torture.

MOLLY:

Sure did. X

I hesitate before sending one letter.

ME:

X

Then I tuck my phone in my pocket and get on with my day, pretending like my guts haven't been pumped full of helium.

———

I END up working back on overtime, which I desperately need but hate every second of, so it's dark by the time I pull up back at home. My nails have been bitten back to stumps, and it takes me a full minute to climb out of my car and go inside.

I have no doubts Molly was serious about attacking me the second I walked in the door, and my want for it is about equal to not wanting it. Things would be so much easier if I didn't feel anything beyond friendship for him because I'd be able to keep the lines clear. Set him straight. Only every time I think about telling him he's ready to go off and date and see if he can find his man, my lungs shrivel up and make it hard to breathe.

Emotions: turning even the most black-hearted people into embarrassments.

My whole body is braced when I open the front door and step inside. There's noise coming from down the hall, so I kick off my shoes, wondering if I'll have time to dump my things, when Molly jogs down the stairs.

"You're home, yay!" Then he launches himself into my arms.

"*Oomf*." I only just catch him. "What the—"

"Hi."

"Yeah. Hi. Umm, any reason you're trying to crash tackle me into the wall?"

He laughs and slides off me. "Just excited to see you."

My face scrunches up. "Why? No one's ever excited to see me."

"Sounds like it was long overdue, then."

"Riiight."

I take in the way he's got his hands tucked in his pockets, shoulders tense and lips downcast. His body language is at complete odds with how happy he's sounded in his messages. "You okay?"

"Yeah. Totally."

Part of me doesn't want to push and have him throw up feelings all over me, but the other part is genuinely concerned. If Xander thinks he'd gut me for hurting him, I'd literally tear someone to shreds if they made him look like this. "You're lying."

"Not really."

I raise my eyebrows. "*Molly*."

"Fine." His face falls. "Can I … Can I sleep with you tonight?"

"Ah …"

"Not sex. Just in your bed. I'll keep my hands to myself and everything."

"Geez. It must be serious if you're promising to behave yourself."

He gives me a hopeful smile that doesn't reach even half the enthusiasm of his usual ones. My protectiveness over him flares to life, overriding everything else.

"Yeah, just let me grab dinner and a shower first."

"I could shower with you," he says innocently.

"Well, that good-boy act lasted a minute."

"Fine." He huffs. "But can I sit in there and talk to you while you shower?"

"Seriously, what's going on?"

"I missed you, is that okay?" he snaps.

Something tells me that isn't it at all. There's no saying no to him though. Ever. "Fine. Not like you haven't seen me naked countless times anyway."

"It's true."

"Come on, then."

To his credit, he doesn't creepily watch me or anything, just sits on the toilet lid, chatting away about work and his designs and how a cafe owner is being a dick about paying him half up front and threatening to complain about him on social media.

"Tell him to kick rocks," I grunt. "You're too busy to deal with that nit."

"I know. But I don't want him to hate me."

"Hate *you*? Nuh-uh. This isn't on you. You have bound-aries. That's a good thing. In fact, you could probably work on putting more of those into place."

"Noted."

I wash my face, hating the idea of someone trying to bully him into waving his terms. "Want me to write back to the guy?"

"No. It's okay. Despite what you might think, I don't need protecting."

And maybe that's true. Molly's made it through this long without me, but that doesn't change the fact that I *want* to protect him. And ... even though I'll never, ever say the words out loud, maybe there's even a small part of me that wants him to protect me right back.

Not physically. I've got that more than covered. But while Xander would quite literally murder someone for me, emotionally, we're both a void of messed-up ideas and triggers. Our way of comfort isn't the norm, and I know it isn't healthy, but it's never changing.

With Molly, he … cares. He's gentle. And I don't doubt that if I'm upset about something, he wouldn't push me to talk about it; he'd just smother me with affection.

I'd hate it.

And love it.

Because if there's one thing I've always known, it's that affection is conditional. It doesn't last. And having affection from Molly, only to have it taken away again, well … that actually might just kill me.

Chapter 28

MOLLY

Seven smells like his bodywash when I climb into bed beside him. I'd told myself not to ask to spend the night with him, to ignore the neediness and the insecurity Dad planted in my chest. Sure, I've made this mistake before, assumed a guy cared about me more than he did, but I know it's not like that with Seven. His and Xander's relationship might not be normal, but I can deal with weird. I can deal with blurred boundaries and sharing affection. As long as I know that sexually and romantically, Seven is mine, he can still give Xander everything he needs. Hell, maybe I can even help him with that.

The problem is that Seven *isn't* mine.

"I'm not used to you being so thinky," he rumbles.

"Long day."

"Can't have been that long if you spent half of it texting me."

"I like telling you things."

That gets me a half smile from him. "I like you telling me things."

Those pleasant little nerves tickle at my gut at the warmth in his tone. No matter what Dad says, I'm not imagining things. Seven feels *something* for me, but convincing him to admit it will be the hard part. Getting him to be vulnerable is something that he'll fight me on.

But I want to try.

Madden's got a date set up for me, but I have no interest in following through on that if I have even the slightest chance with the man lying next to me.

His gaze is steady on me as I burrow under the blankets and wriggle in close to his side. I'm careful not to touch him—I *can* be good, dammit—but it's this closeness I've been craving all day.

"I talked to my dad," I finally say.

"Oh, yeah?"

"And you were right—don't get a big head about it. Maybe I haven't been filling him in as much as I could have been."

Seven gazes warmly down at me. "What did you talk about?"

"My life here. How I'm enjoying it. Filled him in on all of you guys."

"Oh, yeah. Like what?"

"Like how you're helping me not be such an idiot on dates."

Seven cringes. "Not sure that makes me come across in the best light."

I latch onto the thought. "Does it matter?"

"Well, it's not like I want your dad hating me."

"Why?"

"Because … because, well, you're my friend. Obviously."

"Obviously."

He chuckles. "Stop looking at me like that."

I sigh. "Am I being cute again?"

"The cutest. You need to learn how to turn that off."

"Why would I do that when I get to use it against you?"

"That so?" He shakes his head. "What do you want to use it against me for?"

Now, that's a question. There's so, so much about Seven that's still a mystery, but I have to be careful not to push, not to try and take more than he's ready to give.

"Information."

Confusion crosses his brow. "I was expecting sex stuff."

"Nah, I don't need to trick you into that. Besides, I said I'd keep my hands to myself."

"I'm beginning to regret making that deal. I think I'd prefer you to feel me up than talk."

"We could do both. Talk, and then I'll feel you up."

"Don't phrase it like it's a compromise. That's you getting both of the things you want."

I smile angelically, which only makes Seven roll his eyes.

"Ask what you want, then."

"What was your childhood like?"

"A nightmare. Next question."

"You don't have to tell me anything, but you can. If you want to talk about it. I know you have Xander, but—"

"Xander isn't you."

I meet his eyes, unexpectedly thrilled by that comment. "No, I know that, but—"

"I don't think you do." He rolls over onto his side, and I mirror him. "Look, I'm not a big softie or whatever, but I like spending time with you. Just you. While you and Xander might be similar in some ways, you're different in all the ones that matter. You're not like anyone else in my life, and I like it that way."

I tuck my hands under my cheek. "You're making it really hard for me to keep my promise."

Seven laughs. "Yeah … I'm done saying things though, if that helps."

There's a short silence before I end it. "When I was little, I used to think my mom would come back."

He blinks like I've caught him by surprise, but I keep talking.

"I don't remember her all that much. Just this vague sense that if I wanted it enough, it would happen. Dad said I used to ask about her all the time, and I know it killed him because he was the best. I just didn't know it back then." Or now, apparently. "I got cranky with him today when he was worried about me. I wish I could stop taking him for granted."

"I …" He frowns. "I don't know what that's like."

"Was it hard?"

"Yeah. Very. The, umm, the first few homes were only short stays. I barely remember them."

I don't say anything in case he stops talking, but I slowly reach for his hand.

His fingers link through mine, and Seven stares at our joined hands for a moment. "The first place that was long-term … I thought I'd hit the jackpot."

"Why?"

"They were rich. Bought me everything. Got a big room to myself. At thirteen, after spending my life with nothing but bruises and then being passed around places I didn't fit in, it was heaven."

I nod, even as Seven draws a long breath.

"Anyway, it turned out not so great. They had a son who … thought he was entitled. To everything. Even me."

I pick up on what he's saying, and the pain in my chest almost brings me to tears. "Seven …"

"Seriously, don't. His parents found out a few months after it started, sent me back. Said it was for my own good, but they told my case manager it was because I was causing trouble. Took me forever to find a place after that, especially because I turned kinda aggressive at that stage. Even when you're fourteen and have been shat on your whole life, people still want you to act like an innocent, happy kid. Just before I turned seventeen, a couple with experience in high-risk teens took me in. They didn't know what happened, but they knew enough to get me therapy. It helped me not to go totally off the deep end, and then Xander showed up."

My grip on his tightens.

"By that point, he was feral. Lashed out at everyone, stole and broke people's things, but was a complete angel to our fosters. Until they didn't give him attention, and then he'd have one of his attacks. He came from severe neglect, and while these fosters were great, they were a last-stop home. They were kind, and I wouldn't be who I am without their help, but didn't try to be a substitute for parents. They gave us what we needed, booked therapy, helped us with bank accounts and jobs, basically set us up ready for adulthood. They didn't give Xander the connection he needed, so I did. We kept each other safe. But I moved out before him, and his therapist said it was healthy for us to have time apart." His chuckle is dark.

"Let me guess, not so healthy?"

"Xander snapped. He had attacks every other day, didn't stop asking for me, kept trying to leave to come and find me. They had him admitted to a psychiatric ward, but they couldn't hold him because he knew exactly what he needed to do to get out of there. In the end, they let us have visits, and the second he was old enough, he moved in with me."

"Holy shit," I mutter.

Seven's eyes are all shiny. "He's doing a lot better now, but that's why when I say we're for life, I mean it."

"And what about you?"

"What about me?"

"Who holds you together when you can't sleep?"

He immediately looks away.

"That's what I thought."

Silence settles between us.

"Thank you for telling me."

"Yeah, well, you were going on about your sob story. I couldn't exactly let you be the only one who shared, could I?"

"Of course you could have, but I'm glad you didn't." I drag my bottom lip between my teeth. "Can I hug you?"

"If you have to."

"I'm not going to force it on you," I say because I'm almost positive that's exactly what he wants. Pretend like he doesn't want or need affection in moments like this when it's all total bullshit.

He grunts, then lets go of my hand, wraps his arm around me, and hauls me in close. His face presses against my neck. "Shut up."

"Not saying anything."

"I can hear you smiling from here."

I do my best to wipe it off my face because this isn't the time. Seven just told me some super fucked-up, horrifying shit that makes me want to tear the world to shreds. I cling to him, holding him tight, trying to mesh the scarred, damaged pieces of him back together.

"I'm so glad you and Xander found each other," I tell him.

He squeezes me tighter and doesn't reply.

It's not until later, when I'm starting to drift off, that I hear him murmur, "I'm so glad I found you."

Chapter 29

SEVEN

Sleep ebbs away and is replaced by the intense ache between my legs. My usual morning wood is a full-blown boner and—

I'm rutting it against someone's leg.

My eyes fly open to find Molly smiling over at me, hands propped under his chin.

"Don't stop on my account," he says, pressing his leg up higher.

I almost pant at the contact. He feels so good. He smells so good. I know I'm supposed to say this isn't a good idea, and we shouldn't and blah blah blah, but instead, I wrap an arm around him and crash my lips to his.

He sighs into the kiss, tongue twisting against my own, lips so goddamn soft and addictive.

"So much for keeping your hands to yourself," I tease as I nip at his jaw.

Molly shifts his thigh again. "Technically, it's my leg. No hands. Those are all to myself. Like I promised."

I shudder and grip his ass, grinding harder into him. "Think you can get us both off with no hands?"

He grunts and rolls on top of me. "I'll do anything for you."

Oh, fudge.

"One thing for me first though."

"Oh, yeah?"

"Get rid of my pants."

That might just be my favorite thing to do. I hook my fingers into the waistband and strip them off in one.

Molly kisses his way along my bare chest, taking his time over my nipples and as he licks between my abs. He hums and rubs his face over me, getting teasingly closer and closer to my aching length.

"Come on," I complain.

He buries his face in my V. "Want to smell like you."

"Ah. Shoot. Well, carry on with that."

He bites the waistband of my sleep shorts. His arms are crossed behind his back, so I lift my hips to give him a hand. Inch by inch, he tugs them down until my cock flings out, freed and—

Hits Molly in the face.

He jerks back. "Fuck, you almost poked my eye out with that thing!"

I choke on a laugh.

"Not funny. I could have been blind, and then what would I have said to the doctor? Sorry, but Seven's one-eyed monster wanted to even things up in our staring contest?"

My laugh finally comes. "Stop being weird and suck my cock."

"Fine. But only because *I* want to and not because you told me to."

"Uh-huh. Sure. *Riiiiiigh*—" My words turn to a moan as Molly engulfs my cock in one swallow. The hot suction is exactly what I need, and I can't take my eyes off him. His lips stretched wide while my cock disappears in and out of his mouth. The way his pretty eyes water as he rams my tip down his throat, pulling back to gasp down air before doing it all again. He licks and sucks and dips his head to rub his face against my balls before licking a wet stripe up to my tip.

"You love that, don't you? Sucking my dick?"

He runs his tongue over my piercings. "If we were real boyfriends, I'd wake you up every day like this."

"Oh yeah?" I thrust my hips upward, seeking his mouth. "What else would you do? Message me forty times?"

He tsks. "I already do that. I'd message you a hundred times."

"What about?"

His pink tongue dips into my slit. "How perfect you are. How sweet and kind and amazing—"

"You're doing dirty talk wrong."

Molly lights up with the challenge. "I'd send you naked pictures and videos of me jerking off."

"There we go."

"And when you get home from work, I'd have all your favorite things waiting."

I cover my face because while thinking about coming home to him is amazing, it's something I'm also actively trying *not* to think of. Molly isn't for me.

So, I force myself to say the words I never want to say. "When you do find a boyfriend, make sure you suck him off just like this."

He pulls off me with a scowl. "No more talking for you."

And before the guilt can settle around me, Molly pushes himself up, turns around, and straddles my head. His mushroom tip nudges my lips as he leans forward and wraps his mouth around my shaft again.

I gasp, and the second my mouth is open, his dick slips

inside, over my tongue, almost reaching my throat before I close my lips and suck.

Molly moans, hips stuttering, body shuddering on top of me. And because I never promised not to use my hands, I slide them over his hips and grip his ass. I control Molly's thrusts, brushing my fingertips over his hole as I suck him deep and swirl my tongue over his tip, feeling every vein and ridge of his cock as my lips slide over it.

Molly is bobbing up and down on mine, sucking hard, getting me close enough to make my balls tighten, but I don't want to come until his taste is flooding my mouth.

When Molly takes on a challenge, he goes all out. I suck on him like I'll die if I stop, and I wish I was exaggerating, but my head is taking on that fuzzy-edged tinge it gets right before I lose control. When I'm past the point of stopping. Where my body knows what it needs and is on the fast track to make it happen.

I thrust up into Molly's mouth, hips with a mind of their own, and reach around to roll Molly's balls in my palm.

He lets out a muffled cry, and a second later, he floods my mouth with his cum. Spurt after spurt I drink down, loving the taste and the way he's shivering on top of me. It makes my dick ache. Makes my skin oversensitive. Makes the pressure at the base of my spine grow.

Molly softens slightly in my mouth, but I keep sucking, not wanting to let him go until I come. Not when I'm this close. Not when I'm ready … close … about to …

My orgasm swells and hits suddenly, rolling waves of pleasure sweeping over me and pulling me under. I unload into his mouth, and he sucks on my tip, catching every drop. He waits for me to stop before pulling off, and I finally release him too.

I'm panting, sweaty, but so fulloping sated.

Molly settles against my chest. "Can I use my hands yet?"

"Hell yeah."

He cups my face as he kisses me, and it's in that moment I know I've lost. It's in the way I grip him back, the way his body feels like it's supposed to be pressed against mine. I've never had this all-encompassing need before, and I'm terrifyingly obsessed with the way it makes me feel.

But if life has taught me anything, it's that all this good doesn't last. Every time something positive happens, the world has to correct itself and bring the bad down on me again.

So, if Molly makes me the happiest I've ever been, the flip side of that will be a disaster.

The way I see it, I have two choices: either run now and protect myself or prepare for the worst.

Chapter 30

MOLLY

I wear one of Seven's T-shirts downstairs over my briefs. Maybe I should be subtle about all the fucking, but I don't have it in me to care. The whole no-sleeping-together rule is dumb when sleeping together feels this good.

Seven shared with me. A *lot*. And if he didn't see me as anything other than a roommate, I doubt I would have been given as much as he did.

I'm obsessed with having sex with him, spending time with him, going on silly dates with him. But the talking? The real stuff? It's made me feel more connected to him than I've ever felt to another person.

Even my college boyfriend, the one who promised me the world, never made me feel the way Seven does.

I turn on the coffee machine and find two googly eyes staring back at me. "Where are these coming from?"

Seven shrugs. "Just rip them off."

"Okay, killjoy." I study them for a moment. "They're cute."

"You're cute." He sidesteps me to flick each eye off. "They're ridiculous."

"And you're allergic to fun."

"I dunno, what we just did was fun." Seven sends a wink my way, and his deep, rumbly tone makes me smile.

"Lots more fun where that came from. Just tell me where and when."

The teasing slides from his face, and he doesn't reply.

Well, fuck sticks. That can't be good. I almost want to shake the guy, but honestly, I'm tired.

I'd thought we were on the same page. That he had fun with me and that the sex is goddamn incredible. We're friendly. And if he likes the friend stuff and he likes the sex stuff and he thinks I'm cute, *why*, whyyy am I still not good enough?

Don't I deserve to have a man fight for me for once? Don't I deserve to have a man make me feel like I'm everything to them?

Seven takes over making the coffees while I sink into a stool at the counter. I watch him move around the kitchen, back muscles tensed, and wish I could read his mind. The tension between us is growing thick and not in a hot I-want-to-bend-you-over-the-island-and-take-you-to-pound-town kind of way.

"Forget what I said," I manage.

Seven doesn't look convinced. "You know what we are."

"Yeah, for sure." But *do* I? Because Seven acts one way and then gets all cold the next. I hate it. I hate the games and the guesswork and the constant need to chase after people.

I promised myself I wasn't going to do that anymore, and here I am, repeating all the same mistakes.

"Sugar?" he asks, but my brain is already overloaded.

"No, thanks."

He passes over my mug and drinks his at the sink, looking out over the backyard.

"Is everything—" I start, but Madden walks inside and lets out a "*ho-ho*" sound at the sight of me.

"Seeing Damien today," Madden says, pulling up at the stool beside me. "Are you in or what? I don't want to leave the guy hanging."

"Oh, ah …"

Madden, clearly not picking up on the tension in the room, adds, "Think he's ready, Seven?"

Seven turns toward us slowly, hip propped on the sink. "What do you mean?"

"There's this guy I do work for sometimes who's exactly Molly's type. He's got a few houses under his belt, been divorced for long enough that he's not all mopey about it, and when I showed him the photo of Molly, I swear his eyes turned into love hearts. Mols said he was going to check with you if he's ready."

"That's not what I said," I hurry, hoping Seven doesn't get the wrong idea.

"Hmm, pretty sure that's exactly what you said." Madden frowns, gaze swinging from me to Seven and back again. "Everything okay here?"

"Totally." Seven dumps the contents of his mug down the drain and sets his cup in the dishwasher. "I was going to mention that to Molly today, actually. He's ready to get back out there. This Damien guy sounds fan-fucking-tastic."

My mouth drops.

Madden blinks at him. "Dude, did you just swear?"

"I'm going to be late for work." Seven's eyes meet mine. "I hope you find what you're looking for." Then he leaves, and a moment later, I catch the sound of his heavy steps jogging up the stairs.

"Tell me it wasn't just me," Madden says. "But that was weird, right?"

"Very weird."

"Damn, okay, so ... do I tell Damien yes?"

But I'm still staring after Seven, still trying to work out what that was. I'm sure I detected jealousy, *sure* of it, but what if I'm wrong? What if I say no to this perfectly lovely guy and Seven still doesn't want me?

"I've gotta go deal with something," I tell Madden, sliding from the stool.

"Doesn't really answer my question. Yes? No? Maybe? I've gotta leave for work soon."

"I'll text you."

I practically run through the house, wanting to catch Seven before he leaves. There's no way I can get through an entire day without having this conversation, and I'm done with being left guessing.

He gets one chance.

I can't keep putting my life on hold.

"*Seven.*"

He glances up as I let myself into his room and slam the door behind me.

"I have to go to work."

"No, you have to shut up and let me talk."

"No, I don't."

"Yes, you goddamn do. Aren't I at least worth that much?"

His face settles into a passive expression, and he crosses his arms. "So talk."

Oh. Umm ... yes. Talk. Right.

"The thing is ... well ..." Words, Molly. Goddamn, the one chance I have to lay it all out for someone, and it's the one time I don't actually have any words left in me. "I've enjoyed the dates, and the spending time together, and the sex." Yep, this sure is telling him. "Like, *really* enjoyed it. Like, a lot."

"Okay."

"And I know you enjoyed it all too. I know you like me. I know you *want* to keep having sex with me, but for some dumb

225

reason, you won't let yourself. I know you're not in love with Xander, no matter what my dad says, and if it's not him, and it's not anyone else, and you're jealous about me going on this date … *why*, Seven? Why won't you give us a chance?"

"There is no us."

"Bullshit."

"And I'm not jealous. The whole reason for the dates in the first place was to get you ready for this. You knew it was coming. I knew it was coming. I'm sorry if you took them for something they weren't."

My eyes narrow, and my face gets dangerously hot. "Fuck. You. Lie to yourself for all I care, but don't try and lie to me. I'm so sick and tired of getting it wrong all the time, and with you, I know that for the first time in my life, I've gotten it right." My eyes prick with tears. "You're everything I want. Everything. You're sweet and honest and hot as hell. You look at me like you don't believe what you're seeing and touch me like you can't get enough. I know I'm not imagining these things. I know you feel the same way."

He draws a deep breath and, with eyes full of regret, says, "I don't know what you came here expecting, but I've been honest with you from the start."

"You're lying."

"And you would know?"

"Yeah." I step closer, close enough that I'm looking up at him. "I don't know why you're doing this. I don't know why you're fighting this thing between us. We both know that no one in this house will care if we're in a relationship."

He stays resolutely silent.

It's breaking my heart. "I deserve better," I choke out. "If you've shown me anything, it's that. I want someone who's going to fight for me as much as I'd fight for them. Who'll put himself out there for me like I would for him. I don't want to have to beg for attention. I don't want to have to question and guess and never know where I stand. I'm done with that. And … I'm done with chasing you. I'm sorry that I've gone and fallen for you, but that's the only reason I'm standing here right now. This is it, Seven. Your last chance to stop lying to yourself because if you can't admit to yourself that you want to be with me, then I can't wait around forever."

"Tiny …"

I wait. And wait some more. I give Seven all the time to get out the words that his tone is heavy with. But he doesn't.

And that's my answer.

My head drops forward as I try to push back the tears, but they come anyway.

"I guess I should message Madden, then," I say thickly.

I force myself to meet his eyes, and we keep contact the whole time I type out the text, and then I hold it up so he can see.

Tell Damien I said yes.

"I don't want to send it," I whisper.

Seven stares at me, holding my eyes with ones full of regret. His bottom lip shakes as he steps forward, wraps his hand around mine, and presses Send for me. "There. Now you don't have to."

"Why are you doing this?"

He swallows, eyes dropping to the floor. "Because I want you to be happy. So, I'm doing that in the only way I know how."

Chapter 31

SEVEN

The second Molly walks out my door, I want to call him back. Tell him I was wrong. Beg him to understand that my head and my heart and my mouth don't all work on the same wavelength, as much as I might want them to.

Even while I was pushing him away, my heart was yelling at me to shut my trap, but the words—the wrong words—kept coming.

Which goes to prove that it was probably the right choice.

Molly needs a man who can communicate like an actual human, not a grumpy shirt head whose only skill is burying bad memories and pushing people away. At the end of the day, my choice might hurt right now, but it'll be better for us both in the long run.

For Molly, it means not being dragged down by me.

For me, it means not having to face the moment he's sick of me and leaves too.

Because that would goddamn kill me.

Money is the thing that gets me to work, but while I'm

there and do my job, I'm not present. I don't talk to people, don't joke or try to set my clients at ease. I'm just *there*.

The only reason I know I haven't shut down completely is the intense pain burning in my chest, building a lump in my throat. I swallow it down, I ignore the ache, I try to go numb, but nothing works.

I just hurt.

All day at work, I'm wishing I could be home, buried in bed, but when I finally get there, I wish I could go right back to work again. My sheets smell like him.

How was it only last night that we shared a bed?

Only this morning since he made me feel incredible? Since I held him close and got hit by the hard truth of how much I'm starting to fall for him.

Instead of stripping my bed like I should, I roll onto my front and hug my pillow in tight. Inhale his scent and die all over again that it's not him I'm holding.

He wants me, and I hate that I hurt him, but the only thing keeping me going is knowing that I'm hurting worse than he is.

The light knock at my door has my heart driving into my mouth. If it's Molly, I don't think I'll survive seeing him right now, and Xander would have just walked in without knocking.

I feel sick as I call out for them to come in.

I really should have guessed.

"Hey, Aggy."

"Hello, sweet boy." She steps inside and closes the door behind her, then stands there, leaning heavily on her cane and watching me.

"If you're here for a free porn show, you're a few hours early."

That gets a shadow of a smile before it dies again. "I saw him crying earlier."

I flinch like she's slapped me, but I won't acknowledge that I know who she's talking about. "Who?"

"Don't insult my intelligence. You know who. But I don't want to talk about him. I want to talk to you."

I roll onto my back and glare up at her. "Why?"

"Because you're my favorite."

"You've told me I'm out of the will at least weekly since I moved here."

She laughs like she amuses herself. "You really are a pain in the ass, but even with that ..." Aggy walks over, gripping her cane for help, and sits lightly on the edge of my mattress. "When you all moved in here, I thought to myself, now this is either going to be the most obnoxious group of brats I ever met, or I'm going to fall dearly in love with them all." She chuckles. "Somehow, you were both."

"Whereas you're just a brat."

She pats my shin. "Have been since long before you were born."

I groan, not liking that she isn't rising to my disrespect. "What are you doing here?"

"I told you. Keep up."

"If you're going to talk about Molly, you can get out. I'm not interested."

"I'd be lying if I said that man hasn't stolen all our hearts, but that's not why I'm here."

"Then ..."

"You're incredible."

I eye her, waiting for the "but." It doesn't come. "Is that it?"

"You don't hear it enough. You're always there for Xander and the rest of my lost boys. You're the rock in this house. The one they can all count on. Christian can't stay on his feet, and Gabe sees terrible things at work. Rush, bless his heart, makes me want to throttle him some days. I don't understand half of what Madden talks about, and my poor Xander is living in a nightmare. And who's the one who's always there for them all?"

I swallow thickly but don't answer.

"You, Seven. You try to hide it, but you love big when people deserve it. I only wish you could see that you deserve it as well."

"If only the rest of my life wasn't an example of the complete opposite."

"The rest of your life is an example of bad people doing bad things. Are you a bad person?"

I snort. "No."

"And aren't you in control of your life? Isn't that what you're always telling me?"

"I try, but … I didn't want to do it, Aggy. He could be happy with literally anyone—he's that type of person. He doesn't want to be saddled with me."

She gives me an unimpressed look. "From what he told me, that's exactly what he wants."

"Yeah, but—"

"How important is it to you that you're in control of your life?"

I have no idea what she's getting at with that question. "Very."

"Then maybe you should let Molly be in control of his."

My mouth slams closed. I hate that she has a point.

Aggy grabs my hand and squeezes. "You need to do what's best for you, Seven. I love you, Molly or no Molly. I'm not here to convince you either way; I just want to remind you that you're not as worthless as those voices make you feel and hope that one day, before I die, I get to see you happy."

And there's the guilt trip. I sit up and shove her gently. "You almost had me."

She laughs. "I meant every word."

"I thought you were better than that."

"When have I ever led you to believe I won't do and say anything I can to see you boys living your best life?"

Well, she's right about that. Aggy does love us, even if she has a funny way of showing it sometimes—like threatening to take us out of her will. If the house she owns beside ours is anything to go by, being on that will would be a life changer. I doubt it's anything more than a running joke, though.

When she finally leaves, me not being as numb as I was before, I get up and walk over to the stereo system I have set up facing out of my window. Then I put on some music and crank the volume loud.

She deserves to have her windows rattle for an hour after playing the old lady card.

But I'll do it early tonight. Because I maybe love her a bit too.

Chapter 32

MOLLY

My squirrel feeder comes. I'm not as excited as I was when I ordered it. It's a dome that sits in the window and will let me watch the squirrels when they climb inside to feed.

Maybe a cute, fluffy animal will boost me up again.

Because I've never felt so horrible in my life. I've barely been able to work because my eyes have been permanently brimming with tears, and my whole body feels heavy.

I push the living room window up and try to wriggle the feeder into the space. The window keeps slipping every time I pick up the feeder, and just when I'm about to throw the whole thing out, Seven walks in.

He takes one look at my panting, sweaty form, then, without a word, walks over and holds the window open. I bite the inside of my cheek to stop myself from crying as I finally push the feeder into place. Even with the job done, my breathing doesn't ease up. The frustration doesn't stop simmering under my skin.

Maybe this is why we should have listened to the rules and not hooked up.

"Thanks," I manage. Only the one word because anything else and I'll cry. It's the last thing I want to do in front of him because then he'll want to help, and I don't want help from someone who's only giving it out of obligation.

Seven knows I'm hurting without the tears.

Just like how I know he's hurting too.

But I have to respect his choice, and if he's not willing to finally break that guard down for me, then I have to let him go.

After all the date practice we've done, I've finally learned something. Pity the thing I learned was how to deal with a relationship ending, not starting.

"Molly …"

I wait. Give him a chance. Pretend like I'm not doing everything I can to hold myself together.

Instead of saying anything though, Seven snarls, scuffing his hands through his hair before storming out again.

I fill the feeder like he never appeared at all.

Then I head to the office to work, calling Dad as I go.

"Hey, bub—"

"I hate it."

"Hate what?"

"You were right, and I'm in love with Seven and he doesn't want me, and it hurts."

"Molly …"

"You can say I told you so."

Dad swears. "I would never. All I've ever wanted was to see you happy, Mols. Want me to come there? Want to come home? I can have a plane ticket for you in a second."

Hearing how solidly I have his support somehow helps make me feel better about my decision. "Thank you, but I'm not running this time. I'm not chasing. Madden has a date set up with a really nice man, and I'm going to go on it, and on every other date I need to, until I find my person. Because of you, I know there are good men out there. I just need to find mine."

He sighs, and I know he's fighting with himself over wanting to protect me. "Finding a man isn't everything."

"I know." I sit down and turn on my computer. "But it's what I want. What will make me happy." I open the secret project I've been working on and haven't been able to look at all week. It's hurt too much to look at the thing I'd been so sure would make Seven happy and now only fills me with dread so deep I'm choking on it.

"Then I hope it happens quickly. You're a good kid. The best. Nothing would make me happier than to see you settled down."

"Even if it meant I was settled down in Seattle?"

I can picture the exact way his face would soften at this moment. "I hear that's a nice city to retire to."

"The best."

"Love you, Mols."

"Love you too, Dad."

We hang up, and even though the comic pages make me want to curl into a ball and never climb back out again, I shove the emotion aside. It was so close. Almost perfect. And if Seven's going to deny me, he's going to know exactly the kind of devotion he's letting go.

I add the finishing touches to my art, aggressively checking references to the original, and when it's finally done, I print it off, bind it together, and walk down the hall to his room.

I swallow as I look over the Kill Diver cover with the artwork of Seven in Omron's uniform.

Maybe he'll think it's weird.

Or too much.

Or borderline creepy.

Maybe he won't take it the way I mean it, as a way of

showing him that I *want* to make him happy. That I see him as a hero too.

And I don't care.

I'm done with trying to be who I think people want me to be.

I draw a shaky breath, then duck and slide it under his door.

Chapter 33

SEVEN

"Serious question," Xander says, walking into my room without knocking. "Why are you the greatest dumb-dumb head I've ever met?"

"Go away." I'm still curled on my bed with the comic Molly drew me, unable to open it, but the cover was enough. He made this for me. I don't deserve him.

"No, really. Elle, Aggy, and I all voted. We've ordered a crown and everything."

I ignore him because it's the only way to deal with Xander when he gets like this.

"I'm just struggling to understand why my future brother-in-law is getting ready for a date with a human male who isn't you. Why, Seven? Why?"

I groan and bury my face under my pillow whilst flipping Xander the bird. It's been a long week. Avoiding Molly in a house this size should be easy, but every time I want to use my desk, he's working; every time I'm coming or going from the tattoo shop, he's sitting out the front, or standing in the kitchen, or halfway sticking out of a bush trying to tempt Kismet with treats.

And every glimpse of that mop of hair, of those big brown eyes, of his sullen expression, gets me right in the chest.

He has no right to look as irresistible as he does when he's sulking. And he's definitely sulking. We don't talk, we don't hang out—it's like he's suddenly mute in my presence. The puzzle is gone from the dining room table, and there's no more home-cooked meals waiting for me when I get home.

No dates, no laughter, no flirting and teasing.

No phone full of messages.

I miss every one.

Xander flings the blanket off me.

"Urg, what are you doing?"

"Trying to find where the animal died in here because there's no way that smell could be coming from you."

"Kick rocks. I showered this morning."

"Oh. Okay. We're not at that level of heartbreak yet."

"I'm not heartbroken." My voice is muffled by the pillow, but he hears me anyway.

"And I'm not an attention whore. This lying game is fun."

I turn and glare at him. "What do you want?"

"For you to pull your head out of your ass."

"Can't. It's stuck."

"Then let me give you a hand: Molly is the greatest thing that's ever happened to you, and if you don't fix this, I won't even have to gut you, know why?"

"Nope, and I don't care." That doesn't deter him.

"Because living your whole life knowing you could have been with him would be punishment enough."

"Your face is punishment enough," I mutter.

"Aww, there's my baby."

I grunt and fall back on the bed. "It doesn't matter."

"What doesn't?"

"How I feel."

Xander gasps. "Oh my god, you *do* have feelings for him!"

I eye him, trying to work out if he's serious. And I think ... he is. "You really came in with that whole speech when you didn't actually know if I was upset over Molly or not?"

"I was pretty sure, but, well, you're *you*. You like to pretend you don't have feelings, so when you let them show, it's like seeing a unicorn walking down the street."

"A unicorn? You couldn't think of anything else?"

"Oh, I'm sorry, a ferocious fire-breathing dragon, then. Happy?"

"Much."

"Great, now can we get back to the way you're in love with Molly and you're letting him go out with some other guy?"

"Nope."

Xander throws his hands up. "You're impossible."

"And you're still in my room."

"I love him, Seven."

I huff. "Yeah, well, I love him more." And I fudging do. Bone-deep. This stupid, desperate, useless emotion won't let me out of its grip.

Xander bursts into tears, and that's the thing to break through my funk.

"Whoa, dude, it's okay."

"It's not okay." He flings his arms around my neck. "We're fucked-up, Seven. And it's not fair. Why did it happen to us? Why did we have to go through all that? It's not fair that you can't be happy and love Molly and let him love you. And if *you* can't make a relationship work, then there's no hope for me."

"Z, of course there is ..."

He shakes his head and releases me. "No. You're perfect. And if someone like Molly can't even make you see that, then how the hell do I have a chance of settling down? How do I get past all my shit and find my person?"

Whether Xander's doing it on purpose or not, he's getting to me. Digging into those feelings and making them raw. "This has nothing to do with you. You're incredible."

"So are you."

"Yeah, but … Molly is … he's … *incredibler*."

"Not a word. Also, not an excuse. Does he not like you back? Is that what this is? Because he's also walking around like a hot mess, so I call bullshit, but if he said that to you—"

"He didn't. He told me how he felt and, uh, gave me a chance. Said he was done chasing, and I could either tell him how I feel or let him go."

"And you let him *go*?" Xander's voice gets all high-pitched, and he hits me with my pillow. "After all that? After the poor ray of sunshine, the poor *dewdrop* poured his heart out to you like that, and you just were all 'kthanksbye.' What is wrong with you?"

"As we've already established, so many things."

"No. You're not using your trauma to get away with it this time, mister. He likes you. You like him. Don't you think he's worth at least trying to see if you can behave like a normal, functioning adult?"

"Well, obviously, but—"

"And don't you think he deserves to have someone fight for him for once?"

"Well, *yes*, but—"

"And don't you want to be that person?"

I pin Xander with my glare. "Stop it."

"Stop what?"

"Trying to be logical. It's not that simple. You know that. I'm messed up, and *we* work because we've both been through hell, but Molly hasn't. How long until he gets sick of my attitude? How long before he decides I'm too much work? Guys like Molly and guys like me don't belong together. And just because we want it to happen doesn't mean it will."

Xander huffs. "I wish you could see yourself the way everyone else does."

"Just let it go."

Almost as soon as I say the words, the front door slams, and Xander jumps up to run over to the window. His jaw drops.

"The guy drives a Bentley. Are you happy now?"

"There you go. Perfect for Molly."

"Except for one thing."

"What?"

"Molly doesn't want him."

I shrug. "He will soon enough."

"Get over yourself."

"*You* get over yourself. Stop trying to guilt me into this."

"I'm trying to make you see how galactically stupid this whole thing is. Molly doesn't want to fall for that guy. He wants to fall for you."

"Don't worry, I'm sure it won't take him long."

"Why are you being like this?"

"Because he'll hurt me!" I finally explode. "Molly can go out there and be happy and loved by just about anyone. But he's *it* for me. He's my only shot. And I can't start something with him knowing that it's going to end because it hurts enough right now. I don't want to know what it'll feel like once I get that taste of actual real happiness and then it's taken away again."

"Why would it be taken away?"

I sigh, sagging in on myself. "Because it always is."

"Seven …"

"Yeah, yeah. I'm sad and depressing and stupid. I get it."

"Here I was thinking you were doing the whole *it's what's best for him* romance line, but you were actually looking out for yourself. I'm impressed. Look at you and all this selfish personal growth."

Unsurprisingly, none of that makes me feel better.

He sniffs. "Well, at least you've successfully stopped yourself from getting hurt. You can sit here happily, knowing Molly's out there fluttering his eyes at some other guy. Laughing at some other guy's jokes. Hmm … I wonder if they'll come back here to fuck or go back to his house? He drives a Bentley, so probably his. I bet it's big too. The house as well."

I snort. "Molly doesn't put out on first dates."

"Oh yeah, for sure." Xander picks at his thumbnail polish. "But now I think of it … if that's the case, why did I just have this same conversation with him while he was shaving his balls? Huh. Maybe it's a comfort thing?"

It's like the whole last week funnels down into this moment. "He *what*?"

"Oh yeah, we had a great talk."

"Molly was manscaping?" My words are weak, strangled. All the indecision, all the awkwardness, all the moments where I wanted to say something to him this week and couldn't force myself … all for nothing. Because Molly doesn't just sleep with anyone. So if he was getting himself ready, that means he really meant what he said. He's giving this guy a real chance. For the first time, it truly hits me that I could lose him for good … and that's the complete opposite of what I want.

"Manscaping." Xander snaps his fingers. "That's what it's called. I couldn't remember."

"He's going to fuck this guy."

"I would if I was him. He's hot, and he *drives a Bentley*. Keep up, Seven."

"Shut *up*, Xander. Can't you tell I'm freaking out?"

"You're freaking out?"

"Molly's going to sleep with this guy."

Xander blinks at me. "Sorry, but … what did you think he was going to do? Be celibate for the rest of his life? Speaking as a virgin, that doesn't sound like happy fun times for him."

My gut twists, all hot and unsettled, and I try not to rattle out of my skin. Molly dating this guy is bad enough, but him flushed and sweaty, begging with need, all for someone else? That pretty mouth wrapped around another guy's dick?

I think of the messages and the cooking and the puzzles and him cuddling into my lap when things got too much for me. Am I really going to let someone else have all that when Molly was willingly offering it to me?

I grit my teeth, possessiveness boiling through my veins.

"He … can't," I choke out.

"Ah, so *this* is what not being hurt looks like."

Who was I kidding? I haven't done anything to stop Molly from hurting me, when I'm already in worlds of pain. "*Crud.* What have I done, Z?"

"Aside from being a dumbass?"

"Not helping. How do I fix this? I'm not good with words, can never get out what I mean when I'm around him."

"Molly doesn't need words, he needs action. Just give him what he's always wanted—someone who loves him enough to fight for him."

My head spins as I realize that someone is me. I'm in love with him, and the feeling might have snuck up on me, might be completely unwelcome and a total surprise, but now I have it, I never want to give it up.

So time for me to do what I do best. Fight.

Chapter 34

MOLLY

Damien is a perfect gentleman. He looks nice, his smile is nice, he holds the door open for me and even pushes my seat in when I sit down. He's wearing a suit and has his hair styled, and his nails are clean and rounded like he actually takes care of himself.

There's no hint of tattoos or anxiously bitten-back nails or complete and total discomfort at sitting in a fancy restaurant.

"Boston to Seattle was a big move," Damien's saying, and I try my hardest to focus. His smile turns sly. "There was a jilted ex, wasn't there?"

"You are surprisingly close …"

He laughs, and everything about it is comforting and warm. He's exactly the kind of guy I should be interested in, the kind I could see a future with. Damien's giving me all the signs of being interested, and the old me would have jumped on it. Would have been planning to introduce him to Dad and what time of year our wedding should be.

And that's my problem.

That's why my college boyfriend had such an easy time of screwing me over. He didn't promise me the world; he just didn't put a stop to me getting ahead of myself. He's still a cheating dick who treated me terribly, but through Seven, I've finally figured out my type.

Honest.

Even if it hurts.

Even if it's not what I want to hear.

Seven's never backed down on giving me the truth … until the other day. Scared or not, he lied, and I can't wait around for someone like that.

I force myself to refocus on Damien. On the kind of dream man I've always wanted. It hurts, but I owe it to myself to give this a real go instead of pining after a man that might never be available.

"Technically, he wasn't my ex," I explain. "I never got that chance. I thought I was falling for a guy who was falling for someone else, but now that I've had time to get the distance …" I actually laugh at myself because *wow*. How confused and desperate did I have to be to throw myself at a man who was very solidly telling me no? "I was selfish and immature. And I hate knowing that I might have hurt him and his partner, and I'm embarrassed that's who I became."

He plays with the stem of his wineglass. "I have to say that maturity is a big thing for me. Just so you know."

"Yeah, me too. Moving here was the best thing I've ever done, and I've had to face some shitty truths, but I think it was worth it."

"So that's why you ran away, huh? Embarrassed?"

I bury my face in my hands. "So, *so* embarrassed. God, just thinking about it makes me cringe."

"Well, that's a—oh. Hello. Can we help you with something?"

I glance up at Damien's abrupt change, and I suck in a

breath so fast I almost choke on it. Standing over me, tattoos on full display, piercings glinting in the light, sincere eyes burning into mine is—

"S-Seven."

"Hey." He manages a tight smile, then grabs a chair from the table beside it and falls into it next to me. He's in a T-shirt and jeans, hair a mess, shoulders pulled in tight. And even with Seven looking like roadkill next to Damien, my heart almost flutters out of my chest.

But I ignore the needy organ and level Seven with a glare instead. "What are you doing?"

"I got your comic."

My breath catches. "Okay. Good."

"I ..." He flicks a nervous look toward Damien before focusing on me. "I had to see you."

"I'm on a *date*."

"Which is why I had to see you."

"Are you okay, Molly?" Damien asks, once again proving the whole gentleman thing.

I quickly nod. "It's fine. And I'm so sorry."

Seven glances Damien's way again. "For what it's worth, so am I, but I've gotta do this." He shifts his chair closer. "I'm sorry, Tiny."

The way his voice drops, fills with regret, almost softens me to him. "For?"

"For protecting myself by hurting you instead."

"Well, you made your choice," I point out. Because it did hurt. So much more than I've ever been hurt before. So much that it proved to me I'd never been in love all those times I'd thought I had, because losing those other men doesn't compare to how it feels to lose Seven. "I don't need your apology. I just need you to let me get back to my date." I hate how pathetic my voice comes out, but I can't help it. With him here, I can't fool myself into thinking I don't care. I care too much. It's paralyzing.

The softness in Seven's eyes shutters, and he straightens in his chair. "No."

"No?"

"I'm not going anywhere." He waves a hand over the plates. "Continue with your date. Keep talking and flirting and batting those pretty eyes at him. I don't care. I'm not going anywhere because Xander's right. You don't want to fall for this guy. You want to fall for me."

I humph.

"Which is good for me, because I'm so fudging in love with you I almost hate you for it."

I forget to breathe. "W-what?"

"I love you. And if you walk away, it'd serve me right, but I'd never forgive myself if I didn't try. Tonight, tomorrow, next week, next month. I'm here, and I'm going to fight for you. Whether you try to move on with *him* or some other guy, I'll be here. You said you can't wait around forever, but that's fine because I can. Forever. There's no one else for me—I don't want there to be. You deserve to have someone fight for you, Molly, and I'll spend the rest of my life doing exactly that."

Oh my god. Tears spill over onto my cheeks because he's saying everything I've ever wanted someone to say to me.

Seven's hand drops to his chest, right over where his Sevipus tattoo is. "I've known you were special for longer than I realized. I've spent so long not getting close to people, wanting to keep that distance, but the moment I met you, I knew. I can't fight this because it's kismet, baby. And I don't mean the stupid cat."

I choke on a laugh and immediately hate myself for it. Seven left it until I was sitting across from another man to tell me all this, and Damien doesn't deserve it. Doesn't deserve to be ignored like this. I want Seven. My whole soul is begging for us to be together, and I know exactly what he means about kismet because it's impossible to fight.

But I need to ignore it for that little while longer. "I think you should go," I make myself say.

"Gladly." He casts a nervous glance around the restaurant, which only makes me fall for him even more. The timing was fucking ridiculous, but he came here, unafraid to put himself on the line in public, in one of the places he feels the least comfortable, just because he wanted me to know. Seven stands, but as he does, he leans in, lips close by my ear. "But I won't be going far."

I watch him the whole time he walks away before dragging my gaze back to Damien. "I am *so* sorry."

He presses his lips together, frowning slightly. "Yeah, I know you are."

"I had no idea he was going to do that."

"I figured that out too." He licks his lips, and I wait because he's clearly trying to work out what to say. "I have no interest in getting between anything. If you say you want to continue this date, I'll take you at your word, but …"

"But?"

"Every single part of you looks like it's desperate to run after him."

I hate myself because it's true. The last thing I want is for Damien to walk away from tonight regretting it, but what's the point in staying? Seven's offering me a real shot at us, and I know the second I'm free of this date, I'll be going straight to him.

One corner of Damien's lips twitches higher. "Go. I promise it's okay."

"I'm sorry," I say, already half out of my seat. "You were the perfect date. But I think that's part of my problem. I've been looking for perfect, and it doesn't exist. I need someone messy and raw and who needs me because I'm all of those things too, and no offense, but you're not. I literally don't think I've ever met a more put-together, emotionally stable person in my life."

Damien actually laughs. Loudly. "The fact that you think any part of that was an insult is all the confirmation I needed that we wouldn't have worked."

"Thank you."

"I'll get the bill."

But even with my hurry to get out of there and with Damien's offer, I stop and pay discreetly as I leave. Damien shouldn't be stuck paying for a story that he'll no doubt be relaying to Madden next time he sees him.

As soon as my card clears, I jog out of the front doors and toward the parking lot, but before I've barely gotten a few paces away, a strong arm loops around my waist and pulls me close.

Seven's bodywash wraps around me, and before he can say a word, I jump on him, legs closing around his hips as I bring my mouth down on his.

His grunt is surprised, but his hand finds the back of my head and gives me what I want. He deepens the kiss, making those fluttery butterflies explode through me as happiness over-rides everything else.

"You liked my comic?"

Seven gives me a wry smile. "I couldn't open it."

"What do you mean?"

"Seeing the work you put into the cover was hard enough. It ripped my darn heart out, Mols."

"I love you," I tell him. "I hate that it took you so long, and I hate that you thought you couldn't make me happy because you do. Every day, I wake up excited to see you. Wanting to touch you and make you smile and exasperated and so, so happy."

"I was wrong." He touches his forehead to mine. "My

phone's been so empty the last few days. I want it full again. I don't want you to play it cool or hide how excited you are to see me. I don't want you to stop the nervous chatter and the messages, and hell—you can even dribble all over me on any one of our dates. I don't care, Tiny. I just care about you. Exactly the way you are."

A soppy whine gets caught in my throat. "How could you think for a second that you wouldn't make me happy?"

Seven inhales deeply. "I'm scared. I don't want to wreck this and turn you into, well, *me*. I don't know how to be anything other than this grumpy, broken a-hole."

"It's shocking to me that for someone so perceptive, you can be completely oblivious to yourself. Instead of being scared you'll bring me down, why don't you trust that I can handle myself? I mean, fuck. Maybe I'll boost you up instead. That smile you were wearing proves it's possible."

And so help me, the gorgeous smile comes again. "Trusting you is probably the easiest thing you could ask me to do."

"Good. Well, let's start there." I kiss him again. "Because you promised me you'd fight. Forever. And I'm sure as hell holding you to that."

Chapter 35

SEVEN

My heart is full. This isn't a feeling I ever thought I'd be able to have. It's not something I dreamed about, it's not something I was looking for, it's not even something I ever thought I'd want. But Molly makes me want. He makes me hope and dream and brings out so many feelings in me that are tee-totally terrifying.

All relationships are either forever or they end, with the odds being deeply in the *ending* column, so the idea that this could be forever—him and me—I'm not going to bank on it.

I'm sure as hell going to try, though, because I meant what I said. There's no one else for me. No one else I'd willingly tie my life to. No one I'd want to.

Even if something happened and I had the chance to find this again, I'd say no. Molly's the only man I want to experience this with.

He drags me upstairs, glancing back at me over his shoulder, cheekiness lighting up his eyes, and the force of my feelings almost makes it hard to breathe.

Yeah.

Molly's it.

There's no one else like him.

We reach my bedroom, and Molly kicks the door closed, then leans back against it.

"So …"

I smirk and reach for his pants. He's dressed nice. All respectable and stuff. But the only thing this sexy suit makes me want to do is disrespect him in the filthiest ways possible.

"I'm going to fuck you," I say, reeling him in by his belt loop. "Then we're going to hydrate, eat, and I'm going to fuck you again."

Molly's chest hits mine, and he shivers.

"I'm going to fuck you all night until I can't get it up, until there are no more ways for me to show you how much I want you. To show you all the ways you own me. And then when we're done, we're going to tell everyone we're together." He holds my jaw and kisses me. "Because if I have it my way, this is the start of forever. And I want to start us off right."

"I'm swooning over here," he murmurs. "But can you do one more thing for me?"

"Anything."

"Say *fuck* again."

I laugh. "Fuck." I bury my nose in his hair, lips by his ear. "I'm going to fuck you, because I fucking love you, and no one else fucking compares. Fuck."

"I'm going to need you on the bed now."

"Yes, sir."

"*Oohh*, I like that."

I strip off my shirt, but before I can reach for my pants, Molly presses against my back and reaches around for my fly. He works his way down the buttons, flicking them open one by one, and my cock thickens as he brushes it.

"Tell me how you want me," I say.

He kisses the back of my shoulder and tilts his head up

toward my ear. "On the bed, handcuffed, while I take photos of you."

A shiver runs through me, but it's not entirely a good one. "Handcuffed?"

"You love when I hold your wrists, and I haven't forgotten how I found you that day. Let me replace that memory with a good one. Let me put you back in control of what happened."

I turn suddenly, wrap him in my arms, and kiss him like my life depends on it. It isn't even something I thought I needed, but now that he's put it out there, I do. I crave it. I want that feeling of being locked down again, knowing that it isn't going to screw up. That it isn't going to bring all those past vulnerabilities out in me. I want to be able to enjoy it and know that I'm safe.

With Molly, I am.

My kiss turns desperate as I shove down my jeans and then work the buttons open on his shirt. All that perfect, bare skin that I'm dying to get my ink into. To leave my permanent mark all over. He's warm and smooth, addictive. As I grip his shoulders and push the shirt off, my hands follow it down his arms, feeling every muscle and hair on my way.

Molly's already got his pants undone by the time I reach them, so I dip my hands down the back of his briefs and squeeze his tight ass.

He grunts, hips canting forward into mine, hard zipper scratching against the sensitive skin on my cock.

The brief flicker of pain helps me step back. I'm panting, and Molly's lips are swollen and red. The exact shade I love on them.

"Handcuffs are in the drawer," I say, nodding to my night-stand. Then I lie down along my bed and lift my hands over my head.

Molly kicks off his pants and hurries for the drawer. I

watch him pull out handcuffs, lube, and a condom, and just the sight is enough that I almost reach for my cock.

I resist, and when Molly climbs up beside me, my hands are already in position.

He leans forward, kissing me sweetly while he fastens the metal around my wrist, then cuffs the other side to my headboard. When the lock snaps around my other wrist, I almost call this whole thing off—there's a big difference between someone you can easily overpower restraining you and actual handcuffs—but then Molly's thumb lightly strokes the bottom of my palm.

"You're okay," he whispers before clipping the other side to the bed.

He pushes up onto his knees, gaze greedily running over me.

I flex my muscles, wanting to turn him on, wanting him to like everything he sees. There's still that small discomfort swimming under my skin, but all I need to do is look at Molly, and it eases up. He'd never take advantage. All Molly cares about is making me happy, and I feel the same way about him.

He starts off slow, hands lightly trailing my body as he plays with my collarbones, my nipples, and my abs. He lightly skims over my cock, running one finger over my leaking slit and then trailing it down over my piercings.

"These feel so good," he rasps. "Inside me. It makes everything so much more sensitive."

"Good."

"Maybe one day, we could do this without the condom. Just you and me and these incredible piercings lighting up my hole."

"No maybe about it," I growl. "Definitely. I want that." My cock is aching thinking about pressing inside his tight little hole, feeling his skin and his heat wrapped completely around me.

He leans in and presses a kiss to my tip, eyes gleaming as he grabs his phone. "Now, where do we start?"

Ah, crud. Him getting me to list all the places wasn't what I had in mind. "Where do you want to start?"

"You're the one in control. I'm just being a good boy and doing what you tell me to."

Mmphf. Okay. "The handcuffs."

Molly straddles my chest and leans in close enough that I can suck his cock into my mouth. The camera clicks at the same time as Molly lets out a moan, and then he slides back down my body, and his dick disappears.

"No fair."

He grins. "You're in control here."

"Okay," I say, catching on. "I want a photo of my mouth. With your dick in it."

"Yesss ..." He hisses, scrambling back up my body. He grips his shaft and presses his cock to my tongue as he sinks in halfway, and then I suck and lick him through the sounds of Molly taking photos, cock getting impossibly harder at the thought of looking at these when we're done.

He takes every photo I tell him to, moving down my body and over his. When he gets to my dick, he wraps one hand around it, then lifts the camera and lowers his mouth to it. I have a clear view of the screen as he takes photo after photo of his tongue on my shaft, lips wrapped over the tip, big eyes open and directed at the camera the whole time.

"I don't think you could take enough photos of you doing that," I rasp.

"Maybe I should do this, then." Molly switches over to video and then goes to town on the sloppiest, sexiest blow job I've ever witnessed. I want to take over the camera, let him use both hands, or grip his head or *something*, but my arms are tensed above my head, white-knuckling my headboard, hips rocking up to meet his mouth, seeking more.

Molly pulls off with a husky laugh, then runs his tongue from my balls to my tip, and when he batts those lashes at me, my heart stops.

"Urg. Sit on my cock. Sit on it now."

He stops filming and sets the phone down, pouting up at me. "Oh, but I'm not even *stretched* yet."

"Molly …"

"What?" I don't buy into the innocence in his tone for one minute.

"You're planning something."

"Don't know what you mean." He pushes up onto his knees, my cock left cold, wet, and neglected, and I watch in agony as he runs a hand over his hip and back to his ass where I can't see it. "Like I thought, nothing's getting in there." He reaches for the lube and pours a generous amount over his fingers. "Since you're all tied up, I guess I'll have to do it myself."

"Turn around. I want to see."

He pretends to think it over. "Like … this?" He turns and throws a leg over my waist, perfect bubble butt right there, giving me a direct view of his fingers running over his hole.

"Closer," I grunt.

He shifts back over my chest. "Here?"

He's so close. So damn close all I need is him back just a little more for my tongue to be able to reach him. I might not be able to touch him with my hands, but I'm desperate to feel him, to make him feel good.

"Closer."

"I would, but then I couldn't do this …" Molly leans forward and swallows my cock again.

Now that's a point I can't argue with.

He preps himself while he blows me, and I'm a needy, shuddering mess at the sight of him stretching his hole only inches from my face. It's the most delicious tease, and it's taking all my willpower not to take over and thrust into his mouth until I come.

"I'm so close, Mols," I warn him.

"Good because I am too." He grabs the condom and my phone, then takes photos as he rolls the condom down my cock. "I want to ride you facing this way," he says, dragging his fingers over my piercings again. "I want to feel these against my prostate."

"You know I'll give you anything you want, but help me sit up first. I don't want you that far away."

Molly's delighted smile warms me to my core, and he helps me slide the handcuffs to the top of the poles, so I can sit up and hold the headboard behind me.

I'm so desperate and needy for him that when Molly presses a soft kiss to my jaw, it takes a moment to register. And when I do, I melt.

Pure goddamn sunshine.

"You okay with those?" he asks.

"Don't worry about them; worry about my dick. He needs you!"

Molly laughs, then holds my stare as he rubs lube over my cock. The condom makes things the tiniest bit less sensitive, but it's still a tease. Still taunting me. Still making me want to blow.

Then he flips around, knees on either side of my hips, and positions my cock under him.

"Can I take photos of you entering me?" he asks.

My dick throbs, and there's none of the discomfort left. "Hell yeah."

He leans forward as he sinks down onto me, phone reached around, taking shot after shot of me disappearing into his body.

It's hard to think that I almost lost this. That I thought letting him walk away would be so much easier, when everything about us, all of this, is the easiest thing I've ever experienced.

He exhales slowly when I'm fully seated and leans back against my chest. I can't touch him, so I press against him in every way I can, lips finding his neck and his jaw and his shoulder, leaving tiny kisses wherever I can drop them.

"Nothing compares to this," I tell him.

He rolls his hips and lets out a gasp. "Oh my fucking god. Seven." He rolls them again, and a shudder races through him. "This is … *nmmgghh.*"

Whatever it is, I'm left to guess because Molly rocks back and forth on me, building speed, and all he seems capable of is incomprehensible noises. His head drops back onto my shoulder, arms wrapping back behind me as he drives himself wild.

And I'm no better—every time he grinds down, he sends pressure through to my balls. Blindingly amazing pressure, the kind of pressure that could keep building and building, but I need payoff. I need relief.

"You're killing me here."

"Sorry, but this is … this is … so intense." His thighs shudder, and it almost looks painful for him to stop.

Molly holds up my phone, turning the screen toward us, and then hits Play.

He finally moves up and down, and having the view over his shoulder … *gahhhh.*

He jerks himself off as he bounces, holding the phone out, face a wreck of lust and want. He holds my gaze through the image of us on screen, hair stuck to his forehead with sweat, angry red tip of his cock peeking out from his fist with every stroke.

It's killing me not to be able to grab his hips, to slam into him, to give him everything he needs, but seeing Molly take it for himself? Hot as hell.

His angle on the phone is slipping, hips slamming down hard as his thighs start to twitch.

"Close … I'm close …"

Thank froglets for that.

My gaze darts between his face and his cock, not wanting to miss a thing. My own pleasure is building, getting too big to hold back, but I focus on him and refuse to close my eyes. Refuse to give in.

Until … until …

He cries out, limbs locking up as his mouth drops open and he comes.

His ass tightens beautifully around me, and that's all I need to follow him over the edge.

Just like I promised to follow him anywhere.

Forever.

He slumps back against me, a sweaty, panting mess, and I kiss his head. "Love you."

"I know we've had sex before, but that was seriously the greatest sex of my life."

I laugh. "I'm not sure whether I should be insulted for every other time."

He pulls off me so he can turn and cup my face. "Every other time was incredible, except for one thing."

"What?"

"I was always worried it would be the last time. And just then, I knew it was only the first. Knowing I get to experience that again and again meant I could let myself enjoy it. Fully. With you."

And now he's explained it, I know exactly what he means. "Let's see if we can make round two even better."

Chapter 36

MOLLY

Gabe shows up for Monopoly Monday, and I know without Seven having to say a word that he's going to tell them all now. We would have yesterday, but Seven followed through on that promise to fuck me until he physically couldn't anymore. And in between sessions, he flicked through the comic I made him, and it was everything I thought it would be and more. The awe, the sheer happiness on his face as he went through the pages, filled me with more love than I've ever felt in my life.

Then this morning, he went off to work, and I put the puzzle back out on the table, then messaged him between design jobs all day. And when he got home, I fed him all the food I'd spent the afternoon cooking with Aggy.

It's still completely wild to me that I can be over-the-top and extra without having to worry. The insecure part of me worries that I'll scare him off, but that voice is easy to stamp down when I remind myself of all the things Seven said and promised.

Sure, I've been made promises before, but those empty words were just them echoing what I wanted back to me.

Seven told me what *he* wanted, and other than when he was only trying to protect himself, he's never given me a reason not to trust him.

"I'm here, and you buttheads had better not have started without me!"

If Rush wasn't sitting across from me, I'd assume it was him, considering he's always late to everything, but apparently, his boyfriend canceled their plans again, so he's been moping around the house for most of the afternoon.

Elle throws her hands up as she walks into the room. "Yes. I have arrived."

"Sorry, babe," Madden says, counting out the cash. "It's family night."

She gasps. "*I'm* family."

"Not Bertha family."

She jabs a finger toward Gabe. "Technically, neither is he. Anymore."

"He's an *OG.*"

"And he *moved out.*"

Madden shrugs like there's nothing he can do.

"I'll be Christian's stand-in, then," Elle says before she suddenly throws herself forward and flips the box lid with all the cash Madden was counting. Money flies into the air before drifting across the floor. "See?" she says from where she's landed. "Nailed it."

Before Madden can argue back, Seven says, "I invited her."

"To family night?" Rush gasps.

I almost want to laugh at how seriously they're all taking it.

Seven sniggers. "It's not the only Bertha rule I've broken this month, so ..."

My gut swoops when I realize he's about to drop it now. Just throw it out there.

But Xander beats him to it.

"You better be about to tell us that you and Molly are dating."

"Ah—"

Xander whips around toward the others. "And yes, we all agreed not to sleep with each other, but Molly wasn't there then, so technically, they never took the super-solid oath of no Bertha boning about each other. Therefore, no rules broken. And also, if any of you try to make this not happen, you might want to start sleeping with your bedroom door locked."

"Is it actually called the super-solid oath of no Bertha boning?"

"Sure is," Madden says. "I named it."

Rush turns to us. "Is that what you wanted to tell us? That you're together."

Seven takes my hand. "Yep."

Then Elle lets out a squeal and jumps to her feet, moving to stand in front of us. "I'm with Xander. On the doors locked thing. You try to take away my baby Seven's happiness, and I'll hire a hit man. I'll do it. I have the money to."

Gabe raises his hands. "I don't live here anymore, so I don't give a shit."

"I guess that threat's exclusively for us," Madden says, nudging Rush.

"I have absolutely no idea what any of you are talking about. Oath? What oath?"

"Dude, you were there!"

"Was I? Why don't I remember this?"

Elle snorts. "Because you don't remember anything?"

"Huh. Compelling argument."

"Wait a minute." Madden rounds on him. "If you forgot about the oath, why haven't you ever tried to sleep with me?"

Rush blinks rapidly at him for a moment before leaning in and dropping his voice. "Was ... was I supposed to?"

Madden huffs. "No taste. The lot of you."

"I thought we were playing Monopoly," Rush says to no one in particular, one hand making it into his chaotic waves.

"We are," I hurry to answer. "Just wanted to let everyone know about us, and now that we have, and murder has been threatened, and Madden's ego has been knocked down a peg —" Gabe sniggers. "—I think we're ready to get on with it."

"Yes, let's do," Elle says.

Madden crosses his arms over his bare chest. "Nuh-uh. You're only staying if you pick up every note."

She pouts. "Can't I just replace it all with real money to fight over instead?"

"Nope." Madden pops his *P*. "I'm going to thoroughly enjoy you scrambling around on the floor, princess."

She flips him off and, with zero finesse, drops to her knees to scoop the paper up.

I turn to Seven and find him already watching me. Those kind eyes of his will never not make me melt. "That went well."

"It did."

"Even if Xander stole your thunder."

An indulgent smile crosses his face. "Kinda his thing. Being all up in my business."

"And you know I'm okay with that, right?"

"Of course. We wouldn't be doing this if you weren't." Then Seven throws a quick look over to where everyone is bickering and takes my hand. "You're allowed to speak up though. If Xander gets too much, or is too in our business, or does something that makes you uncomfortable, that's okay for you to say. This is *our* relationship, not his. The only thing I ask is that you never try to stop us being friends. Everything else we can handle."

"After what happened last time someone tried to separate you?" I scowl. "I will never do that to him. Or you. And considering how needy I am, it's nice to know that I have you both."

Arms suddenly wrap around me, and Seven's bemused expression strays over my shoulder.

"Listening to all that, huh?" he asks.

"Of course." Xander's voice is right by my ear.

"And what did you hear?"

"That Molly's needy, and he loves me."

Seven looks like he's praying for strength. "And the rest?"

Xander shrugs. "Something about being nosy and annoying. I don't know, it wasn't important."

"Z …"

"Fine." He huffs. "I have to respect your relationship. But Jesus fuck, I already knew that. Put it in my diary and everything."

I glance back at him. "You have a diary."

"If you play your cards right, I'll let you read it one day."

"Interesting …"

Seven sighs. "You do know that playing your cards right means ganging up on me, don't you?"

"Oh yeah, I got that."

Xander laughs, and Seven grabs me, dragging me away from Xander and into his lap.

"My Molly."

His.

I sink into the rush of belonging that one word brings.

All I ever wanted was to be someone's whole world, but with Seven, I've realized how off base I was with that thought. How ridiculous. Friendships are so important, and without them, can any relationship actually work? He'll always have Xander, but then, so will I.

And that's something I won't give up easily.

I've never wanted to be someone's whole world; I've just

wanted to be a priority. Not the afterthought, not the plaything.

Loved.

Seven gives me that and more.

Epilogue

SEVEN

One year later

Hot damn, I'm nervous. Molly's beside me, bouncing up and down, zero chill in sight, all while I feel like I've sweat right through this shirt.

I've spoken to Molly's dad, Keller, and his best friend, Will, a few times over the phone. I know Keller didn't approve of our relationship at first, was worried Molly would get hurt or I'd screw him over or whatever. I still think he's half-convinced that I'm going to run off with Xander any day now. He's not the first to think that, and he won't be the last, but all that matters to me is that Molly knows the truth.

And he's never once been jealous or put out.

"I can't believe we're doing this," I mutter.

"Too late to back out now," Molly reminds me.

"I know. I just … parents scare me."

He presses up onto his toes to kiss my cheek. "I know. But you've also never seen a good one. And I promise, my dad is one of the best there is." His voices softens. "And he's yours now too."

Well, that's getting ahead of ourselves. I still need to get him to like me first.

Molly squeals, latching onto my arm. "There they are."

I glance over to see two men, one tall, tanned, and blond with a backward ball cap and a backpack, who shouts out to Molly and starts running. Molly heads for him too, but I don't even see them hug because my gaze has moved to the older guy.

The man with the longish dark hair, short beard, and all the confidence of a goddamn runway model.

Is Molly's dad … hot?

Will starts to laugh. "I think your boyfriend is broken," he tells Molly.

I'm not quick enough to hide my shock before Molly looks back at me, and his eyes widen comically.

"Oh, no, no, no." He strides over, finger pointed right in my face. "You're not allowed to think my dad's good-looking. No. Nope. I forbid it."

I stare down at my horrified boyfriend and burst out laughing. "Oh my god, I'm sorry."

"Holy shit," he says, stunned. "Our relationship's over. Just like that. *Poof.* The end."

I link my arm around his neck and tug him close. "I'll make it up to you."

"Oohh, how?"

"Yeah," Keller says, crossing his—kill me now—muscular arms over an equally muscular chest. "How?"

This is not going at all the way I thought it would. "I probably shouldn't answer that."

Keller's face screws up. "Mols, I know you're an adult, but do me a favor and pretend to be a virgin for the rest of your life. Okay? For me?"

"Like *you* can talk." Molly steps forward for a hug, but Keller holds out a hand.

"I'm gonna need some space between all this sex talk and a hug."

"You are so weird." Molly looks back over at me. "As you've guessed, this is my overprotective and overbearing dad. Dad, as you've also guessed, this is my Seven."

I quickly hold out my hand, and Keller drags his back through his hair instead. "Yeah, can't touch you either right now. Why don't we do lunch instead?"

Will groans. "Please, I'm starving."

"Come on, then." Molly links their arms and drags Will toward the airport exit, leaving me with Keller.

"Ah, want help with those bags?"

He passes the suitcase over to me with a smirk. "Since you're offering."

We fall into step behind Will and Molly.

"You know, I was worried about meeting you, and I can safely say it's gone nothing like I thought it would. Considering I was prepared for you to tell me to stay away from your kid, I'm not sure if all this is better or not."

Keller gives me the slightest laugh. "I know what you mean. I've only ever met one of Molly's boyfriends, and I wish I could go back in time and punch him in the face after what he did."

"If you ever figure out how, take me with you. He deserves at least two punches for hurting Mols."

I feel Keller study me out of the corner of his eye. "Deal."

Well, hey, that's something.

Not exactly a warm and fuzzy blessing, but we'll get there. I've got years to win him over.

Keller suddenly reaches out and grabs the suitcase, pulling me to a stop. He checks to make sure Molly and Will are still walking. *Oh no.* Here we go. The "you're not good enough for him" speech.

"You once told me you'd do anything for Molly."

I brace myself.

But instead of the words *break up with him*, Keller hands over a card.

"What's this?"

"The number of a local therapist. She's got openings, and I've told her I'll foot the bill."

I frown at him, trying to figure out what he's saying. "You want me in therapy?"

"I want my son happy. And you make him happy. But we're not going to pretend like you don't have your baggage that gets between you sometimes."

Last night was another bad one. Molly sleeping in my lap while I engrossed myself in the forums. He never complains, but it's not healthy for either of us. Admitting I need professional help isn't easy, but taking money from someone—let alone my boyfriend's dad—is even harder.

"I ..."

Keller grunts. "If you're going to tell me you can't take my money, you might as well stop there. I was a teen dad. Had nothing except Molly. If I didn't take handouts where they were offered, I wouldn't be who I am today. Neither would he. Every cent I've worked for has been for him. And helping you helps him, so let me be the dad I've always tried to be."

How the hell do I argue with that? Keller wants what's best for Molly, and so do I. At least that's one thing we have in common. So, even though it feels all kinds of wrong, I nod.

"Okay."

Keller smiles, and *shit*, the man really is hot. "Good man. Now, let's catch up before they know we've been plotting."

I'm not about to argue, so I hurry alongside him, closing the distance between us and them.

And when Molly glances back and catches my eyes, that feeling of unease lessens. Going back to therapy is something I've always wanted to revisit. I started it, and it helped, but when I moved out on my own, I couldn't afford it, so this ... I have to take it with both hands.

Molly deserves to have a stable boyfriend.

And maybe, just maybe, I deserve it a little too.

My life has only improved since Molly walked into it, and I meant every word I said to him a year ago.

I'll always fight for us.

So this is me.

Fighting.

And for Molly, I'll never stop.

THANK YOU SO MUCH FOR READING!

The Big Boned Bertha love stories will continue in in 2024!

And to read my next release before anyone else, see awesome character art, and get bonus content, check out my Patreon: https://www.patreon.com/saxonjames

Author's Note

Thanks so much for reading these gorgeous guys!

The fact you keep showing up for me, release after release, means the absolute world! My dream has always been to have a career as an author and it's mind-blowing to me that I get to live it.

As thanks, I've launched my webstore! You can pick up audiobooks at a great price, website exclusive covers, signed paperbacks, book bundles, and merch.

You can check it out through the link or QR code: www.saxonjamesauthor.com

Author's Note

My Freebies

Do you love friends to lovers?
Second chances or fake relationships?
I have two bonus freebies available!

Friends with Benefits
Total Fabrication
Making Him Mine

This short story is only available to my reader list so follow the
below and join the gang!

https://www.subscribepage.com/saxonjames

Other Books By Saxon James

CU HOCKEY SERIES WITH EDEN FINLEY:

Power Plays & Straight A's

Face Offs & Cheap Shots

Goal Lines & First Times

Line Mates & Study Dates

Puck Drills & Quick Thrills

PUCKBOYS SERIES WITH EDEN FINLEY:

Egotistical Puckboy

Irresponsible Puckboy

Shameless Puckboy

Foolish Puckboy

Clueless Puckboy

STAND ALONES WITH EDEN FINLEY:

Up in Flames

FRANKLIN U SERIES (VARIOUS AUTHORS):

The Dating Disaster

And if you're after something a little sweeter, don't forget my YA pen name

S. M. James.

These books are chock full of adorable, flawed characters with big hearts.

https://geni.us/smjames

Want More From Me?

Follow Saxon James on any of the platforms below.
www.saxonjamesauthor.com
www.facebook.com/thesaxonjames/
www.amazon.com/Saxon-James/e/B082TP7BR7
www.bookbub.com/profile/saxon-james
www.instagram.com/saxonjameswrites/

Acknowledgments

As with any book, this one took a hell of a lot of people to make happen.

The cover was created by the talented Rebecca at Story Styling Cover Designs with a gorgeous image by Michelle Lancaster, and edits were done by Kathleen Payne, with Lori Parks proofreading the bejeebus out of it.

Thanks to Charity VanHuss for being the most amazing PA I could have ever dreamed up. Without you I'd be even more of a chaotic disaster and there isn't enough space to cover the many hats you wear for me.

Eden Finley, you constantly under-sell yourself but I've learned so much from you. You're the bestsest disaster bestie I could ask for, and a queen of a co-author. You're also stuck with me. Lucky you.

To Louisa Masters, thanks for constantly reining in my spirals of doom and reminding me to "stop borrowing trouble". I'd be an anxious mess in the corner at least half of the time without you.

AM Johnson and Riley Hart thank you so much for taking the time to read. Your support is incredible and I really appreciate it!

And of course, thanks to my fam bam. To my husband who constantly frees up time for me to write, and to my kids whose neediness reminds me the real word exists.

Printed in the USA
CPSIA information can be obtained
at www.ICGtesting.com
LVHW050830290823
756437LV00004B/649

9 781922 741271